THE LIGHT OF A BRIGHT SUN

THE LIGHT OF A BRIGHT SUN

By

Thurman P. Banks Jr.

For anyone who has ever felt like they dance just a little bit different, just like me.

How sad it is when the worst cases of disability you have seen in your life, are the poor, unfortunate souls, afflicted with cases of normalcy.

-Thurman P. Banks Jr.

Introduction

Read. Write. Repeat. Read. Write. Repeat. Read. Write—oh shit—I forgot to feed the cat. Read. Write. Feed the cat. Repeat. And so it plays on.

Read: I never planned on writing. Sure, I have always read quite a bit. In fact, the greatest stories I have ever found were the ones sitting lonely on a table, in the books I knew nothing of, but simply, picked up and lived. I have read many of the so called "classics," though, who is anyone else to decide what is a classic in my eyes?

I do not limit myself with genres, as no one genre moves me more than another. While I understand the necessity of it, I find the labels limiting, and that is something I do not care for. A good story has no boundaries. Why try and put walls around it? Is that not the death of creativity? I try to keep my mind as open as the book I am reading. Every book, every genre, tells me as much about myself as the story I am living with each page I turn.

Perhaps, I am crazy.

Write: I am thirty-nine years young, a family man, no greater in this endeavor of putting words on a page than any other. In fact, with every new book I read, I become more and more convinced that I am terrible at it. Somehow, someway, I have found that others enjoy my suffering, so with tortured satisfaction, I will continue.

When I started out writing my first work—Beyond John Dann—I did not live to write. I was writing, because I had lived. My book told itself. My hands on the keys, just the medium to what time and tale had decided to be my destiny. Today, I cannot go a moment without a story in my head. My characters, like prisoners in my mind, follow me into every store, engage silently in every conversation, consuming my breathe until their voice is allowed the freedom they deserve. My eyes, the wardens of time and space, capture every scene as they wander beyond reality.

Madness! That is what writing is in truth—madness.

Repeat: I am never content until I have challenged myself to do something that makes me absolutely miserable until I have achieved it. Every single day, I live the insanity. Every single day, I relive the madness. Every single day, I read, write, and repeat the process. I do not force it. I just do it. It is all with the hope that my books may challenge others to be better people, or perhaps, smile a little easier at their own misfortunes. Despite all that I write about the struggle, the torture, the lack of confidence, I always smile and lead with kindness. I do it for no other reason than it is the right way to be.

With Kindness,
Thurman P. Banks Jr.

CHAPTER ONE

When the days have come that I am gone, and the memory of my life is but a whisper in the heart of those who remember, let it be written that I dreamt in both the light of day and the dark of night, with love in my eyes and peace in my soul, for all of all. My Heart Called Maybe

Present Day:
"Great wisdom arises in mourning. I'm better off like this anyhow, here, a prisoner as I've always been, first to myself, and then to the world. But aren't we all?"
Beep. Beep. Beep.

The drifting daylight falls upon him through the window, its soft touch cascading through the curtains, gently glancing on the side of his tan, wrinkled face, fading his light blue eyes to white with each beam that catches his vision. His once dark hair, now fully white from the top of his head to the sharp trim of his beard, radiates from that one true patch of sunlight that has fully entered her room, that one small vertical crease of enlightenment, showing him that there is still a world outside. He knows that world all too well. He has been born to it, died in it, found breath in the past and the future, over and again.

"Some of the most thought-provoking things I have ever read were written in spray paint on the rundown walls of old, abandoned buildings, their simplistic messages like beacons, calling to me from the face of chaos and ruin. That is why I wrote it over there. My only hope now is that someone with the right vision will see. If only one person finds the beauty, if only one can see the truth and know what must be done, then it will have been worth the risk," he tells her, nodding his head in agreement, his mind convinced, his eyes peering across at his handiwork. "Not too bad for an old stick in the mud."

Beep. Beep. Beep.

"I had to do it today. Do you know why?" He asks her, proceeding without time for an answer, an answer they both knew she could not give. "It's the last day I will ever visit you. Not that I won't want too, but I think we both know it's the last day you will be here for me to see."

Sadness—his voice, his manner, filled with it, consumed with the emotion that comes with a final goodbye. He was nothing to her. She was everything to him. Their bond of one-sided friendship, forged in the abyss of life and death, was complicated and ugly, beautiful and simple, all at the same time.

Beep. Beep. Beep.

I've slipped into the madness again, he thinks, laughing lightly. *So be it if I am in the madness*, he assures himself, *you have to be a little crazy to truly stay sane in this world anyhow.* She could no longer hear him, he was certain of that. Even on the days when she was awake, their conversations had always been one sided. *What makes it through to the soul*, he often wonders, *even when the ears can't hear?*

He had talked to her so many times in the past, without response, without an acknowledgement of understanding, but he never let it stop him before, and he isn't about to let it stop him now.

"I still see their blood, even when I ask my mind to erase it. I try to force my thought to something else, anything, yet all I see is red." His gaze remains out the window, his body, inches from the glass divide. His sight, however, is no longer on the wet red words that adorn the building across from her room. He is in them, lost in the message and memories of the past he long ago accepted, yet can never escape.

Beep. Beep. Beep.

"We shall all go in time. One way or another, we all take our leave from this place. Be thankful you know the end is coming. It is not that way for so many, not that it is unwelcome. Death is like a scavenger, catching them in the shadows, in that dark despair of human hearts and minds, where the clouds of loss and lusts and ravaging winds of hope feed on their every want and desire that never comes true. He takes them from the misfortune they have called life, and for many, they are grateful to go. I wonder if *they* were grateful. I wonder if they were *meant* to go. I had never killed before, not in the physical aspect, at least. Death of emotion, well, that may be a different story. Yet, there I always seemed to be, lurking in the shadows, the Reaper in the doorway."

Turning away from the window, the iris of his eyes regaining their blue hue, he still sees red. "What if I had done things different? Would they all still be alive? Would you be alive?"

Beep. Beep. Beep.

He had just started speaking to her, and had already begun to weep softly. The last few years, faced with the creeping mortality of his own life, had turned the hard man he once took great pride in seeing in the mirror, soft. He wept for her death. He wept for her life. Joyfully, sorrowfully, he wept for the past he couldn't, wouldn't change.

"My life has been a bastion in the fallows. My resurrection in the seedy tides of ripped currents, plunging me without care or want, all at the doing of my own actions. I have murdered, lied, stolen, vandalized, raped the innocence of a child, all of it simply because I could not handle the reality that was before my eyes, so I walked away. How easy it was to torture myself with each step. I knew in my heart it wasn't suffering at all. It was my sanity, paid for at the price of others. How simple to be so cruel, how noble to myself and myself alone."

Beep. Beep. Beep.

Using a tissue by her bed, he wipes the moisture from his eyes. There is plenty of time to wet the cotton however, plenty of time to grieve for his own life, and only a short amount of time to be with her. There is still a story to tell, a life to give breath. She knows it well, she has lived a part of it, but even when we are standing right there, we often miss a piece. We peer into ourselves and like a scolded child testing the sight of the sun, are blinded by the light and sight of what we truly are. But every piece holds its place, whether we wish it to or not. Every second, every torturous occurrence, every blissful memory, create the mystery.

Putting another before himself, the one he holds above all now, he kisses the cover of the book that has remained silent in his hand. Opening it, he begins her journey to heaven.

"In the name of the Father, and of the Son, and of the Holy Ghost."

~ ~ ~ ~

July 27th, 1976:
Kick the can.
Thomas walked slowly, methodically, lining up each swing of his right foot for what he deemed kicking perfection. Each imagined soccer ball hitting the back of the net, or football sailing through the middle of the uprights, destroying his only companion on the road home.

The scraping of the dented soda can against the ground echoed through the sugar maple trees like a crowd roaring in jubilation at his accomplishment, every strike the game winner. He was as all young children—a hero without a cape—living a life of created greatness in an unhurried world and overachieving mind. But those thoughts were about to change. His imaginary innocence was destined to be replaced with the sins of reality; and for Thomas Thompson, it was coming all too soon.

The trees that had conceived the crowd of his arena lined the narrow, cracked road that hadn't been paved once in Thomas's eight years of life. Each crevice, each jagged fracture where the blades of grass had pushed through in their effort to reach up and touch the sun, was a threat from the earth below, warning in surety to open its mouth like a hungry mother and swallow her children, the people of the coastal Connecticut town of Hayward, whole. *Let her,* Thomas thought, *just as long as she leaves the kids and only takes the adults.*

It had been a routine summer day for Thomas and the rest of the kids, full of sunlight they never feared, games on the fly, and friends turned enemies on the field. It was their daily blur, ending each day with the ritualistic setting of the sun, which upon departure, dispersed them like ants back to their origins; each tiny life, racing in an opposite direction to the small homes that graced the large suburban neighborhood of Wood Oaks housing development.

He was alive in a time of unlocked doors, and neighbors you spoke with instead of about; when the necessary last stick of butter or cup of milk was only a short walk across the yard away. The streets, reverberating with the sound of parents yelling "Supper time!" into the orange shade of dusk, to children who always hollered back, and were most often granted, "Ten more minutes!"

He had chosen not to take his bike, a choice he regretted as he watched his friends speed ahead of him. One by one they disappeared, leaving him to walk alone. His decision to walk, something so small and insignificant at the time, was one he would spend the rest of his life questioning. *What if? What would his life be like now if he had been seated in control of those two wheels, pedaling ahead like his friends, gone in seconds?*

It was only a fifteen-minute walk home from the field, which was no great expenditure of energy for Thomas's fit legs. On the occasions he would follow the road all the way to downtown Hayward, rather than take his bike, he walked well over triple that amount of time. Fifteen unwanted minutes can change a life however, and not always for the better. Even fame has a price. Yet, while not taking his bike with him first thing that morning turned out to be the wrong decision, it wasn't a mistake. The only mistake Thomas Thompson truly made that day, was being naïve enough to feel safe and free in a world full of bounds.

His unkempt dark brown hair hung shoulder length, blocking the hazel colored eyes he had inherited from his mother, and concealing his sight from the sides of the street. The brand new Red Sox hat that his father had brought home the previous day, which would have given him full sight if in use, was tucked brim first in the back pocket of his tan corduroy pants—pants that were now stained green from a slide into home.

He had just finished a pickup game of Wiffle ball with the gang from the neighborhood. The slide had kept him just under the catcher's tag and helped clinch the win for his team, the stain that resulted, a battle mark running all the way up the side of his t-shirt. His mother wouldn't be happy, but knowing he had won the game with a head first dive that Pete Rose himself would have been proud of, made it all worthwhile. *Charlie Hustle, meet Thomas the Tank*, he thought, building upon the legend that he had already conjured in his mind.

He was half way home. He knew it when he came to the giant brick buildings that shaded the tattered pavement. The buildings were the property of the Laro School, an eroding institution that had followed the ruins of the road. Out of ten buildings, only the three located in the back of the large grounds were still in use. The remainder were now covered with a growth of vines that wrapped around them like fingers, each one tightening in an attempt to squeeze any signs of man's interference from the landscape.

The dwindling appearance only added to the already haunted view that the children of the town had painted of the school. Stories of ghosts that haunted the grounds and screams heard in the night brought fear to the offspring of Wood Oaks. How little did they know, that while they were sitting around the campfire stoking the legend, real monsters did in fact roam the halls of the buildings that were still occupied, and that many of them, were the people of their very own small New England town.

The place had always given him the creeps, and even more so now that he was alone. Perhaps, it was an intuition, a call to run. Thomas didn't heed the call. He didn't even hear it. Even in his anxiety, his ears were deaf and his eyes were blind to his premonition. Having his hair pulled back by his ball cap may have helped him see the boys that were waiting in the bushes, just ready to grab their prey. But even if Thomas could have seen them, he may never have gotten away.

He was a child who had spent his days in search of adventure, in a world without the fears we live with today. Yet, wicked men and women have always taken in air, their secrets and beady eyes hidden in the bushes, just waiting to pounce. In an average, everyday society, full of no excitement to revel in, these things weren't supposed to happen. But great injustice lives below the sight of the horizon, lower than we wish to look, or ever truly care to see.

Thomas Thompson was only eight-years-old.

Thomas Thompson was only a boy.

"Kick the can. I dare ya. Go on. Kick the can."

The voice leapt at him from inside the shadows of the pine trees just three yards to his right, the wanting nature of the request his first indication of trouble. The aluminum Tab soda can that had just brought such elation to the crowds of his imagination, such unbridled joy to the arena of trees surrounding him, had landed on the edge of the brush, and was now, as silent in his dreams as in the nightmare soon to come.

Move. Keep moving! His mind demanded from his body when they first grabbed and dragged him inside of the enclosed trees. He tried to fight, tried to get away; but even if his adrenaline had granted him the power to overcome one of them, it wasn't enough to get away from them both.

"Hold his arms down tight. I don't want him squirming away," the older boy, the one Thomas deemed the leader, instructed.

"Stop, let me go, let me go!" Thomas screamed.

He had heard stories about the older kids in Wood Oaks beating up the younger members, just because they could. But those were only black eyes, destined to heal. What Thomas had feared was much worse, his thoughts conjuring up the belief that they were going to kill him, perhaps even sacrifice him on the rock hidden behind the circular stance of trees.

He never imagined what was about to happen. Thomas had heard quiet mumbles about such things, knew when and where it was appropriate to touch girls, but no one had ever made him the victim in the stories. As a male, he was always the potential perpetrator, the boy who would someday become a man, the one who needed to learn right from wrong. What he had never been told or ever expected, was that he was destined to be on the wrong side of the story. Thomas didn't need to know what acts he shouldn't commit. What he needed to know was how to get away.

The rock, like a stone altar set in the middle of the pines, dug into his stomach, the jagged edges slicing through his shirt. He wiggled his thin body, fought, screamed, twisted, cried and tried whatever he thought could stop them. He prayed that someone would drive by, that someone would help him. But even if a car did drive by, they may not have seen him through the bushes, and Thomas knew it.

Stop! He just wanted it to stop, but the boy holding him, who was most likely no more than a young teenager, had a death grip on his arms. The one behind him quickly began pulling Thomas's pants to his ankles, then his underwear, which in one tugging rip were gone. As soon as the breeze hit his bare buttocks, Thomas knew what was happening.

"Just relax, you'll like it, we like it now," the one holding him over the rock said in a slurred speech.

"No!" Thomas yelled loudly one moment, his throat straining. "No," he whimpered the next, his resolve, his innocence, gone with the pain. Only tears and terror remained as he whispered in shock to the wind, "I'm a boy. I'm a boy."

Feeling, believing his insides were being torn apart, Thomas wished someone would save him, that one of his friends would be there, or that he would black out. He wished with everything in him to be somewhere, someone, anyone else.

They talked to him the entire time, the sound of their voices only making it worse. *Stop talking*! He screamed in his head, their unrelenting, unwanted words crawling in, molesting the inside of his ears. "You'll like it. It feels good."

Their voices were an echo in the open field behind him, a space that granted him no freedom. Emotionally, physically, he felt every second of his childhood violated. The caped crusaders he had watched with such excitement on television, who always saved the day, were fallacies lost to the tormenting truth of reality. The warm seed of destruction became a part of him, tainted him. At least, that was how Thomas now saw his life. He was dirty, and there wasn't a soap in the world that could take it away.

"My turn," the boy holding him uttered, the excitement leading his hand from Thomas's wrist to the cool metal of his own zipper.

"No. It's getting dark, we have to get inside. You can go first next time," the boy said before turning his attention to Thomas. "You better not say a fucking word or I'll come to your house and kill you and your entire family. You got me?" The words escaped his mouth through a clenched jaw, yet before Thomas could even utter a word of acceptance, he was alone again in silence, their voices still playing in his mind like a skipping record. *You'll like it. You'll like it.*

They left him there, naked and betrayed by his own purity. His fellow children of Hayward, the only ones he had wished minutes ago for Mother Earth to save, were now the demons that had crawled alongside the tufts of grass and through the cracks. Finished with his body, they walked away quicker than his spirit, as if it had never even happened.

From the second they had bent him over the rock, Thomas was changed. His view of humanity, before he could even make an adult decision of it, was in shambles from that moment on. God as he had been born to know and worship, the greatest of all super heroes, was as dead on the cross as Jesus. *Let God be the raped child if he so allows his children to be treated that way, and then maybe we'll see where his faith resides.* It was a thought that Thomas would indulge in anger throughout the years to come—years he would spend trying to bury the pain and shame, to ignore it. But what he could hide from others, Thomas Thompson could never hide from himself.

The little boy whose eyes of winsome wonder had lived so little and so much, was gone forever, imprisoned in the darkness of his own existence, with a pain that blocked out the light, and a heart that refused to shine.

CHAPTER TWO

Present Day:
"Everything changed for me that day. My world flipped like a cheap cardboard game, the pieces of my life scattered and insignificant. I was tired, exhausted really, from the burden of my own belief. I killed God and his son that day. My belief was my first murder. My fortitude, my will, is not now, nor has it ever been, equal to yours, my dear. You have a gift I was never granted, one that I am so thankful to have seen."
Beep. Beep. Beep.

He was pacing slowly as he spoke, his thoughts like footsteps on the cold hard floor, each new step bringing forth a new opinion of the past. His mind—cluttered—had turned each ramble into a new road, each memory into a new story. He was alone with her. He was alone with himself.
Follow the book, follow his story, he fought to remind himself.

"I just couldn't bear to watch him after that day. I was blinded by rage, anger, the shame of it sinking my soul and his into darkness. With my finger pointed at God, I blamed him for the circumstances. I cried to him, *Why me? Why him? Why any of us? Who are you to do this? Have you ever felt this, all of it? Or do you sit there on your paper throne, moving us like pawns on a chessboard, the royal king hiding behind the true rulers of the game, no more powerful than the pawn on the front line. I'll take the rooking over your false castle any day.*"

He stopped for a moment, releasing his hands from the clenched state they had taken. Even all these years later, the anger of the past brought the reaction of his fingers curling into a ball, his muscles flexed, his eyes focused. But it was his legs that betrayed him. They were too shaky to stand up to the heavens, too unstable to stand above God.

Beep. Beep. Beep.

"How petty are we to believe in one another?" He was reliving the question, dancing with the edge of memory and make believe. His body was in her cold teal room, but his mind was walking the old roads.

"How stupid I was to believe in myself. I felt as if I were nothing, a nobody, so unwanted that life itself desired to spit me out. I thought I shall die, lonely, and broken-hearted. Even all these years later, I can feel them inside of me as if I were the one. I can still feel that unwanted pain holding me, using me, the same way they used him—my son, my only boy, suffering at their hands. While I sat calmly at the table eating my lunch, he was being torn apart, physically, emotionally, spiritually. No drink can cure that image. Nothing, nothing can take that away. *Why not some girl?* That was my first thought. A thought that showed the same ignorance of evolution that had kept me from understanding what he was going through—would go through. No crime is better than another, yet that was what I conceived, that it was worse not just because he was my son, but a son and not a daughter."

Beep. Beep. Beep.

The sound of the machine in the background, deaths mechanical apprentice, no longer breaks his stride.

"It was my second murder when I killed his love for me. I couldn't look him in the eyes after that night. I couldn't hold him, couldn't kiss him on the cheek without feeling as if

I had done it to him, as if I had been the one who had taken his innocence."

He had broken from the story he meant to tell, his own life, the lie left floating in the sea of truth was the constant distraction of thoughts he had to remove. His story, his life of wandering, was useless and time consuming, and time was of the essence.

Follow the book.

"I left. I woke two mornings later, but only after doing what needed to be done. Refusing myself the opportunity to look at my wife in the bed or at my own child in his room, I walked out. I walked for nearly six years, never once looking back. Six years of not knowing or wanting to know; six years of getting by, drunk, isolated, with just enough to survive in this world of ours. Though even then, it was more than I truly needed. It was more than I certainly deserved."

Beep. Beep. Beep.

"I could have stayed for him, for her, but how do you go back to a petty life of useless fragility? I had been a good man to that point, a quiet cog in the system, yet, what good did following the line get me? What good did it do for my wife, who was slowly losing her mind well before that day? I didn't want to see her slip like that, but I didn't stop her. She was lost in the boredom of being *normal*, though she never would have admitted it. Most never do. Instead, they choose to embrace the fantasy by making it not only wanted, but their one true need to have and to hold. They find a reason to believe what isn't even there. It's an illusion of wonder, no more than an empty hand and lonely embrace. Madness— that is what our lives truly are—a bundle of thoughts and lies which, like strings, we know are destined to break, yet we still continue to hang ourselves upon."

Beep. Beep. Beep.

"When it happened, I think a part of her let go and, where the Good Lord helps so many, led her to the magical land of giving up by giving it all to him. The young girl I had married left for greener pastures that, at best, were withered dreams called heaven. She was already on her knees when he came home. Even if she wanted to stand, her boy came home changed, and the revelation knocked her right back down on her knees again. One minute spent kneeling for glory, the next for a lifetime of pain."

"I don't blame her. I pushed her to it really. I was the weight that dragged her down. She wasn't always so worn. In all actuality, she was quite lovely once—playful. Then I married her, made her a housewife, went to work and left her with nothing but the boredom of a false world in a box. Slowly, I watched her die the worst death—that of spirit. The young girl who had bounced into my life was gone, rotting from the inside. She had no reason to feel excited. Perhaps she needed the fantasy. She was following the rest of the herd. We are all cattle and nobody sees it, or even more frightening, nobody cares. Well, I see it now. I care. It took something I never wanted to happen, never wanted to happen to him, for me to see, and even then it took years to grasp. In the arms of tragedy, I held the first real piece of clarity I had ever known, while she held you in her own state of revival; though some damage can never be undone."

Beep. Beep. Beep.

"The sight of my life now blinds me to everything but him, the one person who needed me the most; the one person I left. Another son lost to the life of the resurrected—another child reborn in the world of the walking dead."

~ ~ ~ ~

August 1986:
"Not all heroes die in the light of a bright sun, Thomas."

The left side of Willy's face was darkened by his stance in the moonlight, the right side illuminated by the moonbeams that lit his normally pale skin and disheveled brown hair. The words, born from one side of his mouth, crept to the only part of his lips that appeared to be moving, as if the dead half were giving voice to the living.

He held Thomas's gaze for a moment, the spade end of the rusted shovel resting on the dirt, the stained wood resting in his left hand. Thomas returned the look in Willy's direction, though it was the moon just over Willy's shoulder, as if it were resting on the man, which entranced Thomas.

"Yeah, well I wish they would, cause I'm freezing my ass off," Thomas told him, breaking his own lunar trance.

"Watch your mouth. Now help me dig this hole."

"You got it, Willy," Thomas jabbed, adding a sarcastic tone to Willy's name, an addition meant more to pester than to sting. Small jabs had a way of wearing a man like Willy down, and besides Thomas thought, it was a hell of a lot more fun to chip away at Willy's psyche than it was to knock it all out with one blow.

Willy had never cared much for Thomas calling him by his first name, but Thomas never felt quite comfortable with calling Willy "Dad." Not that Thomas should have felt comfortable. Willy wasn't his father. Thomas's father had departed long ago, when he was only eight, leaving his mother alone to raise him. It was a short stay in solitude before Willy entered the picture, his tall thin frame far more appealing than the lackluster masterpiece inside the rectangle of his humanity.

Even in his displeasure, a part of Thomas always felt bad for Willy. He was just the poor slob whose great misfortune was to be single and lonely at a time when Thomas's mother had actually seemed normal, and even in her own way, attractive. The connection Willy and his mother had shared one night at the local bar, had now left Willy and Thomas standing there over a decade later, still with the same discomfort in one stupid little thing like a name. They probably could have had some great bonding moment over it, perhaps chosen to take that next step; but Willy wasn't a bonding man, and Thomas Thompson wasn't evolving into much of one either, at least not when it came to Willy.

William Theodore Crowley, or Willy to those who knew him best (which truthfully, was no one) was prone to cases of personality amnesia, his vision of himself often exceeding the projection of his actual persona. He had been trapped into the life of a family man, the one thing he had spent a lifetime avoiding. But you can't separate yourself from acts that require attachment—it's the entire purpose—and one that carries with it the possible burden of life. Willy, who had prided himself on his life of unattached love, had knocked a woman up, impregnating her with his heir, his seed, or how Willy saw it now, his sacrifice.

Thomas's mother was an easy victim at the bar—lonely, sullen; a fresh lamb in Willy's wolf den; and he knew it the minute she walked in alone. He was a regular predator— the "tall and handsome handful," as he had been dubbed by the barflies who knew his prowess. Always lurking from the stool, he was often most attentive at the sight of new meat. While she wasn't the most attractive woman he had ever seen walk through the doors, she wasn't anything he would ever kick out of bed, either. She was well rounded on the backside, with a handful of pleasure up top. Her face was pretty enough for the dark bar, and an even darker bedroom. After a few hollow compliments and glasses of wine, they found themselves back at her boudoir, comfortably horizontal.

"Just keep your voice down, my son is sleeping," she had told him. He didn't care about a sleeping child in the next room. He wasn't there to be anyone's father or role model. The lust in his pants was the only child he was there to appease. Life and cheap latex had others plans for Willy however, the broken rubber bringing an end to his nights on the prowl—at least, for now.

When she walked into the bar a month later to inform him, "I'm pregnant, and it's yours," he mourned for the part of his life which would die. The remains of his prey had never once saddened him as much as the thought of losing out on the hunt. He could have denied it, said it wasn't his, but somehow he knew she wasn't the lying type; and that in a reversal of fortune, he was the one now caught in the scope.

Made of dirt nobility, he married Thomas's mother, the little shit son of hers being a piece that came along with the parcel. Willy knew the kid would always be a problem. What he hadn't realized was that his heir would cause him an even greater stress and strain. The image he had held, his vision, his savior he expected to beget, didn't quite turn out like Willy expected. The son born of the King was, to Willy, the daughter sired of the Devil.

He shouldn't have been surprised. Tainted illusions were the chosen decorations for his family tree. In Willy's opinion, he had always been screwed one way or the other, which is why he always opted for the more pleasurable side of fornication. His libido, in fact, would easily have scored higher than his own IQ. No matter what had become of the birth he had so waited for, that so scorned him, Willy couldn't walk away. The image would have ruined the greatness that only he could see. He was better than even the greatest Crowley in his own mind, a title that had been granted without Willy's approval to his older brother Steve.

Steve, older than Willy by one year, was the greatest athlete Mazur, Iowa, hell, the entire Mid-west USA, had ever seen. At least, that's how their parents portrayed it. To them, he was Steve Crowley, the gentleman who wooed the ladies with his grace of manner and charm, the framed mane of chiseled features and carved perfection.

Of course, across the table sat Willy—the other brother. Willy, the lazy dreamer, so uncoordinated he would trip over his own feet. Willy, the last piece of chicken handed out at the supper table, while his brother Steve, seated next to their father, arrogantly made sure that Willy got the piece they were told he deserved. Steve was the boy who made crops grow with his hard work, while Willy watched, the drought of the family.

He could still hear his father's voice in memories, "Steve's a worker. He gets things done. Willy just stands there with his head in the clouds thinking about god-knows-what. But it sure ain't the work ahead, I can tell you that."

Behind the veil of greatness there often lies the hidden truth of us all. Willy knew the reality that snuck behind the curtain. He knew what lived in the heart of his brother's prominence. Steve was a false god, a myth created by their own father and mother, one they had spun upon the universe, and certainly in their own home.

As the brothers grew older, so did Steve's legend. He was a hero in Vietnam, named Lieutenant in only two years. Willy was the grunt jumping out of planes, paving the way for the honored men like Steve, just so they could keep their boots clean, the battlefield laden with dead bodies for them to walk across with clean soles. Yet, while boots may stay spotless, a soiled soul will rot a man from the inside, no matter how prominent the accolades or shiny the medals.

Willy survived the worst of the war, while his brother valiantly died for his country, the outcome sealing Steve's fate as the eternal hero. But Steve wasn't an honorable member of humanity, or a man that had graced the world with his presence—though Willy knew his parents would have loved for everyone to believe that. Steve wasn't a god from which the model of life itself should have been sculpted. Steven Michael Crowley was a rapist, shot in the back and killed, his golden penis lodged inside of a twelve-year-old girl when it happened.

The army wouldn't show that side of Steve to his parents, but Willy knew, he had always known his brother's true taking nature. The army dressed Steve, cleansed his body; but the shame of reality doesn't wash as easily down the drain as dirt and blood. Willy knew what the man his mother fell on the casket for was truly like, and when she looked at Willy and told him, "It should have been you, you!" Willy snapped.

It was the last of what he could take, and with an anger that had spent a lifetime gaining momentum, he told her the truth about her treasured boy. He told everyone at the packed funeral home that day. It was a knowledge his parents couldn't accept, wouldn't, and he was greeted with a fist from his father that caught him off guard, though it was the old man's ability to lift Willy by the waist of his pants and hurl him outside that truly surprised him. As if the world itself wasn't cold enough to those who came back from Nam, not a word of it could ever equal the chill of the icy ground upon his hands as he lifted his body, and the biting sting of his father's voice when he said, "Welcome back to the states, Soldier. Now I don't ever want to see your god damn face again."

One moment, one spark in the memory of time can define those who allow it. It was that day and his confession with malice that branded Willy down to his soul. He was twenty then, thirty-nine now. It was the last day he ever saw his parents. Whether they were dead or alive, he made no matter of it. There were occasional disdain laden stories, spit out in a composed anger. Yet, to Willy, they were as dead above the ground as his brother was in it. The thought of death always brought Willy's parents back to life, and here he was, burying Brew, faced with a new loss, the memory of his past creeping back into the present.

Luckily, and unluckily, for Willy, Thomas was always right there to snap him back.

~ ~ ~ ~

"What's a matter, death doesn't go well with Schlitz?" Thomas goaded Willy. He could see that Willy's mind had wandered somewhere else, while his body had slowly continued to go through the motions, each passing second removing motion, until eventually, Thomas feared, he would have been staring at a statue instead of a man.

"Listen smart-ass," Willy piped up, reanimated by Thomas's attitude, "I've done good things in my life, and I've done bad things, but the beer has tasted great during both. Besides, if anything, alcohol goes a little too well. Now just shut up and help me dig," Willy stopped again, this time taking a long swig from his can rather than reminiscing.

Thomas watched Willy take the last pull from his beer can which, upon draining, Willy crushed in his hand and threw carelessly into the ever growing pile he had accumulated; the remnants of his thirst resting on top of the burnt grass that graced the entirety of their back yard. Thomas shook his head at Willy's laziness, a touch of disdain in the young man's composure—some of it due to Willy's actions, some due to Thomas's understandable preference of bottles over cans.

Thomas knew he should have been more compassionate. Willy had just lost his best friend in the world, a companion Thomas had often called Willy's "intellectual equal," (though that may have been a stretch for Willy) to a gunshot wound that no veteran or veterinarian could have healed.

"You were a true soldier, Brew. God will certainly award you in heaven," Willy somewhat blubbered, thanks to the added alcohol, his eyes welling up as they laid Brew in the hole.

They had dug his grave in the left end corner of the small yard, which just got a little tighter now that Brew was going to be there for eternity. Watching him mourn for his friend, Thomas felt for Willy's suffering, though, even then it was tough to completely feel his pain; after all, it was *Willy*, a man that was equally difficult to either love or hate.

"Maybe God will give him his dog-tags for his service," Thomas punched once again, continuing the situation with a disrespectfulness he knew he should have stopped. For whatever reason, when it came to Willy and Willy only, controlling his tongue was like trying to control the weather, a common affliction for most nineteen-year-olds, but one Thomas had normally been able to restrain.

He was hitting Willy in every sore spot he could find. Willy wasn't fond of anything that ever questioned, insulted, or even insinuated that any part of the armed services was humorous. Thomas knew Willy had spent his late teens in Vietnam, jumping out of airplanes. He also knew that Willy didn't like to talk about it much, unless that talk was to defend it, his defenses gaining offense the more intoxicated he became, when the memories of it all would fly by his head like bullets from the Viet-Cong.

Most nights, after the suds of time had gotten to Willy, any sideways word about war was a sure thing to start a battle. He had once given Thomas eight stitches with a cross-hook, just for Thomas's proclamation of being a pacifist. His reaction, Thomas felt necessary to inform him, was quite ironic given the statement, and quite fitting for an asshole who only knew how to follow the soldier before him, rather than be so bold as to stand on his own ground. Thomas was pretty sure that Willy didn't even get his meaning, but who in this world ever gets anyone, anyhow?

With the added event of laying Brew to rest that night, Willy hadn't consumed the amount of fuel it normally took to raise his defenses, so Thomas knew that pushing him was still something he could get away with, and for now, he planned on it.

"You're pushing me, Thomas," Willy said sternly, clearly annoyed, but still not angry enough to declare war. The stitches had come when Thomas was only thirteen, at a time when the boy wouldn't punch or fight back. But the boy was a man now, a man who had developed a build that Willy's ever aging figure, while still quite fit for a man of his years, saw as a challenge to his manhood. With Willy's stubborn, always macho mind however, Thomas figured it was only a matter of time before Willy was going to prod him into action. *Willy wouldn't like the outcome this time,* Thomas thought. He was still a pacifist at heart, but if necessary, Thomas would go to war and gladly beat the living shit out of Willy, with no other reason than attaining retribution for a former crime committed, one that had left a memento of the occasion in a small scar underneath Thomas's left eye.

"Grab your shovel and help me finish burying him," Willy told Thomas rather than asking, his crass attitude seeping from a voice and man who hadn't planned on saying goodbye so early to his earthly companion.

Thomas grabbed the shovel Willy had handed him earlier, giving it the same dumbfounded look it had earned from him all night. There were only two shovels in the rusty shed that graced the side of their house, one was the metal shovel in Willy's hand, the other, a snow shovel, which soon became Thomas's undertaking tool.

"It's all we have," Willy had told him when he first looked at the object. "I'll loosen the dirt, you just scoop it up and move it." Thomas had shaken his head as Willy handed him the tool. Willy was an idiot, but Thomas also knew it would get the job done, whether he liked it or not.

Moving the dark soil that had lay hidden underneath the yellow grass, Thomas wondered what the neighbors were thinking, or if they had even seen Willy and Thomas carrying the sack containing Brew's body. Their neighbors—the Rand's—weren't exactly what Thomas would call stable individuals. Coming from Thomas's collection of humanity, that was saying something.

The Rand family was made up of an ancient grandmother, a haggard looking mother, and two obnoxious sons a few years younger than Thomas. The father of the two boys, perhaps the only one with any sense, was nowhere in sight. Barring an occasionally uncomfortable request for butter, Thomas hardly ever saw any of them, but he heard them plenty. With the houses so closely packed together, all it took was a short walk outside to your car to hear a level of profanity emanating from their house that was mind boggling, especially when it came from the old grandmother.

For the most part, they kept to themselves when outside, which is probably why they avoided it; the stress of public ears hearing the true nature of their everyday speech helping to keep their expletive filled tongues contained. Inside the walls was a different story however, where their verbal attacks at one another were free to roam in the comfort of calling each other an "annoying fucking bitch," or an "ungrateful little cocksucker." After hearing their daily onslaughts against their own family, everyone in Thomas's house was quite content to leave them alone, as well as be left alone by them.

Yet, if they had seen Willy and Thomas, what did they think was in the bag? Would they call the police, ruining Willy's plan of burying the evidence? What worried Thomas the most, and what he expected, was that the Rand's would just ignore it, the same way no one ever complained about the way they treated one another. Their tongues were untethered inside the confines of their own home, while everyone on the outside listening kept their tongues quietly on a leash. They probably didn't care so long as it wasn't one of them in the bag, though judging by some of the things Thomas had heard coming from their house over the years, they may have even been happy if one of them was. Besides, this was the mid-eighties. It was a time well before the tell-all generations, when murder in the burbs came as silent to the lips and hands as the body to the grave.

Thomas helped Willy lower Brew into the hole, somehow able to keep his mouth shut the rest of the time. While Thomas's voice rested, it was his eyes that had become active, their focus on the bag that contained the remains of the family beast. No one could deny that Brew was a good dog, and as he threw dirt over his body, Thomas shed a quiet tear in his memory.

They finished burying their companion, the snow shovel having survived the task. "You go inside and get washed up," Willy told him, his hands wringing the handle of the shovel. "I want a moment alone with Brew. And remember, we don't talk about tonight. What I saw, what he was doing, or what we did. It ain't much of nothing, but it's more than we need to go around explaining," Willy ordered. "We never speak of this again. If anyone asks, he got hit by a car. You hear me?" Willy asked, the added force of not wanting to ever repeat those words inflicted in his voice. "Go on," Willy added, nodding in the direction of the house to Thomas, who had let his lack of words speak for his acknowledgment. "Remember what I said, Thomas. Forget everything but what I just said."

Willy's voice rang louder in Thomas's ears as he walked away, a sure sign that he had understood Willy's message as clearly as he had heard the man's words. But there were some things that Thomas would always remember. So often in life, there are some things that you can never forget.

CHAPTER THREE

Do you weep for me kind sir or madam, as I slip into the
recesses of my mind, into the madness, the mayhem, the
solitude that haunts me? Would you love me if I spoke to you in
this voice? Indeed, I have asked the question, the bared
landscape of my heart placed before your eyes. Do you feel it
beat when you think of me? Or do you forsake me?
A Heart Called Thomas

August 1986:

Thomas's death had never worried him. Quite frankly,
it was his life that crept up and scared the hell out of him at
times. It was August 3rd, 1986 when Brewing Cornelius
Crowley, named after what Willy had called, "The best batch
of Schlitz ever made," left this world, his fate written in time
after jumping at the man who aimed a gun at his master's
chest, the faithful servant of Springer Spaniel decent, taking a
bullet that Willy most likely deserved.

Not all heroes die in the light of a bright sun, were the
words Willy spoke to Thomas. Those words, haunting the
young man like a ghost, forever remained in the background
of his mind after that night. He had dealt with loss before, but
Thomas had never seen it so close. It was his first encounter
with death that year.

Willy wasn't a good man. He wasn't even overly kind;
and at times after talking to him, he left Thomas wondering if

the man had any real redeeming value to make his consumption of oxygen anything but a miscarriage of justice to the rest of humanity. Yet, even crap helps grow crops, and that's what Willy's statement helped Thomas to do. They were words that followed Thomas into the darkness, and led him from it as well.

He wasn't sure if Willy really knew what he was saying, or if it was just something Willy had heard from another, and like a parrot, repeated as if the sole possessor. In all Thomas questioned, as much as it pained him to realize, Willy—as most that he encountered in that year of wrong—was right, and Thomas knew it.

Thomas had found no greatness in his days up to that point, just life—imperfect, wanting, with only brief moments of both the spectacular and horrible, where dull words and phrases, such as, "getting by," had consumed Thomas's time. His life, his existence, had been a conquering of the mundane and sedentary, of the real beasts—his own memory and mind. Thomas's greatest battles of the time, were often against the devilish horror of an ordinary Sunday thru Saturday, his greatest enemies led by his own alarm clock, that tortuous messenger of doom. Every second of every day, the vicissitudes of his life had prodded him along the line of the sane and insane.

Still, he moved, knowing we all move on. Whether we choose to or not, life pushes us forward without care of how the force is wearing on us. We go to our churches, pray to our gods, but no one is ever truly certain what all that gets us. We take jobs and harbor the responsibilities that seem more wanted for us than by us. Breathing in the air, we are given no opportunity to stay without anger, joy, love, hate, pain, or satisfaction. As sure as we take breath, we will encounter the rainbow of emotions. As sure as we live, we will die, long before we ever truly know how to do either.

Thomas had spent the years of his life, and most certainly that one, living as if doomed to speak his mind in a world where others only cared for a false whisper—*hypocrites, that is what all men and women are,* Thomas knew. *In life and even in death, we are all hypocrites*; even those who live above the line, for no man or woman ever truly reaches that pinnacle of perception. If you could open their thoughts like a nutshell, you would find truth—dark thoughts that linger in the twisted coil that, even when suppressed, live and spring in us all. Not wealth, nor poverty, can save any man or woman from the uncontrollable beast that is known as human nature.

His is a story of reality, of flaw and imperfection, for in his life, Thomas had seen none untouched by such fates. From the first atom that made the Adam who, so lonely one somber Eve cried for her creation, to the last days we shall revel in breath, we are never perfect, yet, we are never alone. We are the Father. We are the Son. We are the one, the spirit—the light that shines in each other.

~ ~ ~ ~

The mat adorning the steps to their house read "*Welcome,*" and as Thomas wiped the dirt from his shoes before entering, he made a mental note to add, "*To the Asylum*", when he had the chance, just so it would be literally correct. What sense did it make to hide for show what would clearly be present upon entry? Besides, it would go great with Willy's plaque that hung over the basement door and read, "*This is our old house. Our old house has a lot of imperfections. If you care to point them out, than please feel free to get the fuck out.*" It was,

quite honestly, the only possession of Willy's in that house—
Willy included—that Thomas actually respected.

The house had a strange smell of duality that hit
Thomas's nose upon opening the door. In one breath, he was
treated to the most delicious inhalation of apple pie, while in
the next he was struck with the putrid odor of a damp
basement that had gone far too long unattended.

Mama, or Mumma as Thomas and his sister had grown
accustomed to calling her (the new title courtesy of his sister's
inability to pronounce her name properly as a small child)
was sitting on the couch, the voice of the news reporter
mesmerizing her with a spirit of hope.

"*One hundred-seventy miles of running straight, for
what could be up to fifty hours, resting only on his faith, and all
for the cause of raising money for sick children. What a story of
courage, compassion, and will. Best of luck to you, sir. Diane,
back to you,*" Thomas heard through the old speakers of the
television console, the voices greeting his entrance into the
living room that opened to the front door.

He thought for sure that she would have heard the
commotion of burial services being performed, as well as the
crinkling of Willy's beer cans in the backyard. Walking
through the door, however, it became clear to Thomas that
the only world Mumma was living within was the one inside
of the twenty-inch box, its soft hue erasing the reality that
was alive outside of the house.

His mother had changed immensely since Thomas was
a young boy, her parental and personal fate no doubt
intertwined with his own misfortune. Thomas was well aware
that life had a way of changing people, but for Mumma, the
changes seemed amplified, with her physical appearance
mirroring her inner turmoil.

The long black hair she had once possessed now hung just below her shoulders, and was dyed black to hide the visible grey intruders, which with each passing year, were steadily gaining strength in numbers. The hair dye had never bothered him. Why would it? An unwanted fade to grey was just the natural progression of time. It was the hairstyles of the times that irritated Thomas, especially Mumma's favorite—The Permanent. He wasn't sure how it had come to be named that, or even why. All Thomas knew for sure was that no matter how much he looked at it, all he found himself wishing was that it was only temporary.

Mumma had never been a woman of high fashion, her wardrobe a constant barrage of dull colored dress pants and equally offensive cotton tops courtesy of the Caldor Catalog. But her apparel had never phased him. It was the thought that she was fond of her hair slightly resembling the fur of a poodle, and paying someone to make her look like such, which dumbfounded Thomas. She wasn't alone however, as all it took was one flip of the TV or trip to the local mall to see that Mumma was far from being the only puppy in the litter; though he couldn't help but wish that they all would have just keep that puppy at the pound.

She had only been nineteen when Thomas was born, and was still a young woman at thirty-eight. Looking at the slow droops that were beginning to hang on her slightly aged cheeks however, made it easy to see that they were hard years. Mumma was a woman of averages—average height, average weight, average intelligence, living a life that fit perfectly in the same category. To Thomas, she wasn't overly pretty or ugly, yet he could still see where she may once have been. She was just Mumma to him, and if there was anything about her appearance that stood out most in the years that had passed, aside from her hair, it was that unpleasant reminder of the forces that fight against both sexes, as her rear cheeks had already started to resemble her facial ones in their fight against gravity.

Her life without greatness had begun three towns over in Barton, Connecticut, where Prudence Cecilia Main, or "Prudie," as she was known to her friends (not that she had many) was born to Thomas's Grandma and Grandpa Main, both of whom had passed away by the time he was a small boy. Whereas Willy may have still had parents he didn't want, Mumma had parents she wanted, but couldn't have. Life, Thomas had found, could be cruel that way.

The middle child in a group of three girls born one right after the other, Mumma talked fondly of her childhood, all the stories of how much better the world was back when everyone feared God and people were kinder. "You didn't even have to borrow butter or milk, friends and family just brought it over for no other reason than being polite," she would tell Thomas and his sister on occasion, remembering the magnificent blindfold that she wore. They were glorious stories of childhood happiness and wonder, all of which partially ended for her the day Mumma's oldest sister, Victoria, who avoiding curfew at the age of sixteen (as well as the wrath at her congregating with a black man) drowned in Tuttle's Pond, both of the bodies found two days later when they dredged the dirty water.

There was still fun that came with fear, still good times that came from friendly smiles, even after Victoria died; but there was also an empty void in the family that nothing could replace. Grandpa Main, a fairly modest man who died when Thomas was only four-years-old, and who Thomas remembered best from the stories Mumma told in retrospection, developed a coldness towards humanity after the accident. His greatest displeasures in the world revolving around anything associated with "the niggers," who had stolen his daughter from him.

Mumma said he had never been prone to racial indecency before it, and in fact, was quite accepting of colored people until that day. "Their money is just as good as ours," he would tell his girls. The only real concern Grandpa had was that his lax attitude and open mind had pushed Victoria in that direction, or that others may have thought of him as an outcast whose little girl was dating a "negro," as he called them before the accident. Mostly, he was worried about his grocery business and how Victoria's comings and goings would affect sales—the driving force of their lives.

Grandma Main, who died three years after Grandpa, had been a bit of a spitfire in her own day, though she could never quite understand how anyone could be attracted to "a coon," but if that's where her daughter's interest led her eyes and drove her spirit, she accepted the decision. Watery graves make thoughts change however, and the quiet racism that had lived under his Grandmother's accepting skin, seeped out after Victoria's death like venom from the fangs of a snake, paralyzing any common sense decency, and leaving only hate free to prevail.

Mumma professed that she and her younger sister, Thomas's Aunt Connie, who he had the fondest memories of all from Mumma's side of the family, never once cared to blame the young man's color for Aunt Victoria's death.

"It's this fucked up society," Thomas had listened to his Aunt Connie tell Mumma during the last visit she had ever made to their house. Somehow or another, the conversations between the sisters always seemed to sink back to the topic of

Tuttle's Pond, as if their feet were as heavy in the water as Aunt Victoria and her boyfriend's.

"They never should have felt like they had to sneak around in the first place, but no, heaven forbid you saw a white girl with a black man. It's all hogwash. I've had sex with a black man and I ain't ashamed of it. Hell, it was the best sex I've ever had. Huh." Aunt Connie was close to finishing, before her erratic mind reopened the book. "And what in the world was she thinking? I don't know about Burpee, but we both know she couldn't swim worth a dam. Poor guy was crucified after he died, when you and I both know how much he loved her. Hell, I bet a million dollars he drowned trying to save her dumb ass."

Mumma would just sit there, shaking her head and wincing at the bluntly stated facts that made up Aunt Connie's experiences in the world.

Listening to her, Thomas often wondered if it was the drugs that had dismantled Aunt Connie's filter, or if she had just been born that way. Whichever it was, it was the straightforward, tell-all attitude that he loved the most about her. While Mumma was a "close it all in" type of person, Aunt Connie made sure she let out plenty for the both of them.

Connie had always had a way of making Prudie both laugh and cry, though, it always tended to be more of the latter. Without her, Prudie would never have met Joseph— Thomas's father—who had come to the grocery store one day sniffing around for Connie.

Connie had gained quite a reputation by the time the girls were older teenagers, her availability and eagerness towards sexual advances were well known throughout the small town of Barton. Where her popularity with other girls fell, her fame with the young men of the town had never soared higher.

"It was almost as if she needed to make up for all the men Victoria couldn't touch," Mumma would tell them years later, knowing that Aunt Connie had continued the pace well into adulthood.

The loss of Victoria had been a tragedy for them all, but for Connie it became a severe emotional loss, a void to be filled—one that she was determined to stuff with physical love. Joseph had already gotten her once, and when he walked into the grocery store that next morning, he was looking for seconds.

"What do you want?" Connie had asked, unhappy to see him. Next mornings were Connie's curse in life. Drugs, booze, and sexual indiscretions were the clouds that made up her nights. Yet, even then, she had a difficult time accepting her life in the haze. Seeing her mistakes displayed so clearly in the early daylight only added to the pain she could never completely fog over. It was a continuous cycle, feeding her desire to alter her reality and bury her agony. Her destiny, no different than that of an old time movie vampire, unable to walk without suffering in the light of day.

His name was Joseph Brent Thompson, and while he was smug, arrogant, and chauvinistic to the point of disgust, he had been blessed with one saving grace in Connie's blurry and bloodshot eyes the night before—his chiseled body and stride, one that accentuated his firm rear end in his tight work pants.

"Hello to you," he smiled conceitedly, dropping a pack of gum in front of her register. Where Connie had found his confidence the night before pleasing, especially wrapped in such a nice package, she was now sickened by what he considered the gift of his existence.

Why, Connie? Why? was all she could think to herself as they stood there, a pack of Spearmint gum the only thing between them, and Buffalo Springfield's "For What It's Worth," playing in the background. Normally, the girls weren't allowed to touch the radio that played over the speakers of their three aisle store, but their father wasn't around, and Connie was a constant California dreamer.

Prudie knew why he was there, and that it wasn't for her. Yet, the moment she saw him, she wanted him. Prudie was far from living the loose lifestyle that Connie had chosen, but she was far from the prude her name implied, as well. Connie was ignoring him. Clearly, whatever had happened in the past was a going to stay buried there. At least while Connie was sober.

Unhappy with Connie's disinterest, perhaps too complacent to care, Joseph was ready to leave when he spotted Prudie. She wasn't as fresh as Connie, who had a natural beauty, but she wasn't anything Joseph would turn away from either. Looking at her tight blue top, her cross hanging in between her breasts—perfection curving cotton— filled his eyes.

"Well, well, and how are you today?" He asked, stalking her, knowing in the way that only a man can know, that he had her the minute she looked at him.

"I'm fine, and you?" Prudie returned, reading him like a book, knowing in a way that only a woman can know, that she had him right where she wanted him. She was surprisingly cunning, unsuspectingly sneaky, and she had two husbands that could prove it. Prudie wanted Joe, and she got him.

Nine months later, thanks in part to his Aunt Connie's initial generosity, and most certainly to his mother's finishing touch, Thomas Joseph Thompson was born.

"Her mouth is what killed your grandparents," Mumma would confess after every one of Aunt Connie's visits, her slightly saddened eyes watching out the kitchen window as her sister got into her car to drive away. Thomas knew she didn't mean it, or that it was even possible, but Mumma always worried a little extra after Aunt Connie's visits, and rightfully so.

They were saying goodbye in more ways than one, leaving Thomas to wonder if Mumma knew that her younger sister wasn't meant for the life of an older woman. Perhaps it was just a fear. The drug use had gotten worse each visit, with Aunt Connie's mannerisms and twitching more visible in each sitting. She was beautiful, yet worn-down. Her long brown hair, which had been left straight, had gone from silk to straggly in appearance. Her skin, which had always shone a golden tan, had slowly turned a greyish pale color, the byproduct of her habitual chain smoking and poor blood circulation.

She had developed an addiction to heroin that eventually took her life, leaving Mumma the only sister left standing, and on a pretty wobbly set of legs to boot. The combination of tragedies had cost Mumma both of her siblings, with one sister drowning in the muck-filled water of Tuttle's Pond, and the other drowning in a self-indulgent pool of her own vomit.

The only positive they could find from the loss of Connie, was that Thomas's sister was still too young to understand it all.

"We always ask how. How could someone let themselves get that way or do those things? When we should be asking why and what happened?" Mumma would say, airing the opinion that lived within her, and raising the questions that she regretted never giving a voice while Connie was still alive.

"Can you believe that, Ted? One hundred and seventy miles running, simply amazing," Diane Summers proclaimed, her declaration reaching out from the newsroom to the television console, filling the air of the living room with voices.

"Now that is a true act of God. Praise Jesus," Mumma said.

Her habit of speaking aloud to herself had steadily grown over the years, though in Mumma's mind, the lord was always listening. If the mood was right, she had even taken to giving what Thomas called "Hallelujah High-Fives," in which she would raise both her hands in the air as if she was ready for Jesus to slap her five in acknowledgment for all the kind words and support she was giving him.

As far back as Thomas could remember she had regularly attended church, always dragging him along; but it wasn't until the day Thomas lost religion that she truly found Jesus, as if he was no more than a child lost to the world.

"Have you found Jesus?" Mumma would feel the need to ask people occasionally, to which most would either reply with politeness, "Yes," or simply smile and walk away. There was a part of Thomas that always hoped someone would reply back, "Oh my god, you lost him, God's gonna be pissed," just to see how Mumma would have reacted, though no one ever did.

Why did he have to be found anyhow? Thomas had found himself asking over the years. *And why were people always looking for Jesus more in hard times than any other*? Seemed to Thomas that everybody knew exactly where Jesus was when the sun was out, but heaven forbid the clouds came, because next thing you know, everyone was out looking for him again. The way Thomas saw it, if people couldn't find the beauty in a day full of dark clouds that brought rain, there was no way they could ever truly appreciate the warmth that comes with a blue sky full of sunshine.

Religion had become a crutch for Mumma's heart when she needed it, for the days she never planned on—like the day Thomas had come home different, and the days that followed right after, when his father walked out on them without so much as a goodbye. She had already experienced loss, but those days in between were the ones that damaged her more than any other. While Thomas turned jaded, Mumma turned to Jesus. Thomas knew he wasn't handling it in the best way, though he feared her alternative was even worse, as religion was beginning to keep Mumma from standing on her own two feet and ever truly healing. Mumma's road was paved with good intentions, but even with a heart in the right place, Thomas had begun to fear that she was heading in the wrong direction.

"Isn't that an incredible show of God's strength, Thomas?" she asked, this time speaking and looking directly at Thomas as he took his second step into the small, odiferous house.

Looking at the TV, Thomas wanted to speak his mind on the subject; but there wasn't anyone in that house, with the exception of his sister, that he ever planned on giving that luxury. His sister was the only one who could handle it. Certainly, Mumma could not.

Thomas wanted to tell her that the young man's endeavor took training, hard work, and that while a belief in God may have aided the man, Thomas could gladly point out the countless number of incredible acts that mankind had succeeded in accomplishing with not only other gods, but in some cases, none at all. Instead, Thomas just followed the road to peace, and answered politely with the only response she truly wanted, "It sure is, Mumma."

By the age of nineteen, Thomas had already learned that when it came to talking politics or religion, everyone wants your thoughts, what they don't want, is your honest opinion. It was the double-sided nature of life that made it so beautifully aromatic one moment, and a grotesque, rotting stench the next.

"Come pray with me."

She was so wrapped in the lord that she hadn't even noticed the dirt on his hands, or the blood on his t-shirt.

"Sure, Mumma," Thomas agreed.

"Lord, guide that man on the journey he is taking in your name. May you lift his legs when he is tired and carry him to his destination. This we ask of you, Amen," she prayed. Thomas sat quietly, holding her hand and wondering why she was praying for a healthy man instead of just praying for the sick kids. It wasn't that he didn't believe in the power of kind thoughts, Thomas just found most of them misguided, and often wondered, *if prayer truly worked, would there really be any need to keep praying*?

Thomas was sure that over the course of time people had prayed for just about everything. All you had to do was watch a Miss America pageant to see all the world peace being prayed for. *If God had already blessed those girls with so much beauty, why wouldn't he take it any extra step and answer their prayers*? Mumma didn't want to hear talk like that however, and it wasn't his place to try and change her mind. All Thomas ever prayed for was the allowance of voicing his opinions without someone feeling the need to fix him, the way "Good Christians" always felt so obliged to try and do. But everyone knew the test of time religion had endured, and Thomas just figured there must be a sense of entitlement that came along with the journey. What he couldn't figure out, though, was how everybody seemed to look past all the immoral bloodshed and death that had walked by its side on the path to purity and enlightenment.

　　"Why are your hands so dirty?" Mumma finally asked, looking down as she held them in hers, the soil that had stained his skin snapping her from the trance. Thomas hesitated to answer, which was the unexpected break he needed, as the front door miraculously opened to Willy cursing the bugs that had congregated by the front porch light. *Praise Jesus*, Thomas thought to himself, *this is Willy's mess, let him explain it*.

CHAPTER FOUR

August 1986:

He listened first from the bathroom, where Thomas washed his face, hands, underarms, and privates, all in that order. Thomas had wanted to take a shower, but he knew with the heat in the house that he was going to be sweating all night anyhow. The best the fans ever seemed to do was just blow hot air back on him, so there was no sense wasting all the water. Besides, Thomas was more worried about being fresh in the morning before seeing the rest of a world, a world that, no matter what level of cleanliness he achieved, always seemed finer primped and pressed than Thomas could ever accomplish.

After a quick overall inspection of his body, Thomas put on a plain white t-shirt and old pair of shorts to sleep in. He had been blessed with a slightly above average height, lean, yet somewhat muscular frame, no doubt a gift from his father's side of the family, and one that was aided by age and the steady work out that came with Thomas's daily physical labor. His dark brown hair, another paternal present, hung casually around Thomas's shoulders, framing the day old stubble that had graced his face, all of it seen through the one donation Thomas's mother had made to his appearance— those hazel colored eyes.

Thomas hadn't seen any of the generous genetic benefactors from his father's side of the family in years, not that he expected to. He never really saw them much when his father was around either, as it was only once or twice a year that they had received a visit from his father's Uncle Tom, who apparently, Thomas had been named after.

The family was as low in numbers as they were in fat, Thomas's father being an only child born to a late in life couple—his Grandma and Grandpa Thompson—who had been long deceased before Thomas was even born.

They were his blood, his heritage, yet still no more to Thomas than thin framed images in old pictures that Mumma had removed from the walls years ago. When Thomas was a child, he would spend hours imagining that they were well dressed and pressed people of greatness, quite possibly descendants of kings. As an adult, he imagined they were already lifeless in those pictures, poor folks wearing the donated clothes of another, whose dead bodies had been placed in the sitting position and posed for entertainment as if they were still alive. Either way, Thomas was thankful to share the physical build of those black and white ghosts.

As Thomas cleaned up, Willy was sitting at the kitchen table with Mumma by his side, presenting his story to her, with Thomas trying his best to catch just enough of the details to keep from blowing their cover. He didn't have any great interest in protecting Willy, but Mumma was too fragile for the truth. Every once in a while a glimmer of the woman she once was came to her face, and Thomas wanted to keep it that way, even if it meant keeping secrets from her, not that he enjoyed the deception. Sometimes however, for reasons people think are best, men and women bury secrets the way dogs bury bones. Willy and Thomas were no different than Brew, because they had just buried a bag full of both.

The laundry hamper near the bathroom door was as full as always, so with extra care, Thomas placed the used facecloth in it. He tried his best to bury it below a few other towels and articles of clothes, a small act of respect that would keep Mumma from having to lift a piece of cloth that was just on his neither regions right up in her face at the top of the pile. Turning off the bathroom light, Thomas headed down the short hallway to his bedroom, which is when he noticed the movement from her room.

Thomas wasn't sure how much of the commotion she had heard, or how much he should tell her. Although one thing Thomas had already come to find, was that his sister could handle more than most. Where most people struggled with the realities of life, she accepted them. She didn't have a choice. Her entire life was built on a level of acceptance that most people could never attain. She lived it without thinking anything of it. If only the rest of the world could have been that way.

"What are you doing up, Maybe Baby?" Thomas asked, grinning at her, the Strawberry Shortcake night light he had given her for Christmas the past year, emanating its soft glow throughout her bedroom.

She jumped up, running to give him a hug—Maybe always hugged Thomas upon sight. He was her big brother, her protector, and in many ways, Maybe's best friend. She had been born different; a beautiful affliction that often brought with it ugly and unwanted stares as they walked the streets. Yet there were hidden lives in every corner of their little shoreline town of Hayward, Connecticut, and people who cared more about the appearance of normalcy than the happiness they would have found accepting reality. It bothered Thomas how they looked at her; their sharp glances, like jagged edges that he could never smooth, were always a threat to crude his own attitude.

While they held their noses to the sky, Maybeline couldn't have cared less about keeping airs. She carried her life on her slightly round face and the constant barrage of smiles she offered, even when the person looking back refused to return the gesture. It was a hindrance to their humanity, their own loss. Especially when most people spent lifetimes wanting, trying to make themselves someone special, only to end up with a pocket full of fools gold. Maybeline Victoria Crowley had been born different, but she lived with a richness of spirit, one that had left her better off than most. *How sad it is*, Thomas often thought, *when the worst cases of disability you've seen in your life, are those poor, unfortunate souls, afflicted with cases of normalcy.*

She held on to Thomas as he looked down at her, her light brown hair illuminated with scattered patches of strawberries, until finally, Thomas said, "Thank you, Maybe, but why don't you get back in bed. Here, I'll help tuck you in."

Thomas was only nine-years-old when Maybeline Victoria Crowley was born. After what had been the worst year of his life, Maybe was the one true light in what felt like an eternity of gloom. It was also the end of Thomas's short stint as the man of the house, as Maybe's birth sealed Willy's fate. While Thomas had never cared for Willy, whose company constantly left him feeling like an unwanted nuisance, he was glad to have another man around, even if it was a dipshit like Willy.

Upon first sight, a part of Thomas hated his sister. Looking at her in the hospital on the day she was born, he was no better than the people on the streets. She was different and, to his immature eyes, ugly. Thomas had never seen a baby that looked like her; but there she was, his brand new sister, the monster in his closet.

It was a fear of both the known and unknown that had gripped him, a worry of the world that would forever hang on his shoulders. But even in the fear and anxiety, there was still love inside of Thomas. He knew it after just one small moment of insignificance. When placing his hand near the bundled up creature in his mother's arms, Maybe Baby grabbed hold of his finger, and in one small second in time, changed a piece of him back to the boy he should have been.

Thomas knew right then that Maybe wasn't ugly, he was the one wearing that title. Without any real idea about any of it, Maybe taught her young brother that life is nothing more than a mirror, and that what we see in others, is often no more than a reflection of ourselves. But even a person with sight can be blind, and even though Thomas had been granted the realization, he was still a young boy at the time. Nothing would ever stop him from reflecting his fears upon her, even when it was the greatest thing he would try to avoid.

With her tiny hand wrapped around his finger, her five gentle digits embracing his pointer finger in their first ever hug, he watched as her eyes adjusted to the world. As her focus grew in wonder, the doctors explained to Mumma and Willy that they believed—judging by her features—that the child who would spend her entire life looking up, was most likely born with Down Syndrome.

"She don't look much different," Thomas remembered telling Mumma with optimism in his new found view.

"She's a gift from God," Mumma replied loudly, as if volume would help confirm her love. Either that or she was still coming to grips with it all. "Her name is Maybeline,"

Mumma, who hadn't been able to decide on a name beforehand, stated with tears in her eyes.

Thomas looked at his mother, and for a moment, wondered if they were tears of joy or sadness. Perhaps she needed her hand held, too, he thought. So taking his first ever lead from his sister by grabbing his mother's hand, that's just what Thomas did.

Holding his mother's hand, Thomas proudly told her and anyone else who cared to listen, "I'm gonna call her Maybe!"

Mumma cried a lot the first few weeks Maybe was alive. No matter how many times anyone asked her what was the matter, or if she was, "okay?" she would keep crying and looking at her daughter. Thomas knew some of the tears Mumma had shed before Maybe's birth were for him, most of them over what had happened. She had been prone to water-falling ever since that day, and while Thomas knew she wondered what he thought of their new addition, she never directly asked him. Watching Thomas with her—smiling— she didn't need too.

It had been almost two years since her boy had limped home, and a part of that pain had been replaced by her denial of the act. His father was gone, yet they still never talked about it—ever. They were the only two left to carry that pain, and no matter what reminders life brought them, it was to be carried on the inside. In Mumma's eyes, Jesus knew what had happened, and he was the only person who needed to know. It was their burden to forever keep the secret, their struggle to be right, even when everything about it seemed wrong.

Having to deal with the past, as well as the quality of Maybe's future, was just another kick from life's foot directly into Mumma's stomach—another blow she would ask Jesus to absorb. But Thomas knew in his heart that as difficult as it was for her to accept, that Mumma loved Maybe. He didn't think that anyone ever asked for a baby that was born different. Mumma certainly hadn't. In all the times she was asked, all she ever answered before the birth was, "I just want it to be healthy." She hadn't taken any tests to see what kind of child they were getting, and Thomas was now glad they hadn't. He didn't think Mumma would have changed her mind about having Maybe. Thomas couldn't believe that if he tried. But he wouldn't have put it past Willy to accidentally introduce Mumma to the stairs, had he been privy to the conditions.

Thomas had been entangled in his own web of anger and joy that day—confusion really—yet he still noticed Willy's expressions. Standing a few feet away from the hospital bed, Willy was coming to grips with the hand he had just been dealt. The Royal Flush Willy had envisioned, turned into a pair of Jokers. One he had haphazardly inherited, and one he had picked from his own deck. It's tough betting when the cards that beat you are your own. Still, Thomas knew Mumma truly believed that Maybe was a gift; and with that love, no matter how Willy played it, Maybe had just the hand she needed.

"What are they talking about?" Maybe asked, her curiosity leading Thomas to wonder how much she had already heard. In their little house, hearing things was never much of a problem. The thin walls of the small three bedroom house made sure of it. Noises filtered through the rooms, often peaking questions from Maybe about why Mumma and her father were often screaming at the lord on nights when she thought they should have been asleep, and leading her to figure, "God must get awfully tired having to answer prayers past bedtime."

"What have you heard?" Thomas asked Maybe, not wanting to upset her right before bed if she didn't already know what had happened.

"I heard Daddy talking about Brew. He's dead," she said, a matter-of-fact tone to her words, words that with a slight lisp, the one that had given birth to them calling their mother Mumma, gave all the impression of someone who had their tongue bitten by a bee.

"Yeah, Brew's gone."

"He was a good boy—except that time he stole my Teddy Ruxpin."

"Now, you know he was just playing, and he did give it back," Thomas reminded her, before asking, "You okay?"

"Yeah," she said, as the tears began to form. Even in her sadness, Maybe was still taking the news better than Mumma. Sitting on the edge of the bed, Thomas could hear his mother crying, the sound of her sobs flooding the hallway as they streamed their way into Maybe's room.

"I loved him. He gave good kisses," Maybe said, smiling through the pain, her face scrunched in the same way it always did when Brew would see her, his excited tail showing that a lick on her face was on its way. Brew was always good to Thomas, he was good to everyone in the house; but Brew always loved Maybe just a little bit more. *What a cruel world,* Thomas thought, *when someone like Maybe, who deserved such love, ever had to lose it.*

"I'll miss him," she said, the tears escaping her eyes.

"So will I, but we need to remember those kisses, okay?" he told her, trying to convince her to look at the positive.

"I will. Can we can get a new dog tomorrow?" She asked, showing her age more than her resilience. Even when faced with death, kids always seem to have a way of focusing more on life.

"Maybe, Maybe Baby," Thomas told her, before giving her a kiss on the forehead and walking to the door.

"Thomas," she stopped him with one more question before he was gone, "Brew didn't get hit by a car, did he?"

"No, he didn't," Thomas told her honestly, amazed that at the age of ten, she already had the ability to see through her own father's bullshit.

"I didn't think so," she said quietly, before turning to hug her pillow while fading to sleep, with a tear in her eye, and a memory of Brew that would forever rove in her heart.

~ ~ ~ ~

It had been a rough morning already. Hell, it had been a rough life. His head was dazed from staying up too late, his consumption reaching levels even he wasn't conditioned to handle. It wasn't just the alcohol though, every morning since Willy had meet Prudie had seemed to come with a new difficulty. Even a simple act like reading the newspaper came with subtle, yet scraping annoyances. Most of all it was her, his own daughter, that truly added the salt into the wound of his existence. It was her life that tormented Willy, without him ever speaking a word about it, at least, not ones that he ever remembered uttering the next day.

He had every right to voice his opinion if he wanted. After all, she was just another false god to add to the list his brother had topped. This time however, it was Willy's own mind that had been the creator of the illusion. Long before

Maybe's birth, he had deluded himself with the vision of his future heir—a boy, no doubt—but that's not what Willy got, not even close. *I couldn't even get a normal girl to deal with*, he often scoffed in mental seclusion.

Somewhere, he knew his parents were laughing at him. Somehow, they must have felt his fate. *"Did my revelation shatter your dreams, Mother, the way my own hopes rest in pieces on the floor?"* He asked their images, indulging the despised mirages that still remained in his memory; those false creations with which all madmen speak.

It was five years ago when he had thought about ending it, right after her fifth birthday and another doctor's appointment he had anxiously been trying to avoid. But you can't hide from the truth. Looking or not, it finds you.

"She's hopeless," were the stone cold words that the doctor had used. His less than comforting medical opinion was like an ice sculpture being carved and frozen in Willy's mind. Willy loved her, he knew he did, but it wasn't what he expected. *She* wasn't what he expected.

"Come on, Maybe, let's take a ride to the store," Willy had told her.

It was rare that he wanted to take her anywhere, preferring for the most part to hide her at home, or if they did need to venture out, he would always find a way to pawn the trip off on Prudie. Taken aback by his sudden interest, yet hopeful, Prudie still thought nothing of the mundane act of a father taking his daughter to the store with him. If anything, Willy thought she was happy about it, that she probably hoped he was finally ready to relate with this beautiful gift from God, as Prudie had called her. Willy didn't see it that way however; for him, Maybe was his penance. Every bad act, every small crime, piled into one round face.

He drove to Crystal Hill, a large rock pimple on the face of the earth far away from the hustle of humanity, where the only people he had to worry about finding him were the hikers that occasionally graced the rocks. When he pulled in, he knew he was safe. There wasn't another car in sight.

He looked at her in the rearview mirror before he opened the door. Her eyes, peering out at the trees in wonder, were oblivious to the fact that she was about to die. *Don't look at her,* Willy told himself, quickly getting out the car, afraid that if he waited too long he would chicken out. It was one thing to kill an enemy in Vietnam that was pointing a gun at you; it was another to take a life from someone with an empty hand.

Willy never once felt the car move while he stuffed the hose he had stolen from work into the tailpipe, or when he taped around it in the hopes of creating a greater seal. There was plenty of gas in the car, at least, plenty enough for what he had planned. Standing outside, his duty almost done, he placed the opposite end of the hose in the cracked car window of the passenger front seat, before finally gaining the courage to look at her. Still, she didn't look back. She was abnormally quiet, and for a moment, Willy wondered if somehow the fumes had already taken effect.

Even when he was standing outside of the car in the safety of the fresh air, Willy never once considered staying there. His destiny, his daughter, his shame and sadness born of consequence, was to be in that car with her. He brought her into this world, he would guide her out, and they would enter heaven or hell together.

~ ~ ~ ~

"Daddy? Daddy? Daaaddy?"

Willy wasn't sure how long it would take, or how much longer he could take her talking to him. He had stuffed rags in the cracks of the window that would have led air in from the safety outdoors, but it wasn't the perfect seal he had hoped for. He had used too much tape sealing the pipe, leaving only an empty, useless roll.

"What, Maybe?" He snipped, upset she was still breathing—talking—and that he was with her to do the same.

"Don't the trees look pretty in the wind?" She asked, her head swaying with them.

"Yes," he appeased her, without taking a glance outside, his focus on her alone. "Just keep looking at them. If you get tired, just go to sleep."

He couldn't say that he felt any different, or that anything was happening, it had only been a minute or two, but watching her sway in the rearview mirror, Maybe looked affected.

"Daddy?" She asked again, her voice hypnotically serene, "Do you think one tree knows when it's different from the others?"

Her question surprised him, mostly because he had never thought about it. So why in the world would she?

"I don't know. Why?" He asked, curious where the loss of oxygen had taken her mind.

"Because, they all dance different, just like me."

She wasn't dancing anymore. She wasn't swaying in her own different way. She was looking directly at the reflection of his eyes in the rearview mirror, and for one brief moment, Willy could have sworn that she was looking directly into his soul.

How could I do this? Looking at her, his hurt, his shame bubbling to the surface, *I can't do this.* Within a second he was outside of the car, the fresh air stinging his lungs. He pulled the hose from the window, but it was panic that now filled him, and he was afraid that the act alone wouldn't save them. Rushing to the back of the car, he pried at the warm tape that had begun to melt to the hose and exhaust pipe, burning his fingers as he quickly reached to remove it with his hands.

On his knees, with the torn tape scattered around him in the dirt and rocks, Willy leaned against the car, looked up at the blue sky, then finally over at the trees that he had always seen as exactly the same, each one dancing differently in the breeze. Perhaps Willy didn't quite dance the same either. The man with an iron heart who had walked away from his own parents, the piece of shit son who had survived Vietnam while greatness came home in a box, was the father of a girl who danced different, just like those trees, just like him. Looking at them, enjoying the dance for the first time ever, Willy cried, and when he was done, Willy cried some more.

CHAPTER FIVE

Present Day:
"You were five-years-old the first time I ever lay my eyes upon you. Needless to say, I was more than a little surprised—not of what you were—but by the fact that you were alive at all. Time had stood still for me, as if each day was the same torture, repeating like a broken record. I knew Prudie would move on. Her main objective in life was to follow the line, be a wife, a mother, yet even knowing that, I never expected it to have been so soon."

Beep. Beep. Beep.

Each beep in the background was like a year in time. Each year, lost in his effort to retell the tale, each beep in time adding a new mistake and losing a piece of the truth. He knew his mind rode the edge of insanity like a razor, but even a sharp razor loses it blade over time, leaving nothing more than the dull memory.

"Your condition worried me. He had been through enough, yet I saw him with you. It was simple, easy. He was happy when he looked at you—genuinely, and I loved you for that. I loved that about him. He looked at you the way I should always have looked at him. Still, standing there in the open, still unseen, I was frozen to being the man I should have been. I should have walked over to him. He was my son. Life had separated us, but only because I allowed it. Time, the warden of action, had imprisoned my ability to make it right—I was a coward. I had straightened myself in the wandering years, kicked the sauce, repented in the house of the lord to God and God alone—no other would know my past—only him. Still, standing there, I was alive in hell, determined to live the life of a man lost in the shadows."

~ ~ ~ ~

August 1986:
"Mumma, I think I'm broken."

Maybe's ten-year-old face held the disappointment, while her hand gripped the strap from her sundress, which having come undone, was now hanging from her shoulder.

"Did that darn thing come loose again?" Mumma asked, leaning over the table to adjust it for Maybe, and trying her best not to lean on the syrup Maybe had smothered generously over her waffles. When it came to breakfast, Maybe loved waffles, pancakes, and anything and everything else she could drench in Aunt Jemima.

"I don't know why you even buy her dresses like that, they just keep busting loose. You'd be better off just getting something without all that nonsense," Willy grumbled. He had found a change of heart regarding Maybe's existence on the day he drove her to Crystal Hill, but even a better heart tends to lose its own strap of compassion when riddled with flaws.

He was tired. He had stayed up too late watching Johnny Carson on the *Tonight Show* in between tears and beers over Brew's death; and while Willy didn't dare say it, Thomas knew a part of him was anxious about going to work, as well. Normally, when a man points a gun at you, for good or bad, you never see that person again. Either you go away or they do. Willy wasn't granted that luxury. He had never called the police, as bringing attention to why he was in the situation to have a weapon pointed at him in the first place was the last thing he wanted.

"She loves these dresses. Besides, she has every right to feel just as pretty as any other girl," Mumma told him, actually showing a bit of fortitude, which for Mumma was rare.

Prudie had spent the last ten years putting up with Willy and his grumpy ways, catering to his imperfections. But she had lost one husband already, and while she would never admit it, Prudie felt like a part of Joseph had left years before he ever physically walked away. While Joseph Thompson was gone, Willy was there, a provider for the family. Whether she had trapped him into it was for her to tell, though everyone who knew the situation had their suspicions. All Thomas knew for sure was that whether Willy was a pain in the ass or not, Mumma appeared determined to keep the asshole around.

Thomas stood at the counter by the sink, while everyone else remained seated at the kitchen table. He was trying to butter his toast, and struggling like a small child at the task. He couldn't help but think about how his life mirrored that struggle, the cold stick of butter—much like happiness—an almost impossible task for Thomas to spread in any uniform or convenient manner.

"Why can't you buy the soft butter?" Thomas asked Mumma, frustrated with the clumps, too impatient to wait for them to melt.

"You want the fancy butter, you buy it. You know we can't afford that ritzy stuff. And there's nothing wrong with that butter we have."

"I don't know how you put up with this stuff," Thomas said, his impatience showing in the torn, half-buttered piece of toast on his plate, as well as the mouth full of Puffed Rice cereal he was trying to consume while talking at the same time. Folding the toast over in an attempt to get an even amount of butter with each bite, Thomas asked, with a stuffed mouth, "You want me to drop you off at the center on my way to work, Maybe Baby?"

"Yeeeessss!" Maybe yelled, startling them all a bit, but bringing a smile to Thomas's cereal filled mouth.

"Why don't you all drive in together?" Mumma asked, clearly dumbfounded at why everyone had to drive in separate cars and waste gas. A dollar a gallon was enough to pay for one car, so why pay it for two that were heading in the same direction?

"I think we've had enough excitement driving in together as it is," Thomas said, eyeballing Willy as he spoke.

"Don't you be late for work again. Every time you drive in on your own you end up late," Willy sternly stated, his eyes peering over his issue of the Hayward Daily Newspaper.

"I won't. Besides, even if I am, I'm sure Roy wouldn't hold it against me. Not after everything I've seen," Thomas said casually, but with purpose, noting the leverage he held over Roy.

Roy Brant was the general foreman at Twill Extruders, Thomas and Willy's boss, as well as the man who Thomas had watched aim a gun at Willy the night before; a man whose wife Willy had been shacking up with on the side.

"By the way, anything in that newspaper about gunshots? I could have sworn I heard some last night," Thomas added, with the sole purpose of letting Willy know who the real boss in the situation was, before slurping down the rest of the milk in his bowl and placing it in the overfilled sink.

"Not a word," Willy answered, looking Thomas directly in the eyes, before sinking his own below the paper again.

"It doesn't feel right having breakfast without Brew here begging for food," Mumma interjected, ignoring the conversation the two were having. What was a life and death situation for Willy and Thomas, and death only for Brew, was everyday banter from where Mumma was seated in the conversation.

"Can we get a new dog today?" Maybe asked.

"No, not today," Willy answered quickly from behind the newspaper, afraid if he made eye contact with Thomas that the young man might have had the desire to make Willy reconsider. "Let's let the grass grow over his grave first. We need some time to mourn."

Thomas never would have admitted it out-loud, but he actually agreed with Willy, and thought a bit of healing time in honor of Brew would be for the best.

"You ready, kiddo?" Thomas asked Maybe, who answered by inhaling the last three bites of her waffles as she stood up, causing her to choke, while the rest of them remained unaffected. The normal jumping up to begin the Heimlich-maneuver had faded from their behavior years ago. Maybe had always had the problem, her large tongue and thick neck providing the difficulty, an inconvenience for her that rarely lasted more than a second or two.

"Thomas, can you drop these pies off at the church while you're by the center?" Mumma asked. "I want to make sure they have some, just in case they have any needy folks stop in."

Mumma was terrible with finances, spending most (if not all) of what she made working part time as a cashier at the Tiger Lily Tea House in the Hayward Village, on baked goods for the local church. Willy, on the other hand, was excellent at budgeting; though his greatest monetary skill was informing Mumma of her financial deficiencies.

"More pies?" Willy whined, too tired to go on with one of his usual rants about income over outcome.

Mumma chose to ignore his comment. Besides, she couldn't seem to help herself. She was constantly worried about someone going hungry at the church, as if a gang of starving stragglers was just on the outskirts of town looking for the only thing that would provide them with the sustenance of survival—the lord almighty in the comfort of the Hayward Baptist Church, and Prudie Crowley's apple pies. Yet, the needy nomads, men who fit ironically in the mold of her ex-husband, never seemed to appear. Willy knew they wouldn't, and if anything, he would have bet all the money in Sunday's collection plate that Pastor Carr would have eaten the pies well ahead of any poor stranger's arrival.

"No problem, Mumma, I'll drop 'em off," Thomas told her, bringing a smile to Mumma's face before turning to Maybe and bringing a joyful grin to her face, as well, when he said, "Come on Maybe, let's get outta here."

~ ~ ~ ~

Maybe loved everything about Thomas driving her to camp, but there was one reason that stood out above all the others— the music.

Maybe loved to sing at the top of her lungs, something Mumma never allowed in the car. All Mumma ever had on the radio was the dull, lull-somebody-to-sleep, holy-roller channel.

The tape player in Thomas's six-year-old, two-toned blue, Chevy Chevette was already starting to go, but the slight crack of the speakers weren't even close to bothering Maybe. All it took was one look at her when they stopped at the lights by Benny's Hardware Store, and the giant smile she was sporting as she joined Simon and Garfunkel in singing "Mrs. Robinson," to know that there was true beauty in the world. Watching her, it was one of those inconsequential moments, the kind that meant nothing grand to the world around Thomas, yet, brought his heart the joy of having everything he needed.

Maybe had begged Thomas to buy the *Bookend's* tape the last time they had visited the Monte Cristo Music Store. "Their songs are like butterflies whispering in my ears," she had told him. How could Thomas say, "No?" to that.

The looks Maybe would get while singing in the car were priceless. It was as if people had no idea that someone with an extra chromosome still had the ability to vocalize their enjoyment of music. In the cases where someone looked at her in a disrespectful way, Thomas would gladly ease their disgust by joining her in singing at the top of his lungs, while ever so politely flipping that asshole the bird and a smile.

~ ~ ~ ~

Maybe spent every Monday through Friday during the summer at the Stanton Center, a day camp for kids with special needs. It was a convenient place for them to mingle and play with others who understood life the way they did, not that they saw it any different than anyone else. On the occasions when they did, Thomas couldn't help but notice that they were ones who were usually right.

Sending her there, or anywhere he wasn't, had always concerned Thomas. Leaving her safety in the hands of others always had a way of bringing new light to Thomas's old fears. The center was a fairly open book however, and he had done enough spontaneous dropping in over the years to finally feel somewhat comfortable. As Thomas got older, that sick worry in his stomach slowly gave way to the feeling of ease, though, there would always be that concern lurking in the bushes. That is just how it was.

"Hello, Maybe," her favorite counselor, Jennifer Lynne, said upon sight of Maybe.

"Jennifer!" Maybe yelled back, running to give her a hug as if she hadn't seen Jennifer in a year, even though Maybe had just been there the day before.

While Jennifer joyfully hugged Maybe in return, Thomas awkwardly held true to his normal manner anytime Jennifer was around, by shutting his mouth and quietly admiring her.

Jennifer was a year younger than Thomas, but due to a needed repetition of fourth grade—his—they had both graduated that same year, and when they were younger, had even attended the same middle school. Come high school, Jennifer and some of the other kids of the more well-to-do families in Hayward, left for Catholic School and the comfort of their own version of Jesus being taught at St. Raphael's, leaving the halls of public learning empty of their elegance.

Jennifer's placid presence, one Thomas had missed sorely since the day they went their separate academic ways, was a divinity his anxious heart could never equal. She was the daughter of a prominent doctor and bank executive, and a girl—Thomas was sure—who would never have to worry about delivering apple pies to gain salvation. Jennifer's existence alone was the removal of sin for her, and the damnation for any male counterpart that looked in her direction, all of them with wanting eyes.

With a simplistic style, she enchanted Thomas as she always had. Her sleek chiseled features and dirty-blond feathered hair that shaded her blue eyes, was new age femininity at its finest. Thomas had lost infinite nights dreaming about her; which to his unhappiness, was as close as the two of them had ever gotten. Jennifer Lynne wasn't just out of his league, she was out of Thomas's universe. Still, the dream that she may fall out of her own orbit and into his, was the eventful dream Thomas wished to keep from falling over the horizon.

Jennifer had been working part-time at the center since Maybe was only four-years-old, and while her beauty was unmistakable, it was her kindness and intelligence towards Maybe's condition that truly burrowed into Thomas's heart. *She's perfect, too perfect, at least for someone as unnoticeable as me*, Thomas would tell himself upon sight of her.

"Have a good day, Maybe. Jennifer," Thomas said stoically, as if he were Jennifer's father, pronouncing her name with special care, while goofily waving goodbye, as if all his motor controls had instantly left his body.

Walking with Maybe towards the playground, smiling at Thomas's clear discomfort, Jennifer said, "You too," and returned the wave goodbye with an ease and agility he couldn't muster.

What would it take to capture the heart of a shooting star, Thomas silently asked the universe as he watched them walk away, *while still leaving the heavens untouched?*

~ ~ ~ ~

The Hayward Baptist Church was only two miles down the road from the Stanton Center, and after a short drive, Thomas arrived to deliver Mumma's apple pies. Using the side door, he headed straight to the kitchen, trying his best to avoid walking through the church. Thomas never knew when there was going to be a special service or lone soul praying, and while it wasn't for him, he had no desire to bother anyone who cared to indulge themselves.

He was in the process of taking the pies out of the bag and placing them on the counter when he heard the door. Without turning around, Thomas already knew who it was. The fragrance of her perfume had preceded her entrance, the aroma hanging on his nose like an old memory.

"Well looky what the cat dragged in," she coyly spoke, her lips toying with the words as they exited her mouth.

"Why is it that the wrong girl is always the one there at the right moment?" Thomas asked her, adding a gentle, but needed sarcasm to his question.

"You haven't always thought I was the wrong girl, have you, Thomas?" She asked, her body approaching, her confidence filling the air of the room along with her scent.

"That was before you started dating Roger," Thomas told her, trying to back away; although a part of him, the part that remembered the night he and Mary-Sue had spent together a year before, wanted him to move forward.

"Roger left for the army two months ago, but I'm still here. Are you still here, Thomas?" she asked, filling her mouth with his name, her hand headed right for his member.

Thomas was taken aback by her aggressiveness, though he shouldn't have been. It was the exact reason they had already connected once before in the same exact church. He blocked her hand, but not until she got a good feel for where Thomas stood on the situation. Her perfume had an effect on him, but it was her face and voluptuous lips, framed by her curly, shoulder length brown hair, that seemed to curve her body into a sultry manner, truly stoking Thomas's fire. Mary-Sue, however, wasn't a passion contained to the fireplace. She was an inferno, destined to burn down the house if you let her.

Roger, Mary-Sue's boyfriend for the previous six months (which was a virtual lifetime for the young and the restless) was someone Thomas knew from school, though they were never overly close. Even in a small New England town, most people would be surprised how easy it is for a person to get lost in the shuffle of everyday living. Even a well-known face can walk by without a person having one iota of knowledge about them. Still, in the few encounters he and Roger had shared, Thomas liked him.

When high school had ended that previous spring, Private Roger Burdick had headed to boot camp and a life of rigorously saluting the flag, while Thomas stayed home, only to find himself cornered in the church kitchen by Roger's girlfriend, with Thomas's own private standing at full attention.

The door to the kitchen slowly crept open, saving Thomas from a sure attack on his weak forces of resistance, or what he feared would have been worse given his abstinence since their previous encounter—a friendly misfire.

Mary-Sue stepped back instinctively, the devilish smile remaining on her face as Pastor Carr walked in.

"What are you two up to?" He asked with an untrusting curiosity, his facial expression showing that he was sure it was no good. His eyes weren't fixed on Thomas however, they were focused on Mary-Sue, his daughter, who had earned herself a reputation among the parish. There wasn't a soul who would say anything directly to Pastor Carr, but the low grumble had carried its way to the pulpit, and he knew.

Seeing this as the perfect time to get the hell out of the church, Thomas quickly maneuvered his way towards the door while trying not to arouse any suspicion of the erection in his pants, as he cautiously made his way beyond the Pastor.

"Mumma wanted me to drop off some apple pies," Thomas hurriedly told Pastor Carr, his feet shuffling closer to the safety of the door as he spoke. "Mary-Sue was kind enough to help me get them out of the bag, but I gotta get to work now, so, thank you Mary-Sue," Thomas said, issuing a rather formal goodbye to someone who had just manhandled his manhood. "See you on Sunday, Pastor Carr."

"I'm sure helping was the least Mary-Sue could do. I look forward to seeing you all at service this Sunday," Pastor Carr said, his mood, in an instant, lightened in a way that both comforted and made Thomas uneasy at the same time. "You tell your mother that Pastor Carr and the Good Lord thank her," he said, his smile widening beyond his belt. "Never underestimate the distance one small act of kindness can carry you in the Lord's house," he offered, as Thomas made his way out of the kitchen and into the warm embrace and freedom of the waiting morning sunlight.

CHAPTER SIX

The uncomfortable situation in Thomas's pants that had been created in the church kitchen, helped make him twenty minutes late for work. The last thing Thomas wanted when walking into a machine shop full of greased up men was a raging erection. As for being late itself, he didn't have a care in the world about it. Thomas's boss was no longer in any position to give him the same amount of grief as the other workers, not that Thomas expected special treatment. He just didn't feel the need to spend so much as a second worrying about so called, "time constraints."

Thomas had been working part-time at Twill Extruders since his junior year of high school, and full time since he had graduated that past spring. What started out as a part-time inventory position, stocking parts for the workers on the assembly floor, had turned into a full time Assembly Tech job, complete with average pay, benefits, cranky bosses, and terrible work conditions. Ah, that blessed American Dream.

Willy had gotten Thomas the job, and like everyone else, was constantly telling the young man how thankful he should have been to have it.

"There are adults out there that don't make as much as you do. You should be grateful."

"Grateful? For what?" Thomas would ask. "Grateful that I work my ass off, come home filthy and tired, for an amount of pay that isn't even a percentage of what the machine I'm building makes the guys in the office? You can keep your eyes closed while you dream, but I'm going to keep mine wide open while I'm awake."

"Those people in the offices went college, which last time I checked, wasn't for you, remember? That was your choice. If you don't want to live on your brains than you better learn to rely on the other skills Mother Nature gave you," Willy spat sarcastically. He was right in the fact that Thomas had chosen work over school, work over the armed forces, and work over life. What Thomas still needed to find and choose however, was that one thing that would help him get *over* work.

"Whatever, it just doesn't seem natural to me."

"Ahh, you just don't get it," Willy would finally get frustrated and tell him, even though, in Thomas' opinion, Willy was the one who didn't get it. How could he though? Willy was a third generation grease grunt. He was raised to be just like his father, who had been raised to be just like his. Never once did Thomas ever hear Willy say he wanted to be something more, and Thomas didn't get that. Perhaps, that was because just being there had already made Thomas more than his own father, with plenty of room to grow.

"Glad you could join us today, Thomas," Larry Dean, the four hundred and fifty pound farm boy, remarked as Thomas entered the shop. Larry was using the same ignorant manner in which everything escaped his mouth. He had been given the work area right by the entrance to the shop, which for a man of Larry's copious presence seemed like a bad business choice to Thomas. A lot of things say "buy my product," but to a businessman entering the shop to see Larry's gigantic ass struggling to bend over a piece of equipment that needs to be sold, not so much.

Larry, however, was extremely comfortable with his spot in the shop, his location giving him the whales-eye-view of all the activity on the assembly floor. There wasn't a soul that could arrive late or leave early without Larry being right there, ready to share the gossip of their comings and goings with everyone else in the crew. His gossiping prowess didn't end there, either, as he was also well known for expanding what he saw with the same ease as his waistline. If someone was ten minutes late in reality, they were twenty minutes late when Larry told the story. It was a disposition that had not only earned him the title of "Shop Cop," but Thomas's personal favorite nickname for Larry—"Mr. Miss-Information."

Yet, even knowing how Larry skewed the facts, the men on the shop floor still joyfully ate up his tales, often joining in at lunchtime or secret meetings at their toolboxes, the most common place for small factions to congregate in joint causes of hate and discontent. Anyone who thinks that gossip finds its most comfort in a workplace full of women has clearly never worked in a machine shop full of jaw-flapping men. Thomas had thought that he had finally progressed from the drama of high school, yet there he was, right in the middle of a new system of cliques. There were the Union Supporters, who constantly discussed how the company was doing the employees wrong, the Union Disgruntled, who constantly talked about how the union was letting its people down by pandering to the company, and, the workers like Thomas, who constantly talked about how everyone else was all fucked up.

"Just so glad to be here," Thomas answered Larry as he walked by, smiling, his words dripping with sarcasm.

"Good morning, Thomas," his boss—Roy—greeted the young man as he passed by, using a head nod and false interest in the contents of his clipboard to avoid an unwanted confrontation.

"Roy," Thomas replied back with facetious professionalism while nodding back at the nervous man, trying his best to make eye contact, and working even harder to control his smile. The assembly floor, where men drilled, welded, and constantly operated machinery of all levels of noise, was as quiet as a church mouse. The anticipation of a young punk like Thomas being put in his place was a salivating experience for the older crew. Their lives had been reduced to shop drama as one of their main excitements, spare an occasionally big Red Sox win or another great episode of *Cheers*. People always wonder how Reality TV became so popular, when in fact, reality entertainment has been the driving force for thousands of years; and if you don't think so, just feel free to ask Adam and Eve.

A reprimand for lateness, a confrontation between the boss and the employee, which was in high hopes for all that had miraculously stopped laboring at the same time, was not to be. Some of them scoffed, some of them muttered, "I'm not surprised, Roy's a pussy supervisor," but all seemed slightly disappointed. Apparently, the Red Sox had lost, Sam and Diane didn't have enough real-life drama for them that week, and no one was in the mood for reading the biblical re-runs.

~ ~ ~ ~

The heat in the machine shop was demanding enough in the summertime, but welding only made it worse, with the hot flame of the torch and melting metal radiating off the beam.

Swathed in a steady stream of sweat that only added to the discomfort under his welding jacket, Thomas felt a tap on his shoulder, which was all the excuse he needed to stop. Thomas expected it to be Roy, quietly wanting to discuss his tardiness without a crowd of onlookers watching. It wasn't Roy however, it was his current co-worker, former classmate and friend since kindergarten, Ralph Gaccione.

They had graduated together, both following the workingman lead of their male role models, Ralph's being his father, and for Thomas, the dumb-ass referred to as Willy. Thomas knew why he hadn't gone to college, he hated school and always had. Why Ralph had chosen a dirty machine shop over the cleansed collegiate ambiance however, Thomas didn't quite understand. Ralph was the smartest person Thomas knew, and while Ralph's grades at Hayward High were just average, everyone knew that if he had had any desire to try, he would have easily finished top in the class.

"Hey, I can't believe Roy didn't give you shit for being late again," Ralph said, trying to sound surprised, but clearly digging for something Thomas may have been hiding. It would have bothered Thomas if anyone else had asked, but he could trust Ralph. Whereas ninety-nine percent of the people Thomas met were like open vaults with any and every kind of knowledge, Ralph was perfectly content to close the door and be the only one who knew the truth.

Ralph wasn't surprised to hear that Willy had been sneaking around with Roy's wife. It wasn't the first time Willy had strayed, and it wasn't the first affair Roy's wife had been suspected of either. Ralph was, however, shocked and saddened to hear about their meeting at Jefferson Park, and Brew's unfortunate death. "Willy deserved that bullet more than Brew did," he said, correct in his line of thought as

Thomas saw it. "I'm sorry, I know how much Maybe loved him," Ralph added gently. Ralph had been a good friend to him for the last couple of years, and had always shown Maybe the kind of compassion she deserved, which was something that always stuck out with Thomas.

"Wanna meet up later, get your mind off of things?" Ralph asked.

"Sure. What you got planned?" Thomas asked back, curious to see how the rest of the world was living.

"Me and Holtzer are going to meet up with some girls down at the gravel pit, maybe even throw a few back, you in?" Ralph asked with an enticing raise of his eyebrows this time.

"Yeah," Thomas told him, "let me just make sure Maybe is all set after dinner and then I'll meet you there around eight."

"Sounds good," Ralph said with a smile, before heading back to his machine, leaving Thomas to carry on with the hot flame, unaware that the burn of hot flame was only hours away.

~ ~ ~ ~

It had been a productive day at work based on what his low-level standards of "work production" actually meant, which for Thomas, was getting to the end of the day without attempting a self-lobotomy with his drill gun. It didn't really take much to appear productive in the *real world*, anyhow. After all, Thomas was working for a company with the motto, "On Time, All The Time," when in reality, it should have read, "On Time, All the Time, Sometimes," because they rarely ever succeeded with the, "On Time," part of the equation.

Thomas's greatest accomplishment of the day had come when he caught Roy and Willy having a conversation behind the piping bins. They were discussing the events of the night before, trying their best to keep their voices down, but by crouching behind the cable wire in the adjacent aisle, Thomas could not only see them, but he could hear every word.

"I don't want to see you anywhere near Melanie ever again, do you hear me? It took everything in me not to go tell Prudie what you've been up to behind her back," Roy threatened, his normally melancholy voice giving way to anger. It was a normal anger though, not the "point a gun and think about killing a man" anger this time, which for Willy, was a good thing.

"I'm sorry, Roy. I truly am, but in my defense she came on to me. Things ain't been really hot at home lately...." Willy was whining as if that was the excuse Roy wanted to hear.

"Don't give me that bullshit. Just don't say another word about it. You don't bother me, and I won't bother you. Got it?" Roy told him, doing his best impression of a stern supervisor, a role that never quite suited him. Willy nodded his head in agreement, affirming his performance, when Roy asked, "You don't think Thomas will say anything, do you? If he keeps coming in here late I'm going to have write him up." His statement came with a look of rightful concern. Roy feared what Thomas may reprimand *him* for and how the young man may go about it in return.

"I doubt it," Willy told him, with a slight air of confidence that Thomas didn't quite care for. "He just feels big right now because he's got something on us. Give him a couple of weeks, he'll forget all about it," Willy's ignorant, stupid ass told Roy. *Seriously*, Thomas thought, *one man slept with the other's wife, who then in turn tried to kill him for doing such, leading both to be responsible for killing an innocent dog.* All of those things, Thomas surely would not *just* forget.

"Good," Roy said with a sigh of relief, before adding, "Sorry about your dog," with an actual twinge of remorse in the statement.

"He was good, but he was just a dog. I'll find another."

Just a dog, Thomas angrily thought. Just a soldier when Willy wanted to call him one. Just his best friend when no one else wanted to listen. Brew, unlike Willy, never strayed. Willy had been right the night before. Brew was a hero who had saved a man's life. Brew was a soldier protecting his territory. Brew was a friend, a companion who took the bullet meant for another. If anyone involved in that entire ordeal was *just a dog*, Thomas knew, it was Willy.

CHAPTER SEVEN

Willy surprised Mumma by staying home that night, rather than his usual evening indulgence of cocktails after supper was finished. Normally, he would leave as soon as his plate was clean and head down to JJ O'Malley's under the guise of, "watching the Red Sox" or some other game, though he spent more time sniffing tail than keeping his eye on the ball.

Mumma was oblivious to it, and while Thomas often made hints about it, she just ignored them. Some people see only what they want to see. Mumma probably could have walked in on Willy with another woman and still been blind to his ways. She had Jesus, baking, work, and Maybe, all in that order. What Mumma lacked, was a set of eyes that truly saw the world, and unless you have a good pair of those, you might as well have none of it.

Of course, Thomas wasn't surprised a bit that Willy had stayed home that night, or that the next night he would probably be back out again. Thomas was sure that Willy would listen to Roy and his warning for a little while, but he also figured that Willy would forget about it pretty quickly as well.

"The Red Sox aren't on tonight?" Mumma asked Willy as she cleared his empty plate of spaghetti.

"Yeah, they're on. I just felt like staying in tonight to watch the game," Willy answered, an edge to his response that showed his distaste in staying home.

Thomas and Maybe talked about her day as they ate seconds, Willy only interjecting with an occasional guttural displeasure of their conversation, and Mumma adding her two cents to anything she agreed upon, with a, "Praise the Lord." Aside from Willy being home, it was a normal night in their household, with Thomas and Maybe alone on an island of sanity, while the inmates—when they were home—just mumbled from their cells.

Thomas would have been lost in that house without Maybe. His baby sister was the only thing that saved him at times. Still, he was nineteen, and Thomas couldn't spend every moment with her. Whether Thomas felt he deserved one or not, he needed a life with others, a life of his own to experience. If only the world would have shown him then what he couldn't see, Thomas may have just been better off staying home.

It was eight o'clock when he tucked Maybe into bed with a copy of her favorite book, *The Small One*, and gave her a kiss goodnight. Mumma was sitting at the kitchen table reading the bible and taking notes while waiting on some cookies she had in the oven; all the while an irritated and fidgety Willy watched the Red Sox game and downed a twelve pack.

"Where are you going?" Willy asked, the disappointment that Thomas was going somewhere while he was stuck at home showing in his tone.

"Out," Thomas told him, showing defiance. Thomas was a grown man now, he had a job, and Willy didn't need to know anything that wasn't his concern. "See you later, Mumma," Thomas told her, more out of routine politeness than anything else, not that it mattered, she couldn't hear him with the words of her deceased savior ringing louder and with more volume in her ears and mind than any living person could ever achieve.

~ ~ ~ ~

The gravel pits were owned by the Tuttle's, which was the same local farming family that owned the pond where his Aunt Victoria had died; though the two sites were quite a distance apart. At one point the Tuttle family had possessed a great share of Hayward, cultivating it for all they could. But as the years rolled on and land elevated in price, they sold more and more off, while still keeping far more than most.

They shut down the work in the gravel pit at dusk, leaving only an easily removed rope in front of the dirt road entrance to stop people from entering, not that they truly cared. Teenage gatherings were a part of life, and as long as no one messed with the equipment, it didn't seem to bother them when youngsters took advantage of the location. Noise didn't travel too far from the pit, and as long as the party didn't stray far from the area, most everyone, the police included, left the kids alone.

The center area of the pits was the main choice for gathering. Secluded by large mountains of cut rock and sharp ledges that were destined to be chiseled down to small stones, it made the perfect spot for teenage antics and anarchy. There was a larger crowd than Thomas expected when he arrived— much larger. Ralph had mentioned Holtzer and a few girls, but what Thomas had walked into was a full-blown party. He recognized most of their faces, even though Thomas didn't know most of their names.

There were people who he had just graduated with, many on the verge of leaving for college, mingling with future seniors, and even a few older kids, still holding on to a piece of their youth. All of that humanity, and Thomas, the man-child destined for the path of the beaten—work, eat, sleep, and repeat, until one day chiseled down to his own slab of stone. So many futures lay ahead of those unknown faces in the pits; while Thomas stood there in envy, with the feeling that he was on the assembly line to the grave, no different than the large rocks ready to be crumbled to dust.

"Hooooo, there he is," Ralph yelled when he spotted Thomas approaching the crowd, a beer extended in his friend's direction.

"I didn't know there were going to be so many people," Thomas told him, not that he minded. Large get-togethers had their benefits. For someone like Thomas, who had always felt more comfortable keeping to himself, large crowds made it easier to hide in plain sight. It wasn't that Thomas hated people; in fact, he had always enjoyed the thought of having company, at least, right up to the point where he found himself smack dab in the middle of it.

"Where's Holtzer?" Thomas asked.

"Holtzer?" Ralph asked, repeating the question as if he hadn't heard Thomas correctly, a sure sign that Ralph was already on his way to a rather fulfilling evening of drinking. "He's right over there with his date," Ralph said, pointing towards the largest mound of rock in the pit, where the largest gathering had accumulated. It was the way of the party. One small group usually began it, growing into one larger group, which over the course of the night, dwindled back down into smaller and smaller circles of humanity.

"I'm gonna go say hi real quick, I'll be right back," he told Ralph, who was already back to the conversation with the young lady he had his arm around, by the time Thomas was two steps away.

Walking over to see Holtzer, Thomas didn't expect much, just a quick hello to a good friend, one Thomas had known since he was seven-years-old. Strange things happen in the moonlight however. Holtzer had his back turned to Thomas and was engaged in a very typical, crowd consuming story. Some people have a presence for things like that, and Holtzer was one of them. He had been bred that way.

Thomas couldn't quite hear the punch-line of what he knew must have been an epic tale, but the laughter of the crowd was the trademark sign of another crowd pleasing, Holtzer grand finale. People were patting him on the back, the enjoyment of his company on their face as the crowd slightly separated. Holtzer's back was slightly turned, but Thomas could see there was enjoyment on his face as he leaned down to whisper in the ear of the girl standing next to him.

"Hey, Holtzer," Thomas said, slightly raising his voice in hopes that it would carry over the crowd.

Thomas knew that his greeting had made its way to Holtzer's ears when his friend joyously hollered, "Ziggy!" in Thomas's direction, bringing the attention of others upon them.

Anyone who could bring forth that type of acknowledgment from Bradley T. Holtzer was somebody people wanted to see. Holtzer was the top of the social mountain. With a persona that reeked of his father's social and business savvy wherewithal, plus a body and face that replicated his mother—who looked herself like she had just stepped off the cover of *Vogue*—the tall, tennis-fit, black haired, blue-eyed boy of privilege was always oozing and entertaining with every ounce of modern day preppy perfection. Holtzer was the type of guy that if you didn't know him, you instantly hated him; the kind that could wear a turtleneck and sweater in July and still look cool in every way. Unfortunately for those who had turned around, Thomas was the only person they saw Holtzer addressing, and sporting no more than his usual unkempt hair, plain t-shirt, worn looking jeans, and knock-off Puma's. Most of them looked away quicker than they had looked towards.

Holtzer had been calling him "Ziggy" since the first time he had ever read the cartoon; and while Thomas's appearance was far from the short, big-nosed cartoon character, Holtzer felt the bland personality was a dead ringer. What Holtzer called bland however, Thomas called reserved—a reservation Holtzer's out-going personality never accepted.

"How you doing?" Thomas asked, smiling and extending his arm out for a handshake.

Thomas was glad to see Holtzer. They had both been busy with life. Thomas had been working, while Holtzer had been getting ready to leave for Yale in the fall, and they had failed to make the time, though they were clearly an odd couple of friends anyhow. Thomas had been born on the dirt side of the tracks, the poor, working class side of Hayward. Holtzer had been born on the ritzy side, like Ricky Schroeder with *Silver Spoons* in his mouth, while Thomas had to learn how to get by with nothing more than a rusty fork.

Holtzer was first class heritage with private school privilege, while Thomas was public school poor with second-rate lineage. When Holtzer was at the prestigious Pine Point Academy, Thomas was at the dilapidated Freeman Hathaway Public School. When Thomas was getting by in high school at

Hayward High, Holtzer spent his days ensconced in higher learning at the upscale Fountain School.

The two of them had only one connection, town baseball, where no amount of money could keep Holtzer from having to mingle with the likes of Thomas. The mere love of a sport had put them together as kids, and had kept them together during every summer since. Having a fairly equal amount of ability on the diamond—Holtzer the clean cut pretty boy shortstop, and Thomas the get it done dirt-dog catcher—they formed a strange bond that, even to them, was somewhat perplexing. It was less noticeable when they were kids, but age and knowledge had a way of changing things; and Thomas feared that Holtzer was starting to see his friend's true place, well below the horizon.

"I'm doing well, Zig. Did you see how well the Hayward Little League team is doing? That Dann kid is a beast at the plate. Little rat dropped a big pop fly in center yesterday though. Can't let that happen again," Holtzer said, slumming it with a common ground conversation.

"Who knows, maybe the sun got in his eyes," Thomas offered, giving the kid the benefit of the doubt.

"Good old Ziggy, always making excuses for everyone else. You're only holding yourself back by doing it," Holtzer returned.

"Well, maybe the sun gets in my eyes too," Thomas said with a gentle smile.

Holtzer grinned. "How is Twill Extruders treating you?" he asked in his usual Holtzer manner, putting a caring emphasis on the company name, while not really appearing to give a crap at the same time. Thomas had never thought much of it. Holtzer had been that way since he was a little boy, and even baseball coaches that had demanded respect throughout the years always got just a little less from Holtzer.

It was his nature to ask a considerate question, and then look everywhere but right at the person as they answered. Thomas had always attributed Holtzer's behavior to a mind that wouldn't stop, even when all signs pointed to the fact that he should.

"It's a job," Thomas answered, allowing his tone to show the displeasure he felt with his working class status. He thought about adding a statement out of Willy's playbook and saying how he was grateful to at least have a job, that many would have been lucky to have the opportunities Thomas had been granted. Then he thought about saying how the money was good, and how *that* was perhaps the only thing that made it worth it, but talking money with Holtzer was a losing battle, and Thomas knew it. No matter how much Thomas made at Twill Extruders, it would never be enough to impress Holtzer.

"Well, we can't all be Ivy League," Holtzer said after a moment, this time adding a little punch to his words, and a direct look that straightened Thomas's stance.

"No, I guess we can't," Thomas smiled back, relaxing his upper body with a calm breath, allowing Holtzer the verbal jab, while hoping for peace's sake that it was just a poorly made joke.

"Not that you wouldn't make a fine Ivy-Leaguer, Zig," Holtzer calmly, more politely recited while raising his clear cup full of beer in a semi-toast to Thomas, a gesture Thomas returned with a half-smile and raise of his own glass.

"Oh Ziggy, where are my manners. I would like to introduce you to the lovely lady who was so kind as to join me tonight, a future Yale scholar as well, Miss Jennifer Lynne,"

Holtzer suavely uttered, pouring the charm on thicker than Maybe poured Aunt Jemima on her waffles.

She had been standing right next to him, her head slightly turned, her face and hair hidden under the brim of a felt hat. At first, Thomas didn't know if she was a snobbish or shy companion of Holtzer's. His Ivy-League bound friend had a penchant for going through girls like Pac-Man went through pellets; and with Holtzer's all-encompassing taste, no one ever knew what kind of a girl or woman he would be sharing his time with. All they knew for certain, was that as soon as they gave Holtzer a boost with their fruit, he was going to turn them into ghosts, consume them, and they would never be seen again. In Holtzer's world, there was no room for a Ms. Pac-Man.

Holtzer could see that Thomas and Jennifer recognized each other immediately, and with casual curiosity asked, "You two know one another, I take it?"

"Yes," Jennifer answered first, "I take care of Thomas's sister Maybe, at the center," she told him in a somewhat meek fashion.

"Jennifer is Maybe's favorite counselor," Thomas awkwardly added, with a slight smile on his face, his focus fully on her. She was avoiding Thomas's look, which struck him as odd. Perhaps, outside of the boundaries of the Stanton Center and Maybe's presence, Jennifer was just shy, though, the two had never spoken much anyway. In fact, the last great conversation Thomas and Jennifer had ever engaged in was back in elementary school, when she had politely handed him back a stray Frisbee on the playground, sparking a two minute conversation about her dog who loved to play fetch. It was a tiny moment in time, but Thomas could still see them there holding opposite ends of the Frisbee like it was yesterday.

Since then, however, Jennifer hadn't said very much, and only spoke sparingly on the occasions when Thomas dropped Maybe off. *Why should this be any different?* Thomas dejectedly asked himself.

"Well, it is truly a small world," Holtzer jumped in, happy to steer the conversation. "Jennifer and I met down at the Eastern Yacht Club. Her parent's boat is in the dock right next to ours. The minute I saw her I knew I had to ask her out. This isn't quite the place I envisioned for a first date, but good friends and good drinks are always great company. Am I right?" He confidently asked Jennifer, widening his smile, his body language making it clear that no answer was necessary— or wanted.

Thomas could sense that Holtzer was suddenly scanning him, which was out of the norm for Holtzer, yet Thomas still couldn't stop looking at her, even though he knew he shouldn't have been. She was there with Holtzer, not Thomas. Why would she be? Thomas was just a nobody. While Holtzer had boats and Yacht Clubs, Thomas had a beat up Chevette and grease stained jeans.

Releasing his stare, Thomas broke the moment of silence the three of them had been indulging in. "Think I need another. If I get lost in here somewhere, you guys have a good time," he stated, waving his hand in regards to the large crowd that made up the impromptu gathering.

"Come on back and chat some more with us," Holtzer said, enjoying every chance he had to see through Thomas.

Looking at Holtzer and Jennifer wasn't an activity Thomas had any desire to spend his night engaging in however, so Thomas lied and said, "I'm sure I'll be back around, gotta make the rounds saying hello to everyone first."

Holtzer grinned at the remark. He knew Thomas well, too well; and he knew that Thomas wasn't a "make the rounds" kind of guy. Thomas was a quiet, talk to the few close to him, observer. The only hope Thomas had, was that his smile had showed that he wished to let Holtzer have some alone time with Jennifer, even if it was the last thing Thomas ever wanted to think about. It was her life however, and other than their connection to Maybe, Thomas was beginning to see how little he and Jennifer had in common. Thomas could have been a jealous man and tried to warn her, but if Jennifer had said yes to spending time with a guy like Holtzer in the first place, than maybe she deserved the outcome.

~ ~ ~ ~

Thomas spent the rest of the night alone in the crowd, occasionally finding himself in small talk with largely intoxicated friends, like Ralph, who had gotten so drunk he took off all his clothes and decided to climb a gravel mountain. Ralph never ceased to amaze Thomas. Here Ralph was, the smartest, wisest of them all, and still the most prone to acts of sheer frivolity bordering the line of stupidity. He almost made it to his destination and title of King of the Mountain, until someone climbed up behind him and pulled his underwear down to his ankles, to which Ralph reacted by covering his privates and falling backwards down the pile. Thomas was worried that Ralph had hurt himself, but jumping up after the fall, not realizing that his underwear were still at his ankles, Ralph proudly showed that he was at least alright physically, and with all body parts still fully intact.

It was taking everything Thomas had in him not to watch Holtzer and Jennifer, and occasionally, he failed. Once, Thomas even caught her eye, and for a moment, she even held the look. She was the most beautiful thing he had ever seen, and Thomas wanted what Holtzer had, now more than ever.

The large crowd and cold beers helped move the time—as well as his suffering—forward at a faster pace than Thomas initially realized, and it was one in the morning when most of the people started to leave. Holtzer and Jennifer had left a little after eleven. They had looked for Thomas, hoping to say goodbye, but he had snuck behind a rock cutter to avoid them.

Ralph was in good hands with his date, who had her hands full with Ralph. He was in an effervescent state of intoxication, spending his last few minutes at the party walking around gibbering and telling everyone how much he loved them.

Thomas said goodbye to him after replying, "I love you too, man," and agreeing with Ralph that they were more like brothers than friends, and that everyone else that worked at the factory was, in fact, "a fucking dumbass."

Thomas had parked off to the side in the small family graveyard that was right outside of the pits, where he had left his car hidden and alone with the tombstones. It wasn't alone however. There was a body lying on the hood, one that Thomas couldn't fully make out in the dark; though he could clearly smell and see the smoke rising from a joint.

"Get off of my car," Thomas said, somewhat peevishly. He hadn't paid much attention to how much he had drunk, and while Thomas was far from the level of inebriation that

Ralph was currently manifesting, his words gave way to a slight slur.

"I saw the way you looked at her."

He knew the voice right away, her silhouette playing in the moonlight as she sat up, her lips seductively blowing a puff of smoke into the nighttime air, the sweet smell of marijuana dominating her perfume.

"What are you talking about Mary-Sue?" Thomas asked, though they both knew exactly what and whom she was talking about.

Reaching for the keys in his pocket, Thomas dodged headstones while hoping his careless attitude would help him do the same with Mary-Sue's questioning. The mass of people and starless night had kept her hidden from Thomas. *How long had she been there, and where*? These were thoughts as mysterious to him as the lives beneath his feet.

"I've seen her around town before. She's pretty. A little too wholesome for me; but I can see why you were looking at her like that." Mary-Sue was confident in both her assumption and delivery.

"She takes care of my sister at the center, that's all. She's a nice person," Thomas told her with an inflection of annoyance, one that came with describing the woman he longed for as a "nice person," and the thought that he was most likely mirroring the exact label he had been given by Jennifer.

Leaning against the car in frustration with his current existence, Thomas looked at the fading name on the headstone in front of him. Richard Talbot Walker, 1792- 1865, was now a moss covered piece of stone that was threatening to topple over from the rages of weather and time. *I'm only a young man, Richard, yet here we are together, in pretty much the same condition*, Thomas thought.

"Being a nice person ain't going to get her anywhere with Brad," Mary-Sue said, hitting an already tender nerve.

"Just leave it alone, Mary-Sue," Thomas scornfully told her, showing an anger in his voice and violence in his hands, which in one swift motion, had grabbed her wrists and pulled her off the car.

"Touchy, touchy, Thomas," Mary-Sue said, unaffected. "You haven't grabbed me like that in over a year."

Her lack of acknowledgment towards his anger should have enraged Thomas more, but they both knew he wouldn't take it any further. Thomas relaxed his body back on the car and, without any resistance from Mary-Sue, took the joint out of her mouth and took a hit, inhaling deeply, before blowing the smoke out in a mock ceremony of released tension.

"I'm lonely, Thomas," her breath was on his neck, her perfume, mixed with weed, now creeping up his nose and into his head. She slithered her body in front of Thomas, one hand on his shoulder, the other around the small of his back, both breasts pressed against his chest.

"You know I can't do this," Thomas said, never once making an effort to stop her.

"Oh, I think you can," Mary-Sue said back, looking directly in Thomas's eyes, luring him in.

A part of Thomas wanted to stop her, wanted to say how he couldn't do this to Roger—that Roger was a friend—but something kept Thomas from saying Roger's name out loud; and in an instant, Thomas had erased the memory of Roger from his mind.

Thomas grabbed her again, but this time with a force of passion, around the waist and lifted Mary-Sue onto the hood. Her hand found the mark it had reached for earlier that day, only this time, Thomas had no desire to stop her.

"Ummm," her voice and body rumbled, feeling Thomas's excitement through his jeans, "Brings a whole new meaning to a stiff in the graveyard."

"Shut-up," Thomas said, only wanting their bodies to do the talking, his lips moving from his words to her mouth; his hands exploring her body, in a search she was more than willing to oblige.

Of all the places Mary-Sue and Thomas could have let their passion take them, they let it have them right there in that small cemetery outside of the gravel pits. Surrounded by death, they created a life. A life, but for only one brief moment, Thomas would never be destined to know.

CHAPTER EIGHT

"It is he who provides for us, enriches our souls in hopes that we will rise up to his greatness and join him in righteousness. Thank you, Lord Almighty, for giving this congregation the strength to persevere and prosper in this sinful world. We are humbled, and grateful for the kindness you shine down upon us. May we someday meet you at the mountaintop, stripped bare of our earthly shortcomings, and overcome with the joy and thankfulness that comes with standing tall by your side. Amen!"

"Amen!" the crowd repeated back to Pastor Carr's long-winded and rousing sermon, an extra emphasis and bar on the volume chart reached.

"And now, we welcome all who have given themselves to Jesus Christ to take part in the sacrament."

On cue, the organ rang through the church, while the activity of gathering the body of Christ began up front. Church Servants, a title in which Thomas had occasionally been volunteered for by Mumma, respectfully began to dole out the offering as soon as Pastor Carr was done blessing it with his expanding divinity.

Thomas couldn't say that he ever truly felt either comfortable or awkward in church, even after the comfort of knowing that he didn't believe was apparent. After all, there were plenty of decent people, like Mumma and Maybe, who were staunch believers, and just because Thomas didn't believe didn't mean other people were wrong because they did. *Who truly knows?* That was how Thomas looked at it. Because he couldn't give a definitive answer either way, Thomas left it at that. Yet, he still couldn't help but laugh at the absurdities that sprung from it all, and apparently, Thomas wasn't alone.

"What is this?" he heard the young woman a few pews in front of them ask her female companion.

Thomas figured from their resemblance that they were sisters, but whatever their relation, he suspected that they were new to the church. Thomas had never seen them before, and from the sounds of the younger woman's questions, she was quite new to the Baptist way.

"It represents the blood and body of Christ," her companion told her, trying to keep her voice down.

"No, that looks more like grape juice in a medicine cup along with a bunch of crumbled up Saltine crackers," the woman said sarcastically. "It's even served on a silver platter. Isn't serving Jesus up on a silver platter what created this entire fiasco to begin with? Who are they honoring here, Jesus, or Judas?"

"It's a Baptist church, they're more relaxed than the Catholics," she told her as she looked around to make sure no one could hear them. Aside from himself, Thomas didn't think anyone did.

"It just doesn't seem right to me," her friend responded. "Besides, if Jesus was going to be a cracker, don't you think he would be something more wholesome—like a Triscuit or a Wheat Thin?"

"Just be quiet and take it," her friend commanded, ending the inquisition.

Thomas had spent that Sunday's sermon looking from Pastor Carr to Mary-Sue, who always sat up front. Her mother had once sat next to her, at least she had until cancer had taken her four years prior, leaving Mary-Sue a newly turned teenage girl without a mother. Thomas often wondered how the loss had affected Mary-Sue. She had always seemed so quiet and timid before, and now, well, Mary-Sue was just different—much different.

The oldest parishioner in the church, Ethel Pratt, had taken it upon her crotchety old self to take the seat of Mary-Sue's mother. On that particular Sunday, her giant hat (one that looked like something out of Mrs. Howell's wardrobe closest on *Gilligan's Island*) was blocking Thomas's vision of Mary-Sue. He had expected her to look back, or at least make some effort to see Thomas, but her eyes never moved from her father.

He hadn't seen her in a couple of nights, not that Thomas expected to. They had taken care of a need and nothing more. With their physical pleasure fulfilled, they left each other that night without a kiss goodbye, and not one single word spoken.

Thomas's family had spent every Sunday in that church, Mumma beaming full of the grace of God as she imagined Jesus nailed to the cross. She would bring her usual basket of baked goods to serve afterward, and Pastor Carr would spend his time devouring and thanking her for them, the flattery only making Mumma want to bake more. This was clearly Pastor Carr's intention with the compliments. Even Willy could tell, as he would often roll his eyes when Pastor Carr started in, "Um, um, um. These are the best cookies I have ever had in my entire life, Prudence."

Mumma never noticed Pastor Carr's true intention. All she saw was her path to heaven, laid out in a trail so sugary that Willy Wonka himself would have been jealous. Thomas knew her heart was in the right place, thinking she was doing good by the lord; he just wished that every once in a while, her mind would have met her halfway.

"You think you could save some of this good cooking for next Saturday night? Mary-Sue just found out yesterday that her boyfriend Roger is coming home for a liberty weekend before shipping off to A School, and I would love to give a proper get-together for a young man that has so honorably chosen to serve his country." It was a question Pastor Carr asked Mumma, knowing all too well that anyone in their right mind—and even Mumma—who wanted so desperately to look respectable in the eyes of her lord and country, would never say, "No."

"It would be my pleasure," Mumma beamed. "You know, I tried talking Thomas into joining the forces, especially with everything going on in Libya and that Muammar Gaddafi, but he didn't want any part of it." She frowned, throwing her son's pacifism to the troops for supper, while serving his Patriotism up to the alter for sacrifice.

"Mumma, you know I could never shoot anyone," Thomas quickly replied in childlike defense.

"He doesn't have the toughness to survive in the military," Willy interjected, scoffing at the thought of Thomas wearing the same uniform Willy once wore so proudly—and disgraced so regularly with his behavior ever since.

"Well, Thomas, there are plenty of other careers in the military that don't require firing at an enemy. I myself was a pastor in the Vietnam War, and while I wouldn't have minded firing away, I never had to," Pastor Carr added, his mind filled with visions of medals he believed he could have won, the loss of all that unclaimed glory painting his heart purple.

Mumma, Willy, and Pastor Carr stood there massaging each other's egos for a few more minutes, while Thomas stood there politely smiling as best he could, feigning interest with an occasional, "Wow, really," that only seemed to keep them wanting to talk about themselves more. His mind was still on Mary-Sue however, her desire to ignore Thomas making more sense with the news that Roger was coming home.

Thomas hadn't expected anything from their night in the cemetery, except perhaps the guilt he was now feeling. The guilt that he would never have thought she would feel; yet clearly she was. It should have stopped them in the first place, but some forces push beyond control. Thomas watched her smile politely, the same fake smile he had been wearing, while her father shared the news. Mary-Sue was feeling her share of the shame.

He had waited for Jennifer to look him in the eyes that night. Right now, Thomas was glad that Mary-Sue wouldn't. Sometimes there are things you can't remember, while at other times, there are things that you just need to forget.

~ ~ ~ ~

After seeing her with Holtzer, Thomas had all intentions of avoiding Jennifer, but both Willy and Maybe's schedules had other plans. Willy asked him to pick up Maybe at the center after work, to which Thomas reluctantly answered, "Yes." Willy's concern about "watching the Red Sox" at the bar had apparently worn off after only one week, leaving Thomas to wonder what animal was going to end up in a hole in the backyard next.

The children were playing an afternoon game of kickball with the staff on the small field behind the center, the cheers from them all reverberating throughout the field. Maybe was in right field, twirling under the bright sun, the soft breeze jostling her hair. She had a giant smile on her face, which instantly brought a smile to Thomas upon sight of her.

He hadn't noticed Jennifer walking along the chain link fence to greet him. Thomas was too busy basking in Maybe's joy, the same way Maybe was busy in the outfield, with rays in her hair and not a cloud in her mind. She was oblivious to the game being played, and as Thomas looked out at her, apparently so was he.

"She loves dancing in the outfield." Jennifer's voice, while slightly startling Thomas, was as gentle as the breeze in the trees that lined the outfield fence.

Giving his best effort to appear as cool as the Fonz—an impossible task for Thomas, especially around Jennifer—he calmly replied, "She loves music, even without the radio she still hears it in her head."

"I think she hears it in her heart," Jennifer quietly spoke, her eyes unafraid to meet his for the first time ever, which in an act of unanticipated role reversal, forced Thomas to look away. "We should all be that lucky," she added again, softly.

"Aren't we that lucky?" Thomas asked, trying to sound curious rather than confrontational, while casually resting his arms on the fence.

"I think a lot of people with perfectly good ears and hearts can't hear a thing," she said with a matter-of-fact confidence, her sky blue eyes looking directly at Thomas—into him—for the first time ever. He was afraid to look at her, yet this time Thomas couldn't look away, even if he had tried.

It was a look he wasn't prepared for and his tongue numbed, not allowing him to speak. Although, it didn't really matter, as there wasn't a proper response anywhere in Thomas's mind.

Unable to reply with something deserving, in an act of pure sabotage and betrayal to no one more than himself, Thomas asked her the wrong question. "How's Holtzer doing?"

Her eyes quickly retreated back to the field, while her voice paused before answering, "He's doing fine, I guess."

The fact that she didn't know how he was doing both inspired and saddened Thomas. *Was Jennifer indifferent towards him, or was she just another discarded female on Holtzer's path of self-indulgence?*

"He's something," Thomas said, hoping to sound mysterious and understanding. Whichever way her feelings were headed, Thomas wanted her to know that he would follow.

"You've got that right," Jennifer said, returning Thomas's mysterious manner and leaving him without a clue, not that Thomas needed any help.

"Nice talking to you, Thomas."

Jennifer walked away after saying it, leaving Thomas with the odd feeling that he had just talked to two different people. One moment she was gentle, kind, and Thomas had almost believed that she was interested in him. The next, she was quick with her answers, cold, forcing Thomas to wonder if she gave a shit about him at all. *Women,* Thomas thought, *catching Haley's Comet would probably be easier than figuring one of them out, and probably only happens about as often as that comet comes around.*

CHAPTER NINE

Present Day:

"I never cared for your father. He was a womanizer, ignorant, in all common sense and words. To put it bluntly—he was an asshole. But he was there, inside, with all of you. While I choose to lurk in the bushes like some peeping Tom, your father was there. Even after the nights he spent with other women, he always came home. In fact, my greatest fear was that he wouldn't come back, leaving me to make a decision. Would I enter the doorway? I'm thankful he never left me the choice. For all his shortcomings, he always came home. While in all of mine, I always walked away."

~ ~ ~ ~

August 1986:

"I don't think your sister's the only retard your mother gave birth to."

He was shit-faced drunk; his words slurring from too many "one mores" down at J.J. O'Malley's.

"Just get the hell out of here before I throw your worthless ass out," Thomas warned him. The young man was still a pacifist at heart, yet, Willy was mistaking Thomas's kindness as weakness, and his open hand for one that wouldn't close.

"What are you gonna do about it, Boy." Willy spit the last word out, hoping to get a rise out of Thomas, but there wasn't anything Willy's ignorant ass could say about Thomas that was going to cause him to make a move. Willy knew what button to press however, and the longer that he stood there swaying, the more inclined he felt to push.

"Maybe we should send you to that school with your dumbass sister."

"This is your last warning," Thomas told him, staring him down man to man. Willy didn't hear Thomas however, he was too far gone.

"Both of you!" Willy yelled in the direction of Maybe, his own daughter, who was in her room crying, "Are nothing but worthless pieces of shit!"

One punch—that was all it took to finally shut Willy up. It was the quickest fight Thomas had ever been in, which was pretty good considering it was the only one he had ever chosen to be in as well.

Mumma, who had been praying silently on the couch for the confrontation to stop, ran over to Willy on the floor, the spot where her son's right cross had left the man to reap the silence his mouth had sowed. Thomas had always done his best to avoid physical anger, which at times had been difficult while protecting Maybe from the cold people in the world. If he had to admit the truth, it felt good to hit Willy— real good. Apparently, Thomas was a pacifist with a taste for anger, or perhaps, he just wasn't a pacifist at all. After all, all men and women have that animal side in them. The one that lurks in the back of their mind, suppressed. Thomas had unleashed the horned beast, and even if only for one strike, something about it felt pleasantly natural.

"Just throw some ice on him. If he wakes up, put him back to sleep. If he doesn't want to go to sleep, I'll make him," Thomas arrogantly told Mumma, an animalistic power running through his body. Willy's actions had warranted an ass-whooping for a long time and for a multitude of different reasons; and now that Thomas had broken the seal, he was feeling quite content about keeping the can open.

"I think you should just leave before he wakes up," Mumma said, her focus remaining on Willy as she avoided looking at Thomas.

"Not until I make sure Maybe's alright," Thomas said, using a stern inflection to let her know that he was in charge of where and when he would go—not her—not Willy— not anyone.

"Just get out!" Mumma yelled, showing a strength and rage she seldom used. All of the might she could muster was aimed at Thomas, the lone one who had defended her only daughter, his sister, yet Thomas was the one she chose to flex her only resilience at in anger.

"You know what Mumma? You belong on that floor next to him. You're both just a couple of beaten dogs," Thomas told her, this time making sure she was looking directly at him. Lost in anger and eager to give her what she asked for, Thomas left without even saying goodbye to Maybe, who had been left alone crying in her bedroom. Willy wouldn't apologize. Mama wouldn't console her; and Thomas had stormed out in a shroud of his own bitterness.

Maybe was alone in the world, and it wouldn't be the first time Thomas left her that way, but he couldn't stay. He was a time bomb ready to explode, and Mumma and Willy had just made damn sure that his fuse was lit.

~ ~ ~ ~

"Thanks for letting me crash here."

Thomas didn't know where to go, so he called the first person who came to mind, and when Ralph didn't answer, he called the last person he should have.

"It's no problem, come on over," Holtzer answered.

The house in which Holtzer had spent his years growing up was a mansion compared to the Thompson/Crowley homestead. While the magnificent size of the place always impressed Thomas, it was the smell of fresh flowers that greeted his nose upon arrival that he appreciated the most; a far cry from the usual nasal invasion Thomas had become accustomed to at home.

He was struck with the same old feelings as he walked through the entryway. Every time Thomas had visited Holtzer's house in the past, a part of him felt like he should have been there to either clean the floors, dust the house, or landscape the grounds. Holtzer, rightfully so, was properly suited to live in the well-to-do home, while Thomas always felt like someone who belonged in the more uniformed comfort of the help.

"Make yourself at home Zig. My parents aren't even here. They're on a ten day Alaska cruise. I could have gone with them, but I figured I would stay home this time. We just went to Alaska two years ago and it was boring as shit if you ask me. Oh well, they enjoy it, and I get the house to myself, which is nice," he said, the last three words spoken in an attempt at mimicking Bill Murray in *Caddyshack*—an attempt that failed. Besides, if Holtzer was anyone from that movie, he was a lot more like Judge Smails.

Holtzer was always different when someone was alone with him. He was more down to earth than when he was in a crowd, making him much more pleasant to talk with. Thomas had always attributed it to the lifestyle his family lived. When your parents hold an elite status, there are certain stipulations of behavior a person is expected to adhere to in public, many of which he broke by spending time with broke people like Thomas. It wasn't that Holtzer's parents ever treated Thomas any differently than all of Holtzer's other friends, though Thomas did always feel as if they had a bit of remorse for him regarding the family he had been born into. Frankly, Thomas did as well.

They sat outside on the second story balcony, smoking cigarettes and drinking Johnny Walker. Thomas wasn't much of a scotch man, but Mr. and Mrs. Holtzer had a cabinet full of it; and after the events that had just occurred, Thomas was glad to drink it down.

"You know what your problem is Ziggy," Holtzer, the undercover psychologist began, "you let that household of yours hold you back. You could go to college, do something good with your life; yet, you choose to stay in this little town and settle for a little life." He took a long drag of his Marlboro, along with a quick swig of his scotch. "Not me, Zig. I'm going to do big things in this world. People are going to know my name, and if they don't, I'll make sure they never forget it."

Holtzer was feeling the alcohol, but unlike Willy, who was a droopy drunk, it raised the shoulders on Holtzer's frame, invigorating him. Thomas was uncomfortable, mostly because he feared Holtzer was right. *How could I leave Maybe?* Thomas had often asked himself. It was the question that had kept his feet planted in Hayward. *Is it really for Maybe, or am I just using her life as a reason to play it safe and never try to accomplish anything with mine? Am I afraid to leave her? Or am I just afraid to fail? Perhaps, what I fear the most, is to be caught living after the pain?*

"You're probably right, but how can I leave Maybe with them, especially when I know how they are?" Thomas asked aloud, this time hoping for an answer he could never seem to find.

"You left her tonight," Holtzer stated, bringing up an uncomfortable truth. "She could survive without you. She may even be better off if you were gone."

"How?" Thomas asked aggressively, as if in a world full of possibility, Holtzer was stating the one thing that was impossible.

"She may learn how to deal with them on her own. You can't protect her from life, Ziggy, no matter how close you are. At some point, she's going to have to learn how to fend for herself." Holtzer said it with a casual confidence, the kind that comes with a mixture of arrogance and knowledge.

Is that what drove my father away, Thomas wondered, *the thought that no matter what, he couldn't protect me, hadn't been able to? Why bother staying? Maybe that was his conclusion. Yet, should it be mine, does it have to be? Is it truly better not to be there at all than to be there unable to protect her, my only fate being to watch her suffer? If I can't stop the tears in the first place, what good is it to be there just to catch them?* Even if that was his father's choice, Thomas still didn't think he could do that to Maybe. He wouldn't. One night out, worried about her, was tough enough. Thomas couldn't bear to imagine a lifetime.

"You're pretty smart Holtzer, no wonder you're the one going to Yale," Thomas said teasingly, ready to talk about something else. After all, it was a lot to think about, not that he hadn't already run that train of thought around the tracks. Still, now wasn't the time to let the wheels roll. Thomas had left her alone tonight, and he was already feeling the guilt that came with not knowing who had tucked her in—if in fact, anyone had at all. For all he knew, Maybe had cried herself to sleep, or worse, was sitting in her room with tears in her eyes, while Thomas sat with Holtzer, contemplating both of their fates.

The two sat quietly for a minute sipping their drinks, taking a moment to collect their thoughts. It was easily accomplished with the view from the balcony overlooking the well-manicured lawn. The sure work of a professional was soothing to gaze upon, each blade of grass the pure essence of a subdued earth bowing on its knees in peace. Each side of the long yard had been lined with star magnolia trees and flowerbeds that were lit up at night with lamps, any darkness that threatened instantly sent retreating back to the celestial beauty of the nighttime sky; the entire trance-like scene a moonlit dream come life.

How different it all was from Thomas's normal view of a small, messy suburban nightmare, complete with dead dogs and faded toys that had collected too much dirt from having been left outside too long. It was the work of an idiot—Willy. While Thomas knew he could have helped out more with the yard work, he was comfortable with the fact that he did mow the lawn on occasion. Besides, Thomas was fairly confident that it was more than Holtzer or his parents ever did to physically participate in the making of their backyard reverie. *Hell*, Thomas thought, *even Willy can sign a check.*

Holtzer lit up another cigarette, the flash of the flame illuminating his clean-shaven face, reminding Thomas of the day's stubble he was still presenting as his picture to the world.

"So what do you think of her?" Holtzer asked uncaringly, his face returning to the dark shadow the house was casting, and to the one spot the moonbeams couldn't breach.

Thomas tried to pretend that he didn't know who Holtzer was talking about, and feigning stupidity, asked, "Who?" a question and effort Holtzer saw right through.

"Oh, don't be so coy, my friend. You know who— Jennifer," Holtzer said, leaning in closer as he emphasized her name, a slow grin appearing on his face.

"I know Maybe likes her," Thomas answered, avoiding the real question, an act that Holtzer wouldn't allow.

"I didn't ask what *Maybe* thinks of her, I asked what *you* think of her." His tone was relaxed, yet still, Thomas felt like Holtzer was goading him. However, with the events that had already occurred that night, Thomas also feared it was only his nerves.

"She seems nice...pretty enough," Thomas added, as if Jennifer was a run of the mill, everyday girl.

"Pretty, he says!" Holtzer chuckled loudly to the sky, laughing harder as his words collected in the clouds. Looking at Thomas, his grin as large as the Cheshire Cat's, Holtzer said, "Pretty? She's beautiful! Heather Locklear would be without a *Dynasty* if the producers ever saw Jennifer's smile."

He slapped Thomas on the back as he said it, and while his words appeared gently teasing, Holtzer's hand hit Thomas's spine hard—too hard.

"Well," Thomas returned, trying to ease the tension Holtzer's actions had him feeling, "You are the one most likely to be the future Blake Carrington, so I guess if anyone was an expert, it would be you."

Holtzer ignored the comment and continued talking. "She asked about you the night of the party," a serious voice returning, "All kinds of questions. If I hadn't of known any better, I would have thought she had a thing for you." Holtzer took another nonchalant sip, changing personalities as easily as he changed conversations. As Thomas watched his friend take a drink, his mind instantly roamed to the idea that Holtzer was a lot less like Blake Carrington, and quite a bit more like J.R. Ewing.

Thomas thought of all the questions Jennifer might have asked. Not wanting to seem eager, he asked with a confused smile, "What do you mean, *if I didn't know any better?*"

"There is always a chance that I'm wrong, but most girls our age don't usually put out if they're interested in someone else. Especially, girls like Jennifer," he said, an air of pride and accomplishment surrounding him.

"You would know better than I would," Thomas scoffed, trying to hold back the level of disdain he had for Holtzer's womanizing, something Holtzer most likely saw as jealously alone.

"You should have seen her naked body, Ziggy," he began again, pouring salt into a wound Thomas didn't want to acknowledge was even there. Who was Jennifer to Thomas anyhow—just someone who took care of Maybe, nothing more than a dream, like all of his dreams, unreal and untouchable. If only Thomas could have planted that thought to the point where it would grow roots, he may have been able to fool himself into believing she meant nothing. But Thomas knew there was no use watering a dead plant. He wanted her to be more. At the very least, more than just another one of Holtzer's used memories.

"I've been with a lot of girls, even a few women, yet her body was the most perfect one I have ever seen." Holtzer was reliving the moment, reveling in the scotch and the conquest, his eyes moving back and forth from the memory to the increasing displeasure that had crept upon Thomas's face.

"Her tits, Zig, they were...." He was cupping his hands, adding a visual aid, when Thomas jumped in, "Okay, okay. I don't want to hear any more about your sex life," Thomas told him. But it was Jennifer's part in the excursion that bothered him to hear about. Whether Holtzer's descriptions were just amusement and bragging, or meant in some way to bother Thomas, he had succeeded in both.

"Woo, woo, sorry, Ziggy. I didn't realize you were such a prude. What's a matter, all backed up?" He asked, with fake pity in his voice.

It was a childish chide, meant only to tease and perhaps demean, but Thomas fell for it. Without sense or prejudice, he changed everyone's life with one reply. It was one little secret that Thomas should have kept, that in a moment of juvenile pride, derailed more lives than just his own. Perhaps the everyday course of time and events would have brought the same results. Yet, Thomas couldn't help but think that his one little answer, that one little time he should have shown restraint—that seemed so insignificant—was in fact, his mark on history. After all, Thomas knew that as adults we create our own production, leaving everyone who enters just another player on the stage.

"Not at all, I spent that night with Mary-Sue."

Holtzer's face broadened with a devilish approval of the statement.

"You dog, Ziggy! Playing with another man's toy heart—a Pastor's daughter, nonetheless. I think I've underestimated you all along."

Thomas shouldn't have told him. He knew nothing good would come from it, and Holtzer's instant ragging was already more than he wanted to bear.

"You can't say a word, to anyone. It was a mistake." Thomas was looking directly at him, trying to use a stare to show the seriousness of his words. Holtzer understood, yet he still smiled back at Thomas, the spotlighted character that hid behind the flash. On the outside, Holtzer was the silver platter. But as Thomas would eventually find out, on the inside, he was no more than a crumbled, lowly Saltine. How cruel a fate, when those we dance with on the floor of the production, we often times bury on that same floor and stage.

CHAPTER TEN

Thomas made himself comfortable in the same guest room he had used when they were children, in one of the handful of times he had stayed the night. It had been longer than he could remember since one of those boyhood sleepovers, when late night movies and talk of girls had still remained innocent. Unlike Thomas and Holtzer, the room hadn't changed. Every knickknack, every piece of furniture, every color, stood still. It was old-fashioned elegance, with dark, cherry stained wooden nightstands and dressers.

The wood throughout the room was softened by the off-white beaded décor on the bed sheets which, even when not in use by guests, appeared to be laundered daily, the fresh smell releasing in the air upon touch. Thomas took a moment and gently brushed the palm of his hand over the sheets. When you come from a world of less, it never ceases to amaze you how something so simple as a freshly pressed sheet can create such wonder. The difference between Holtzer and Thomas was most prevalent in that one touch. Holtzer most likely thought nothing of it. *"They're just sheets, Ziggy,"* Thomas imagined him saying. But they weren't "just sheets." They were like touching a beautiful world Thomas could see, feel, and if only for one brief moment, live within.

Would Holtzer ever run his hand across the sheets at my house? Thomas wondered. If Holtzer ever did, he most likely wouldn't have had the same epiphany. If anything,

Holtzer would probably have been more inclined to want to head home and wash his hands.

Thomas expected to have trouble sleeping, his worried mind racing beyond his control with thoughts of Jennifer's naked body. The innocent object of his infatuation as a schoolboy, had turned sultry in an ominous way. A sleepless night however, wasn't to be. Within minutes of resting his head on one of the King's pillows, Thomas drifted off to slumber, leaving the pawing pain of reality for another day.

~ ~ ~ ~

Upon waking the next morning, Thomas immediately headed for the guest bathroom attached to his room, following Holtzer's demands that he make himself at home. The soft, hot stream of water was a welcome luxury, as the hard water at Thomas's own house never quite seemed warm enough for him to scour his body. It was a good beginning to what he feared would be a tumultuous day. Gathering his thoughts while the perfectly scented soap ran down his body, Thomas allowed his mind to rise with the steam that had emanated from the hot water, which at one point, threatened to burn the young man. The heat never seemed to be able to reach that scalding level however. Even at Holtzer's, Thomas could never reach the level of hot and clean he longed for, and he feared that if he couldn't find it there, that he never would.

After drying off with a towel so soft that it momentarily transported him into another universe, Thomas got dressed for work. Walking through the house in his work uniform, feeling like one of the help, Thomas decided to take full advantage of Holtzer's hospitality, so he helped himself to one of the bagels in the bread rack that sat on the kitchen counter, placing it gently in a toaster that looked like something out of *The Jetson's* kitchen. Thomas even opened the fridge for shits and giggles, and without surprise, found the soft spread butter there for the taking.

He would have enjoyed taking the day off from work to lounge around Holtzer's house, but the thought that he may need to find a place of his own to live was present in Thomas's mind. Besides, if anyone should have taken the day off to hang low, it was Willy—again.

~ ~ ~ ~

He arrived at work right on time, which for Thomas was the usual ten to twenty minutes late.

"Thanks for joining us today," Larry Dean greeted Thomas with sarcastic enthusiasm.

"Hey, thanks for getting even fatter over the weekend," Thomas returned, clearly not in the mood for Larry—not that anyone ever was.

"Hey, I've been on a diet," Larry whined. "It isn't easy you know. I'm trying to lose weight."

"Ya, well, no one's ever won a medal at the Olympics for trying," Thomas quickly retorted, shutting Larry up as he slowly walked away.

The usual eyes were watching as he walked down the aisle of the machine shop, his presence causing Roy's head to turn. Thomas knew Roy had seen him. Still, Roy pretended to be looking towards the opposite side of the shop at the exact same time that everyone else's sight was directly on the late arriver. Thomas was looking for Willy, and all it took was one glance in the direction of the man's work area to find him.

Willy's right eye looked a dullish yellow, widening the smile Thomas held on the inside, even while keeping his face stoic.

"Thomas," Willy cordially greeted the young man, going against his normal grain.

"Willard," Thomas said, returning the uncommon hello, but only with the mannerism of a completely comfortable asshole.

The shop had reached its usual state of silence, with each late arrival building on their hopes of viewing a confrontation between Thomas and Roy, the lack of action bringing groans from the crowd. Feeling the need to stand up for himself, but having no desire for it to come at Thomas's expense—which could ultimately be his—Roy flashed the managerial prowess they were always accusing him of lacking, when he instructed the crew to, "Get back to work." If anything good had come from Willy's wandering and Brew's death, perhaps it was the needed development of Roy Brant's backbone.

Willy looked serious, more serious than Thomas could ever remember, and in an act of uncommon kindness, the young man eased up, willing to meet him halfway.

"Listen, things got a little crazy last night. I know we both said and did some things we regret..." Willy trailed off. He was unsure of how to apologize, and showed his inability to do so by adding a regret that Thomas didn't feel. Still, Thomas let it go. Showing a resolve that caught the young man off guard, Willy spoke, "I just want to say, I'm sorry."

Thomas looked at Willy for a moment, ignoring the apology, and asked, "How's Maybe?" She was his main concern, the one that had led Thomas to raising a fist to Willy in the first place. Looking at the discolored state of Willy's eye, now, without the anger he had felt the night before, Thomas listened to Willy speak.

"She was quiet this morning. Wouldn't say a word to me when I dropped her off at the center. She never talks as much as she does when you're around anyhow. Your mother wasn't very talkative either," Willy said, his eyes looking at a scene that only he had watched. "Just come home after work, for them."

"I don't want to hear you talk about Maybe like that ever again," Thomas warned, feeling the underlying dominance that he now held over Willy. It was a dominance that Willy would never accept, even while slowly realizing its existence.

Willy didn't agree to stop. How could he? He knew his drinking tongue often over-ruled what, in his mind, he knew was right from wrong. All he could manage was, "You know I love your sister."

It wasn't the response Thomas wanted, or even close to what Maybe deserved. Yet, it was the best Willy could do, and Thomas had no desire to make him be a better person than he could be. He couldn't make Willy say the right thing. All Thomas wanted was for him to stop saying all the shit he shouldn't have, and if Willy was at least willing to try, so was Thomas.

"You gonna come home tonight?" Willy asked, "Your mother really missed you this morning. Not that getting your own place would be a bad idea. I was already in the Army by the time I was your age."

Willy had to take a warm moment, at least by their standards, and added the cold reality he held with such heated passion.

"I'm sure Mumma was all torn up," Thomas said sarcastically, knowing that Willy was out cold when Thomas had last spoken to her. "I'll see you at home," Thomas told him, leaving it abruptly at that before heading in the direction of his own work area, and like a crated beast, subserviently entered his own daily cage.

~ ~ ~ ~

"We're all prisoners, Tom, it's how we've been raised. We shackle ourselves, while calmly placing the key in our pocket and crying for our own freedom, all at the same time. The worst part is the way people handcuff their children. It's the most legal and even encouraged form of child abuse there is. They put the cold iron of the institutions that society has taught them to revere around their little wrists, kiss them on the cheeks, and lock their minds and spirits in the cage. And there isn't a single person who isn't guilty of the deed—our parents, and someday us, as well."

It was nice to see Ralph upright, even if he was on one of his rants. The swerving around side of him was starting to become a regular occurrence, and Thomas feared Ralph was following his father's footsteps.

Mr. Gaccione—Ralph's father—had a heart that was as big as his thirst, a genetic dehydration that Ralph had clearly inherited. While Mr. Gaccione was always on the side of joviality when it came to drinking, his over-consumption was often apparent. Thomas did have to admit however, that without all that alcohol, there wouldn't have been nearly as many good stories in that machine shop; and Ralph's father had some whoppers.

Thomas's personal favorite came when Mr. Gaccione got so drunk that he forgot which exact house he lived in. Somehow maneuvering his large pot belly through the house of the happy couple who lived next door to the Gacciones, he plopped himself right in between the unsuspecting, loving couple in bed, who's first names just happened to be Todd and George. It was this incident that had earned him the nickname in the shop of "Gangbang Gaccione," and the mere remembrance of the story often led the chorus of assemblymen to sing, "Gaycations all I ever wanted..." Spoofing the hot at the time, "Vacation" song, by the Go-Go's.

"I think all the drinking has made you crazy," Thomas said, both joking and seriously.

"Funny, I always thought it was all the crazy that made me drink," Ralph said back with a smile.

"I just feel, stuck," Thomas admitted, rewinding back to the thought that had sent Ralph off on the tangent.

"I hear you. I just wish I knew what to tell you," was the best Ralph could do.

"Ah, I'll get through it, thanks for listening." Thomas halfheartedly smiled.

"Hey, yo, no problem, Rock," Ralph teased, raising his hands as he mimicked Rocky ready to knock out Drago. Ralph had come over in search of the story behind Willy's black eye, gladly adding the material to his already overstuffed vault, before leaving with the pleasure of busting his friend's balls.

Thomas spent the rest of the day reflecting on his life. *It's almost surreal how glorious it's turning out*, he noted to himself with a heavy dose of sarcasm. It was his however, whether Thomas had chosen it or not. It wasn't the good sheets, the silver spoon or lining that Holtzer undoubtedly saw every time he opened his eyes. Yet, for Thomas, knowing he could touch the sheets on occasion seemed to be all he needed to keep balanced, at least, as balanced as Thomas would ever get. Barring death there was no getting out of his life anyhow, no matter how much Thomas wanted it to change. All of that thinking may have been different however, if Thomas had known just how close he was coming to facing the eternal grave.

~ ~ ~ ~

Maybe wouldn't speak to him when he first got back to the house, and even turned her back and headed to her room when she saw Thomas had returned. "No hug today, I guess," Thomas said aloud, hoping it would stir her. The one night reprieve he had taken at Holtzer's had been like a one evening prison sentence for Maybe, and she viewed Thomas as the judge, jury, and possible executioner.

Mumma was home, and regardless of what Willy said, she was treating Thomas with the same warmth as Maybe. Apparently, caring about others had bit him in the ass as far as popularity in the house was concerned. *What a sad day,* Thomas thought, *when I have to wait for an asshole like Willy to come home just so I have someone to talk too.*

Work had left Thomas hot and sweaty, so when he said, "Hello," to Mumma, and only got a cold shoulder, he took it as compensation for a hard day's work. She kept her attention on the television; and while Thomas knew she had heard him, there was no reason to try and make her speak, or try to apologize to her—not that Thomas felt he should. Besides, Thomas was sure that Mumma had already been on her hands and knees pleading to the Lord for his salvation, the same way she had been on them the night before, wiping the corners of Willy's mouth and catching his saliva. Within a day or two, Thomas was sure she would be asking him to pray with her again, and Thomas knew he would. It was their normal routine—destiny perhaps—that always seemed to calmly and complacently return them to the comfortable level of dysfunction they all shared and embraced.

Thomas knocked on Maybe's door, creating a shuffling of feet and the muffling of her voice. He could tell by the sound of Maybe's voice that she had been using her My Kid Sister doll to speak her thoughts aloud. Maybe had always enjoyed a good conversation with herself, and using the doll added the extra comfort of pretending someone else was listening. She loved that doll, and had even made Thomas keep the counter part in the collection—My Buddy—in his bedroom, but not before a short period of following the toys' theme song and taking the two dolls everywhere Maybe and Thomas went. Thomas felt like an idiot carrying that thing around, as if his high school years weren't tough enough with a special sister, crazy mother, drunk ass stepfather, and a past that had remained hidden. The last thing Thomas had needed was all his friends, friends like Ralph, singing, "My Buddy, My Buddy, wherever I go..." *The things we do for those we love,* Thomas thought.

"Maybe Baby, it's me, can I come in? I want to talk to you." She still wouldn't answer.

Thomas could have just walked in. The lock on her door had been removed after what Thomas had called the, "*Three's Company*, but Fours a Fight," fiasco. Maybe had gotten so mad at Mumma one night for making her take a bath when she wanted to stay up and watch the show, that Maybe had barricaded herself in her bedroom, screaming her displeasure for what seemed like hours. Since that night, the lock had been gone. Still, Thomas didn't want to push open the door. It would have felt like he was pushing her to forgive him, when what Thomas really wanted, was for her to arrive at that destination on her own.

"Well, if you decide to forgive me for leaving last night, I'll be in my room listening to the Beatles." He didn't consider it a push mentioning one her favorite bands from his album collection. It was more of a slight musical nudge. Maybe wasn't budging, however. Standing outside of the door, silent, Thomas felt the hurt radiating from her room. He wanted to stay there, wait for her, but he knew Maybe would come around. She always had, and in his heart, Thomas knew she always would.

~ ~ ~ ~

Thomas was grateful that the Hayward County Fair was only a once a year event. What Maybe loved, Thomas despised like the plague, and as their feet moved across the dirt beneath them, all he could think about was getting away.

There had always been something ominous for Thomas about the fair, a frightening sickness that threw off what little balance he held. From the time he was a small boy, the rumors of girls being raped behind the trailers that housed the Carnies had riddled Thomas with an anxiety that even the bright lights of the rides—rides thrown together by traveling thieves—couldn't lighten. It was a shadow of fear, one scarier than anything the haunted house roller coaster could ever summon, that hung over Thomas. He knew better than anyone, rape wasn't "just for girls."

He was older now however, and although Thomas felt safe, he worried tenfold about Maybe. Perhaps there were good men and women that roamed the grounds, good Carnies and patrons alike. But human nature has a way of blurring the soul, especially one that has already been blinded; and everywhere Thomas looked, all he could see were potential predators, lost boys and men, their mouths filled with lit cigarettes and toothless smiles. All the darkness of human hunger that comes with living on the edge of survival, staring at them, calling them as they walked by; yet still, nothing seemed frightening enough to keep fathers from bringing their sons and daughters, uncles from bringing their nieces and nephews, or Thomas from bringing Maybe.

"Step on up. Everyone's a winner!" The words spoken a sure sign of a lying man.

Thomas could hear the amusement in the Carnies voices, the salivation growing with each repetition. Thomas could see it in their eyes, mannerisms, as he and Maybe walked by.

Drooling with excitement, they leered in Maybe's direction, their faces creasing with insidious smiles after spotting what they believed was an easy target. Still, they never made eye contact with her, avoiding it, like Maybe was Medusa herself.

Yet, even in those disgusting looks of pleasure, Maybe wasn't the victim they preyed upon. Thomas was the one they wanted. Maybe was the game they played, but Thomas was the one who stocked the stand, each gamesman locking him in their sights, sure he would respond with his wallet to their beckoning calls and stares.

"Make her happy. Make her forget what she is. Make her feel like she's won."

Thomas wouldn't stop. Even if Maybe had wanted to, he wouldn't.

"Keep going, Maybe, we'll play one of the games on our way out."

"Fuck you, anyway," Thomas heard the self-proclaimed "Balloon Master" mutter behind him.

The sign over the man's booth—the one declaring his title to the world—was as bright in the night as the lights bouncing off his freshly shaved head. Where his head lit the world however, like a man who had stumbled out of a cartoon with a great idea, the rest of his face put the world to rest. He wasn't middle-aged, his body was too fit for those kind of years. Yet, his cheeks and neck were scrunched together in layers, as if that part of his head had grown twice as much skin as necessary, the excess resting on his black t-shirt and leather vest, giving him all the look of a man with a body in its ripe thirties, and a face in need of circumcision.

He had made no attempt to keep his words, like the dull darts in his dirty hands, hidden. It was clear from the Balloon Master's confident stance, that he wanted Thomas to hear him; he wanted Thomas to see.

"Why don't you take your date to the freak show tent where she belongs, I don't want that bitch over here spreading her stupid anyhow."

The last word whistled through the space created by the Balloon Master's missing front teeth, and as soon as it pierced the ear of the young man, Thomas took a step towards the Carnie. Normally, outside of his low tolerance with Willy, Thomas's control was better. He had heard it all before, accepting that he would have to fight the entire world if he began swinging after every sideways comment about Maybe. Still, Thomas didn't like it one bit. Each insult, each slur, was like a small axe, chipping away at him, leaving

Thomas with the fear and thought that one day, he was destined to snap.

What truly bothered Thomas, was that the man had said it loud enough for Maybe's ears. Thomas knew trying to protect her was impossible, yet, to be so close and to know she could hear it, killed him inside.

It only took a step or two by the young man before the Carnie had hopped over the table to confront him; and only a step more for a few of the Balloon Master's coworkers—if that's what you call them—to be right there by their fellow Carnie's side. Thomas didn't know what to expect, not that he was thinking about much of anything. The Carnie was quick, cat like, and before Thomas could even decide where this was heading, the toothless Balloon pioneer took control of the situation.

With one swing of the man's arm, Thomas felt the sharp pain of his jaw being misplaced, along with the thud of his body hitting the ground—one side of Thomas's face stung by the Carnie's fist, the other from the bouncing of his cheek on the hard dirt surface.

"What are you all standing there for, go ride some rides. And you, why don't you go back to your sleazy little life." Thomas heard Jennifer say, her arms struggling to roll him over.

"You better watch it little girl. Fighting ain't the only thing we're good at it, and you're fixing to find out. Come on, get back to work," The Balloon Master told the other Carnies, who were lost in laughter at Thomas's expense. "Pleasure meeting you with my fist, boy," he aimed at Thomas as he headed back to his mastery, landing one last verbal jab when he said, "Good luck with your retard and your whore."

If Jennifer hadn't been holding Thomas's head up, she may have started round two, but she settled on a burning look instead, the "lord have mercy" kind that only a woman can make.

When a moment had passed and she was done shooting laser beams through the Clown's mouth, Jennifer turned her disapproval to Thomas. "What are you doing getting yourself into this mess, getting Maybe in it?"

She was upset, and so was Maybe. Thomas could see his sister pacing back and forth next to them.

"It's okay, Maybe," Jennifer told her.

"I want to go home," Maybe replied aloud, to no one more than herself. "I wanna go home."

"So much for her fun night at the fair," Thomas said, raising his body off of the ground with Jennifer's aid. His legs were wobbly, his head, pulsating with pain.

"You only have yourself to blame for that." Jennifer scoffed.

"Well, he started it..." Thomas stopped, knowing that he sounded like a child, even while he still wanted to say it.

"He did a pretty good job of finishing it too. Haven't you ever been in a fight?" Jennifer asked disgustedly, as if fighting should have been a normal part of Thomas's existence.

"No, I'm sorry Mrs. Ali, I haven't," Thomas answered, his childish sarcasm leading the way this time.

"I wanna go home," Maybe continued, her repeated words drilling into his already bored head.

"I better get you both home, I don't think you're in any condition to drive."

Jennifer was right. Thomas's eyes were blurred, the light of the festivities, causing them an extra sensitivity. She put her arm around him, balancing Thomas. "Come on Maybe," Jennifer said, "We don't want to give these dirt bags any of our money anyhow."

Thomas looked over at the Balloon Master, who was smiling—smugly—delighted by the exit he had caused. Feeling a need to regain a piece of his manhood, or at least, any piece that he hadn't already left on the ground, Thomas reverted to playground antics, and waved goodbye with his middle finger.

The Balloon Master just shook his head in pity at Thomas. Whatever satisfaction Thomas thought he would gain from flipping the man the bird, never came.

"Where'd you come from?" Thomas asked, suddenly aware of Jennifer's appearance, one he hadn't expected, and one that seemed to come out of nowhere.

"Some friends talked me into coming. I didn't really want to; I've never been too fond of these types of places. But I figured it was better to come than sit at home, floating around." Her lips gently gave way to a smile, while her eyes were glowing like orbs of light. *She's an angel,* Thomas thought, an odd line of intuition for someone who thought it was all nonsense.

"I'm just glad I was here, or you might be laying on the ground still."

The points of her smile broadened this time, showing her enjoyment of having rescued Thomas. Either that, or she was sickly delighted in the thought of him breathing in the dust.

Thomas wanted to say something sarcastic back; yet, his mind held it before it got to his tongue, allowing only, "I'm glad you were here, too."

He didn't recall walking, yet, suddenly, Thomas realized that they were standing outside of Jennifer's car. "That was quick," he muttered. He knew his mind had been slightly clouded by the hit, but the thought of losing time seemed wrong—very wrong. That was just the beginning.

Looking around, Thomas saw that they were no longer alone. Somehow, the Carnies had beaten the three of them to their destination, the bald head of the Balloon Master shining in the moon and shadows. But it wasn't the stance of the man that brought the fear of God into Thomas's heart. It wasn't the toothless smile on the sweaty man's face that scared Thomas, or the sight of the Carnie's balled up fist. It was the soda can that landed by his foot, which stopped the world; the same Tab soda can from his childhood.

"Kick the can. Go on. I dare you. Kick the can."

The world was happening in flashes, *spinning*, leaving Thomas no more than a helpless child stuck on a merry-go-round gaining speed with each revolution.

Spinning—he saw Jennifer grabbed by the tracers of the Balloon Master. Her shirt was torn off in seconds—her bare breasts fondled and free; while her pants rested on her ankles, her naked behind sliding back and forth on the trunk of the car in rhythm with the bald Carnie. He looked at Thomas as the young man flung by again and again. The Carnie's body was one with Jennifer, but his eyes were inside of Thomas.

Spinning—his stomach already on the verge of purging its contents from the Carnie's stares, he saw Maybe being tossed into the backseat of the car, her clothes flying over the front seat and disappearing in the distortion of color, her naked feet, separated by the man in between them, pointed at the roof of the car.

"Help me, Thomas, help me!" He heard Maybe's screams trail off into the night.

Thomas wanted to run to her, save her, yet the steady pull of the ride was holding him in place, forcing him to relive their pain turn after turn. But it wasn't just the ride that was holding Thomas.

Move. Just move!

Spinning—Thomas felt his arms, the grip on and around his wrists, the same as the force of gravity from the ride, too strong to break. Suddenly, Thomas felt the unsettling and all too familiar sensation of his uncovered backside touching the wind.

"Just relax. You'll like it. We like it now," he heard whispered in his ear.

The words were a memory from the past; a nightmare brought back to life.

Thomas tried looking at Jennifer, her body gliding on the trunk, her face, once hidden, was now aimed in his direction. There wasn't any suffering in her look however, no struggle or force. With her blues eye wide open, she smiled and told Thomas, "Just relax. You'll like. We like it now."

"No!" Thomas yelled, closing his eyes, hoping to make it go away, even when closing his eyes was the exact thing that had gotten him into the situation.

"No!" Thomas yelled again. Opening his eyes, there was only one person in his sight this time—Maybe—now fully clothed, sitting as stoned faced on the merry-go-round as the horse she now rode, both of them, mocking Thomas with their stares.

"Maybe Baby, no," Thomas cried, but neither Maybe nor her plastic horse moved.

He tried to move his arms, free himself, but he was a child again, uselessly struggling. Looking up at his captor, Thomas saw that it was no longer a Carnie from the night, but a vision from the Laro School. The young boy that had held him once, now held him again. It was the vision Thomas couldn't escape.

"You'll like. We like it now," he heard Jennifer mocking from the trunk, her soft body, now as hard and grotesque as her voice.

"You'll like it," he heard the boy from the past whispering in his ear.

"Just quit talking!" Thomas yelled, snarling this time as he looked up at the boy. This time was different. This time, it wasn't the boy from behind the pine trees that was holding him. This time, it wasn't a Carnie out for some form of sick revenge. The person holding Thomas, their hands around his wrist, was his Maybe Baby.

"No!" Thomas yelled at her. "No, Maybe! Noooooooo!"
Creak.

~ ~ ~ ~

The sound of the door awoke Thomas with a jolt, his heart thumping in his chest. Maybe, the girl who had just held Thomas down in his dreams was now opening the door to his bedroom, and saving him with her reality.
7:45 P.M.

It had been two hours since he had arrived at home, exhausted. The nightmare, the memory, just another scene for Thomas to live out with his eyes closed. Normally, they weren't as vivid, but the emotions of the past few weeks had piled on him, breaking him, perhaps.

Thomas could see that Maybe was still upset, with her face—sucked in at the cheeks—showing her desire to maintain a wounded appearance. Thomas knew her all too well however, and the fact that she had come to his room meant she was already over it. Still, Thomas indulged Maybe's sorrow by trying to keep a glum expression.

She was carrying her My Kid Sister doll, and after moving her pigeon toed feet through the door, asked, "You wanna play?"

"Sure," Thomas answered, even though playing with dolls was the last thing he really wanted to do. He unhooked the headphones that had dropped onto his shoulders when he fell asleep, and turned the music back on, happy to let the sound of the Beatles fly through the room.

Grabbing the My Buddy toy from a wooden rocking chair that had been squeezed into his small, already constricted bedroom, Thomas held it up as if it were standing on the bed. Using a fake, childish boy's voice, he said, "So, tell me Sister, what's new?"

"A lot," her My Kid Sister doll said with a smile, while Maybe remained stuck in a frown.

"Tell me about it," My Buddy added.

"I'm sorry you know." This time, Thomas was the one talking, looking around My Buddy to see her face more clearly. She was sitting on the edge of the bed, and instantly made a hand gesture to let him know that My Buddy was supposed to be talking to My Kid Sister. Playing the game, Thomas used My Buddy to speak, and apologized again. "I'm sorry. Do you forgive me?"

My Kid Sister continued to smile away, while Maybe had begun to think about it. After a moment of reflection, My Kid Sister hugged My Buddy, and then Maybe hugged

Thomas. She held him extra tight, the strength of her embrace showing how scared she must have been. *How could I ever leave?* Thomas thought. A part of him knew that Holtzer was right, but how do you hug someone who needs it more than anything in the world, only to let them go? Inside, Thomas hoped all the worry would get better as Maybe got older. He hoped that someday he could leave. *Will I grow to resent her if I have to stay? What kind of a person am I for even asking?*

When she let go, Thomas saw her tears, turning every thought he had just entertained into a tiny knife stabbing at his soul.

"Are we ever going to be happy, Thomas?" Maybe asked, her wet cheek dampening the top of her doll.

It was an odd question for Maybe, who even with the bouts of humanity that plague every person, had always seemed to find more happiness in life than most. Thomas had asked that same question at least once a day for his entire life, but he had never the felt happiness she possessed, at least, he hadn't in a long time.

"Of course, we are," Thomas lied, unsure if anyone is ever truly happy, and wondering why she had even asked a question that she normally left up to faith. It was a faith that, with Mumma's aid, of course, Maybe had been grooming at Sunday school for the better half of five years; though it really wasn't until she was seven-years-old that she actually started to get something out of it.

"Her delay is keeping her from fully understanding the beauty of the lord," Pastor Carr had told their mother. Mumma, to no one's surprise, adamantly agreed with him.

In all reality, Maybe was just a curious child at the time, and the bombardment of religion had left her with all kinds of questions.

"Mumma, if Jesus is the son of God, why in the world would he just allow him to be nailed to a cross?"

Her somewhat slurred speech in no way dulled the pristine clarity of her thought. Taken aback by the question, Mumma had answered in a somewhat stuttering manner herself, "Just, just...because. Because he was dying for our sins and God wanted to show just how much he would sacrifice for us."

"Sounds like a bad Daddy to me. If I ever see you and Daddy with a wooden cross I'm outta here," Maybe said, dead set in her opinion, one that had caused Thomas to spit out some of his dinner in laughter. Mumma just shook her head, while Willy remained quiet, the silence of a man who had nearly attempted a similar act of sacrifice, keeping his lips tightened.

Even in the questions of God's actions that came with her age, Maybe slowly started to believe without asking them anymore. A part of Thomas missed her curious nature and wished she would have kept asking those questions, but Thomas didn't blame her. Most adults had never even asked once. Comfortable in her belief and wanting to share it, Maybe would often ask Thomas to pray with her at night—as with Mumma, Thomas always obliged.

"Our father, who art in Heaven, hallowed be Thy name, Thy kingdom come...." The little version of Mumma would always lead the prayers. The older Maybe got, the more adamant she was about saying them. In fact, if it wasn't for the beauty Thomas saw in Maybe's questions first, and then in her belief, he may never have gone to church again. But he

saw a certain beauty to everyone having their own questions
and beliefs. Where the beauty was lost, he often thought, was
in the condemnation of others for viewing things differently,
those selfish protestations that sour humanity by claiming to
have the only opinion that can possibly be right.

"Thomas."

"Yes, Maybe."

"Does God love people like me?"

She had heard her father the night before, saying
things she was starting to understand all too well, and it was
clear, they had hurt her. It was every reason Thomas had tried
to stop Willy. Her own father's words had damaged her to the
point that her faith was left shaken, which for Maybe, was as
deep as the cut could go. Thomas wanted to cry over the fact
that she had been injured enough to ask. God had always
been her first option for a difficult day, her rock of answers.
Thomas was no more than a second hand selection, full of
unwanted and rocky revelations. Still, he couldn't leave her
feeling that pain.

"He loves you more, because you love him more. You
love everyone more, and it has absolutely nothing to do with
how you were born, and everything to do with who you are in
your heart. *That*, Maybe, it was makes you special," he told
her.

It wasn't the most eloquent, soul-enriching
compliment Thomas could have given her, and if he had been
granted more time, Thomas probably could have come up
with something more comforting for her. But that's not a
luxury we are given in the moment, especially when we are
asked questions we never expect, for the mere fact that we
have never asked them ourselves. Thomas never thought
Maybe would question her difference. He only saw her from

his own view, and if there was a god to give love, Thomas knew, Maybe was one of the only people who actually deserved it.

CHAPTER ELEVEN

"When life gives you a million reasons to quit, give it a million and one reasons why you never will."

Roger was indulging his new found bravery, and rather sickeningly sharing it with the entire congregation that had gathered to welcome him home. He had made it through boot-camp, yet, by the stories he was telling, people probably thought that he had single-handedly won a war.

Thomas had always liked Roger. They had, and still did, call each other friends. The events with Mary-Sue however, everything—life—were beginning to turn Thomas fickle, and for the moment, he couldn't have cared if Roger had been on the Challenger when it blew up. After every sentence Roger began with, "And then the drill sergeant said," Thomas would actually spend a moment wishing his friend had been.

"And then the drill sergeant said..."

"Somebody call the Rogers Commission, I think we have an over-inflated ego causing O-ring damage," Thomas mumbled behind the cookie he was using to shield his insults.

Once Thomas was safe, or rather, once he was comfortable that everyone was safe from his slurs, Thomas shoved the cookie in his mouth, and was instantly greeted by a pat on the back that almost caused him to choke.

"Ziggy! How are you?" Holtzer asked, joyful to either see Thomas or to have almost dropped him to his death, another loss caused by a chocolate chip and M&M treat.

It took Thomas a second of swallowing to get the cookie headed in the right direction. With a throat allowing air and a mouth still full, he asked, "Holtzer, you trying to make me choke?"

"Not at all, sorry about that. You shouldn't be so skittish. You wouldn't have choked if you hadn't of jumped," Holtzer chortled, cheerfully making Thomas' startled nature seem like the perfect explanation for bringing about his demise.

Thomas didn't think he would be at the party but, typical Holtzer, he was a surprise guest—the only one who could have saved the Challenger and made the story even more appealing than Roger. Thomas had a sickening feeling that he was going to be stuck listening to Roger and Holtzer duel with stories the way the *North and South* had dueled on both the battlefield and the soft glow of ABC programming.

"Oh, that damn rap music the kids are all listening to. Mark my words, that foolish noise won't last," Willy's voice carried across the room assuredly. He was rambling on with the same conviction that had kept him from buying stock in, what Willy called, "Some cockamamie computer nonsense called Microsoft. What the hell kind of a name is that, anyhow?" He had laughed at his newspaper, as if it had the capability and memory to care.

"Ziggy, you remember Jennifer, don't you?" Holtzer asked with a smile, knowing all too well that Thomas did.

"How you doing?" Thomas offered, without care.

"Good," Jennifer replied back, with faint pleasantry.

"I don't know how you spend your time with these insufferable bores," Holtzer sneered as he surveyed the crowd, showing no desire to keep his voice down. His breath smelled heavily of Johnnie, no doubt removing his normal desire to show only the highest of airs. Liquid fuel often provided that removal of upper echelon oxygen.

"I do it for my mother. It's not like I enjoy it here either," Thomas told him, honestly.

"You sure you don't come here for the company?"

Holtzer made sure Thomas was watching as his eyes made their way to Mary-Sue. She caught them both in the look, Holtzer with his devilish stare, and Thomas with a look of perturbed trouble. Mary-Sue and Thomas hadn't spoken one word to each other since the night in the graveyard, the act they had engaged in as dead as the bodies in the ground beneath them. They had used one another, their lust served and satisfied, and they were both content to leave it at that. Somehow, seeing Holtzer, Mary-Sue knew that he was recreating the act, his minds' eye creeping in the graveyard, and that he was a threat to bring the act to light.

"I'm going to grab a cigarette," Thomas said, hoping Holtzer would stop staring at Mary-Sue and follow him outside; but it was Jennifer who chimed in. "I'll join you."

"I think I'm going to stay inside and say hello to Roger. Catch up a little." Holtzer was going out of his way to make Thomas uncomfortable, much to Thomas's displeasure. Holtzer's teasing about the situation was one thing; his reveling in it was another. Yet, the last thing Thomas needed to do was make a scene. Besides, Holtzer had kept secrets before, and this was most likely just some type of domineering stand on Jennifer's behalf. Thomas was uncomfortable, but like it or not, he had to trust Holtzer.

"Why don't you two get to know each other better, anyhow," Holtzer said with a smug grin on his face, and the smell of alcohol heavy on his breath.

Without uttering a word in return, Thomas directed a *don't say a word* look at Holtzer, then slowly stepped outside, never turning to see if Jennifer had followed.

~ ~ ~ ~

It was quiet in the darkness outside of the church, just the way Thomas liked it. The lightless street only visible from the headlights of the occasional car that passed by and the houses that were fifty yards away. The brightest light came from inside the church. Thomas walked away from them. Even though he knew he couldn't walk away from everything, a momentary escape was on his mind. It seemed like getting away was all he could think of lately—not to college like Holtzer, not to the Army like Roger, but from Hayward itself. *Anywhere*, Thomas thought, *has to be better than this.*

The black of night was alive behind the church. In the direction Thomas was walking, there a small makeshift dock swaying in the lake that graced the backside of the property, as if the large moon overhead was pulling on it. Lost somewhere else—in the world of the moon and water—as if he was holding the sheets from Holtzer's house in his hand, Thomas hadn't paid attention to see if she was following him, although he hoped she had. Tired of always feeling helpless, Thomas wanted the power of walking away from Jennifer as she followed him.

Slowing his stride, Thomas heard Jennifer behind him. The sensitivity of his ears was always heightened at night. Thomas wanted only to love the dark, but a part of him had always feared it since that day. His monsters had hidden in the open light of the daytime, but it was the nighttime sky that often brought their faces back to life—faces that had a way of staying out of focus in the dark, showing only who they truly were when up close. Thomas did his best to make sure it never got that far. *No one gets too close.* It was his fate to accept. Everyone has something however, and Thomas knew it. So, he took that fear and forced himself into the night, just to show that he wasn't going to let those faces of the past win.

"You know he's jealous of you, right?" She said from behind him.

Thomas kept walking, knowing he was right—twenty yards away. That was how far he had determined she was behind him by the sound of her footsteps and the exact distance Jennifer's voice had traveled. It was a gift that came with suffering. Had Thomas ever decided to join the armed services, perhaps he could have excelled with his controlled fear and the ability it had given him.

"Why in the world would Holtzer be jealous of me? He's got everything in the world he could want: money, a future in politics to cushion himself even further, you."

Thomas didn't want to say the last part of it, but his mind let it escape from his mouth. "What do I have—this?" Thomas asked as he walked closer to the mirrored surface of the lake water, using the light at the end of his cigarette to point out at the trees.

Unable to walk any further, Thomas stopped on the dock. Many times, this one included, he had contemplated the idea of walking right off and giving up the struggle. As the shadows of the surroundings played on the watery edges of the dock, Thomas couldn't help but wonder, *Would Aunt Victoria be there to guide me into the afterlife?*

"What is your problem, Thomas? What do you want from life? What do you want for Maybe? Do you just want her to see you miserable? Huh? What good is that going to do her?" Jennifer was asking questions that Thomas didn't want to answer, couldn't. So, he did the usual—what he was best at—and just shut up.

In his silence, Thomas thought about how he didn't care for the way she was speaking to him. It was like listening to the other half of your brain, the side that only shows you the opposite of every decision you make, especially when it's the wrong one. Normally, that would have been fine for Thomas, but Jennifer had no right to question to him like that. She wasn't his savior. *Who had asked her for her opinion anyhow?* If Jennifer really wanted to help, she could just shut her mouth. The only problem however, was the fact that Jennifer knew his answers well before she had asked. It was Maybe, no doubt, who had most likely been inserting ideas about who Thomas was into Jennifer's head, telling her everything she needed or wanted to know. *Thank God Maybe didn't know about the past,* or Thomas feared that he may have been confronted right then.

"Don't you have dreams, for you, for her? I've seen the way she looks at you. She idolizes you, and I can see why. You're good to her. You genuinely love her and she loves you. But what does being miserable and settling in life show her?"

She was standing right next to Thomas, against him, looking directly in his eyes. Jennifer had come to the party with Holtzer, but she had come to the party to see Thomas. He knew it right then, saw it in her every movement and stare. A second became an hour...an hour—never enough.

Time lost its hold on the world, and no matter how long they actually stood there, next to one another, all Thomas knew was that he wanted more.

"Don't you dream, believe, want things?" Jennifer was now asking in a soft, caring voice. "What do you see when the lights go out at night, Thomas?"

Face to face, where Thomas thought they were alone, he spoke his curse aloud when he answered, "Only darkness."

It was that black which had grabbed Thomas years ago and had held him ever since—that was now calling Thomas once again, its cold voice whispering to him as the rock hit his head, and his world faded. In an eternity of instants, Thomas woke up surrounded by the darkness that catches the living, immersed in the water that renews the dead.

~ ~ ~ ~

Thomas wanted to die right then. After all, he was already dead in so many ways. The only thing left was to make it official. He didn't want to come up, but he had to, for her— for Maybe. It's a sad day when the only life you can think of living for belongs to someone else. That, however, was exactly the case. Surrounded by the darkness of the warm water, Thomas couldn't imagine anything but giving up, letting go of any effort to swim, and just sinking to the bottom. His heart had been breathless for so long, that his body was asking him to join it.

Let go, Thomas. Why fight? Why go back up to the surface and a life that has done nothing but kick you around like a soda can from your youth? That's what you are—a crinkled, mangled, shredded can being knocked around for everyone else's pleasure. There is nothing left in you to quench the thirst of life, so stay down. Raise your arms to the side, relax your legs together, let out your last breath, and let go. Go gently. Float to your death, Thomas, and let none be the worse for it.

His life, his every indiscretion threatening to flash before him, yet it was the indiscretions of others that floated in the water with Thomas, those memories that could never drown, be killed, or revoked. They floated with him, mockingly caressing his warm cheek. Inside and around him, they were the water of life, and if this was his, *than take me.*

Death however, much as life, doesn't always work on command. As Thomas's body sank, he felt something, his spirit perhaps, crying, *"NO! Move. Just move. When no one is there to hold you, just move and be free."* It was in that instant that Thomas opened his eyes, and without thought, pushed through the water until he broke free and felt the beauty of the air entering his lungs. It was as if Thomas had never taken breath before, and he rejoiced. But in that salvation of the summer air, there was still the reminder of reality, and that someone up above may not have wanted Thomas to resurface.

~ ~ ~ ~

He had never been one to put himself in situations where he was getting hit over the head with things, though life seemed to be making sure Thomas was, anyway. He didn't know exactly how long he was in the water. All Thomas knew is that as he pulled his body up on the dock, the last thing in his mind was how good he would be in the army.

Jennifer had taken his attention to an entirely new level, and whoever had struck him over the head had crept up unbeknownst to Thomas. He tried instantly to think of who it may have been. Was it Holtzer, caught in a jealous rage? Had Roger found out about his sordid excursion with Mary-Sue in the graveyard? Was Willy seeking retribution for the knockout blow he had landed? The more Thomas thought about it, the more he was beginning to realize that he was giving life plenty of good reasons to knock him around. The person Thomas didn't expect to see standing over him however, was Mary-Sue. Yet there she was, fuming as she hovered over his drenched body, a vision of death in a maroon sundress.

Thomas watched Jennifer try to grab the grapefruit-sized stone away from Mary-Sue as he raised himself, careful not to fall back into the water, only to see Mary-Sue pulling her hand away from Jennifer while raising the rock in a don't-try-it fashion. He was woozy. Turned out Mary-Sue could pack quite a punch when equipped with Neanderthal weaponry.

"You son of a bitch!" Mary-Sue screamed.

While it wasn't quite the greeting Thomas was looking for, it was certainly better than hitting him upside the head with a rock, so he gladly took the improvement.

"What the hell, Mary-Sue?" Thomas asked, straightening himself up and checking for blood. There was a thicker-than-water stream rolling down the side of his head, but not nearly as much as he thought there would be. His wet hair had captured the rest, and while Thomas felt for a cut, he only found a decent sized bump with a slight opening.

"You told Holtzer about us, that's what the hell," Mary-Sue loudly announced.

"What do you mean, *about us*?" Jennifer asked aloud, trying to keep her five foot distance from Mary-Sue, while still approaching to see if Thomas was hurt. At least, that was Jennifer's plan until the question had sparked in her mind.

"Shut-up bitch, this doesn't involve you," Mary-Sue told Jennifer, indignantly throwing her words around like skipping stones toying atop the water before finally sinking in.

"Just put that damn rock down," Thomas said, more concerned with taking another dip in the lake that he wasn't ready for. He wasn't overly excited about the first one.

"What is she talking about, Thomas?" Jennifer asked, directing her question right at him this time.

Thomas had already been hit upside the head to the point of a momentary black out, possibly left to drown—as apparently no one had cared enough to attempt to jump in and save him; and yet there he was, finally up on the stand for questioning.

"It's nothing. Mary-Sue and I....the night of the party at the gravel pits..." Thomas trailed off, though Mary-Sue was more than happy to inform Jennifer of the rest.

"Nothing?" Mary-Sue asked snidely. "Why don't you tell little Miss Goody-Two-Shoes here about how you fucked me on the hood of your car?"

Mary-Sue was happy to ruin Jennifer's image of Thomas, if in fact that was even possible. It was definitely information she was sharing with that intent. Mary-Sue wanted to hurt Jennifer, why, Thomas didn't know.

It was clear however, when Mary-Sue looked at Jennifer and said, "He ain't nothing special. Neither is your boyfriend in there. Go ask him what I had to do to keep him from telling Roger about Thomas and me. Ask him!" Mary-Sue shrieked into the night, using the rock to point towards the church. "Don't worry, it ain't the first time I've been rabbit-fucked in my father's office," Mary-Sue said, grinning at Thomas as she recollected their first encounter a year ago. "I'm sure it won't be the last, either. I might as well fuck the whole town in there. You can't get pregnant twice."

Mary-Sue smirked as she looked right at Thomas again, her anger and staunch disgust for her life holding back her tears.

"What are you saying?" Thomas asked, calmly walking closer to Mary-Sue. He feared what she was implying was true. Thomas hadn't used a condom the night in the cemetery; neither alcohol, passion, or Mary-Sue had cared to stop him from plowing forward without one. Still, Thomas wasn't ready to be a father, and he certainly wasn't ready to raise a child with Mary-Sue.

Jennifer, who Thomas had come inches from kissing only moments before, was slowly walking in the opposite direction, away from Thomas and Mary-Sue, her dismay from the night's news and events written on her unsuspecting face. What a life Thomas was living, when everyone he touched, or wanted to touch, only found grief because of it. Perhaps everyone would have been better off if Thomas had never resurfaced. He may not have had a machete, but Thomas was doing more damage by the lake than Jason Vorhees on his favorite Friday night. Thomas had chosen to live, and it was killing everyone around him.

"I'm telling you right now that I am having *Roger's* baby," Mary-Sue said, her face showing the anger she had embraced. Mary-Sue would have been better off if she had allowed herself to cry; but she had made her choice, and was displaying her fervor towards keeping it at the forefront.

"Then why?..." Thomas asked, only for her to interrupt.

"Because I don't want you to ever, *never ever*, bring up that possibility. Do you understand me? Nothing good will ever come from questioning whether you're the father. You got that?"

She was pointing the rock at Thomas, using it as her exclamation point, knowing she wouldn't need to use it.

The moonlight lit Mary-Sue's eyes as she looked at Thomas. A world of unhappiness radiated from her physically attractive face, as if the beams only reflected the inner anguish of a tortured soul. *What did Mary-Sue see when the lights went out at night?* Thomas wondered. *Did she pray to God before or after she closed her eyes?*

"This is the last we will ever talk about it," she said, throwing the rock down as she headed back inside to Roger, who was most likely too involved in building a stepstool out of a military issued machine gun to notice she was even gone.

"And make sure that little bitch doesn't say a word either," Mary-Sue commanded. She turned around and asked out of satisfied curiosity, "What was she doing out here with you anyway, Thomas?"

Her face distorted with the slight movement of her head, and in that moment, she reminded Thomas of Willy the night Brew had died—half of her head in the light of the night, the other half in the shadows. Mary-Sue was finally showing a bit of happiness, but it was for all the wrong reasons.

Thomas didn't answer. He didn't know what to say. That was Jennifer's question to answer.

"You sure are something else, Thomas Thompson," Mary-Sue commented on Thomas's state of unnatural being, before disappearing into the background.

Thomas lit another cigarette and grabbed his head while staring into the water. His reflection was distorted—his life pretty much the same. He took a step towards the end of the dock, the face looking back keeping Thomas from jumping in. Where Thomas had just seen the ruins of his life in the water, he now saw Maybe, smiling, the joy in her face coming from the baby she was holding in her hands. It was a vision that saved Thomas, and a vision that troubled him. Maybe wasn't holding Thomas's child. She was holding her own.

CHAPTER TWELVE

Present Day:
"I never much cared for that Mary-Sue girl, or her father, for that matter. Some people just seem wrong in certain ways, though, even when we have the feeling, we still tend to question the validity of it. Our feelings are so often mistaken that we forget how to trust, leaving our own truth to suffer. How can people believe in Him, when they can't even believe in themselves?"
Follow the story.
Beep. Beep. Beep.

"I wanted to jump in and save him, but I couldn't. He needed to fall—we all do at times—and as much as it pained me to wait, I held my ground, hoping that he would come back for you; and he did. I thought he would, we all breathe in the water, not in the literal sense, yet, we are one when surrounded. Every day the air surrounds us like that water. The only difference is the thickness. We feel the water on us. The air of life is no different, we just don't feel the swell of it on our skin, though trust me, like the father, it is always there, yet never seen."

~ ~ ~ ~

August 1986:

"You're back early," Nadine Wilson, the only babysitter who Maybe had ever actually gotten along with, stated.

"Why are you all wet?" she asked, snapping her gum and looking at Thomas as if he had just stepped out of a lake, which was, in fact, the case.

Thomas liked Nadine, aside from a personality that was a little too bold for a girl of only fourteen, and a mismatched colored wardrobe that made her look like she was auditioning to be Punky Brewster's double, she was a good kid.

"I got bored at the party and decided to go for a swim," Thomas told her, putting a bag of peas he had just grabbed out of the freezer on his throbbing head.

"Why didn't you just take your clothes off and go skinny dipping?" Nadine smiled devilishly, raising her eyebrows while looking Thomas up and down. "Me and my friends go pool hopping on the weekends in our underwear."

"Yeah, well, I prefer to keep my clothes on, thank you," Thomas said, chuckling at her youthful playfulness.

He had long suspected that Nadine had a young girl's crush on him. Thomas had once had his own kiddie crush on her older sister, Linda, who in a reversal of fortune, had been Thomas's babysitter years before. Linda had never fallen spontaneously in love with Thomas like he had dreamed while alone at night in his bedroom, and in keeping with the tradition, he wasn't about to fall in love with Nadine. Her sister had always been sweet to him, however, so Thomas always tried to treat Nadine the same.

Linda would often get stuck watching Thomas and Ralph at the same time, the two boys like little dogs in heat looking at her. Yet, it wasn't just her beauty that attracted them both to Linda. She was the cool older kid who, once their parents were out of sight, would hand them cigarettes in exchange for not ratting her out about having her boyfriends—and there were several—come over. Once, she even let the boys watch a porno, a bribe Thomas and Ralph had offered in exchange for not telling any of their parents—hers especially—about the funny smelling cigarettes she would smoke out on the porch after they left.

Watching that video was going to be one of the greatest events of Thomas and Ralph's life. They were finally going to see what they suspected Linda and her boyfriends were doing when they snuck in the bedroom. Thomas knew what they were doing. Unwanted experience had taught him the lesson. Still, he never told Ralph, and besides, he was curious to see what sex looked like when it was wanted.

Unfortunately, the momentous occasion of watching the movie was ruined by the modern day technology of the time; and instead of watching *Debbie Does Dallas*, the boys ended up watching Linda and her boyfriend sweating bullets as they tried to remove the jammed VCR tape with a butter knife. They never did get the jammed movie out, ruining a perfectly good piece of history, and the VCR player, as well. It was the last night Thomas and Ralph's parents ever used Linda as a babysitter.

"How was Maybe tonight?"

"Oh, she was good," Nadine said, snapping her gum at the realization that Thomas wasn't going to pursue naked aquatics with her and her friends. She turned around on the couch to see what was happening on *The Golden Girls*, before turning her focus back to Thomas. "We watched TV, painted each other's toe nails, talked about boys." Nadine smiled excitedly as she said the last part.

"She's getting close to getting her period, you know," Nadine continued in her usual straightforward manner, causing a sip of the soda Thomas had begun drinking to go down the wrong pipe. He didn't want to think about things like that, and the last person Thomas wanted to talk about periods with, was Nadine.

"Yeah," Thomas coughed, trying to regain his poise and fresh path of breath, "I'll be sure to let my mother know."

"She doesn't want to talk to your mother about it, which is why she asked me, and why I'm telling you. Do you know how it all...works?"

For a moment, Thomas contemplated giving God a hallelujah-high-five if he would make her stop talking to him about menstruation, which was causing his brain mental constipation. Thomas was far from a prude when it came to feminine hygiene. Mumma had been sending him to the store to buy tampons and maxi-pads since he was Maybe's age. It was the thought of Maybe growing older, along with that strange image his mind had projected into the water, that had Thomas skittish.

"She'll get by, don't worry," Thomas rushed, with no desire to continue the conversation.

"Suit yourself, Big Shot," Nadine snickered. "I would be glad to show you how it all works if you would like," she stated with another grin, knowing Thomas had no intention to take her up on the show.

"Gross, Nadine."

"Alright, but don't say I didn't ask. I guess you're just not the big freak I always heard you were," she teased, knowing she would peak his interest. Thomas didn't want to bite, but his head was still woozy, so he nibbled.

"Oh yeah, who said I was a freak?"

"My mother. She said you and that other little freak Ralph Gaccione are why we spent three years going to the movies rather than renting them at home. Something about dirty movies getting stuck in the VCR one time my sister babysat you two."

Nadine was speaking to Thomas as if she was the adult and he was the troublesome kid.

"I think your sister just may be the pervert your mother should be talking about," Thomas told her.

"Huh. You kidding me? My mother thinks Linda's an angel, as pure as the driven snow. If only she knew just how generous Linda is, especially with all the men at college." Nadine smiled, enjoying the fact that she knew how her sister truly was. Thomas smiled back as she stepped out of the front door, knowing from Linda's past record that Nadine was most likely right.

"Goodnight, Trouble. Be safe," Thomas told her.

"Goodnight, *Stud*," Nadine said, trying her best alluring voice on for size, right before smacking one last bubble, and walking herself the one block it took to get home.

~ ~ ~ ~

There are certain things we expect in life. We expect to be happy, though most of the time we struggle. We expect to have money, yet we never seem to get enough. We expect to, at the very least, be treated like we matter, and with kindness, yet we constantly ignore one another and pass by without even so much as a small, "hello." What we never expect, is to be used in the most appalling of manners.

Thomas Thompson was living proof of that. The physical desires of two young men, eleven years earlier, had changed him in a way he accepted he would never be able to fix. He was broken, damn near physically, and with all absolute of emotion. Thomas tried not to think of it when the lights went out at night, however, he always saw the darkness of the past. It used him like a lustful teenager getting out its frustrations. Thomas wanted to stop it. He wanted to kill it and never allow it to breathe in his mind again, but he could not. No matter how much Thomas wanted—needed—it to go away, it never did. It never would until the day he took his last breath, and after that, Thomas knew it was up to heaven to decide if they both remained. It lived inside of him. Even when he was so blessed to forget, feel normal, it pushed Thomas down and grabbed hold of him, leaving Thomas to scream, *"Let me go! Let me go! Let me go!....let me go....let me....let..."*

Thomas could not—would not—ever leave Maybe. Not just for the valiant reason of being her protector. At times, even he believed it was all horseshit. Thomas wouldn't leave because he knew he would never be a man. He would never be able to just suck it up and deal with it. At least, that's how Thomas felt on the days that held him down. They crept in more and more as the realization of his existence, the worst of all things imaginable, stepped into the light.

What will I be ten years from now, if I stay like this? Will I be my own father? No, Thomas both asked and answered himself. *I will die here rather than walk away. I will be so miserable that even Maybe herself will look for happiness, leaving me here alone, the true one in need.*

His true essence was no more than the pile of bills Mumma kept collecting in the mail every day, just putting aside unopened and forgotten, with the one true hope that they would just vanish away. Sitting there that day, it was the first time in his life that he thought his father had been right to leave him. *How much suffering had he saved himself, just by giving it all away?*

These were the ruminations that rattled in his mind as he entered the church that day. The water in the lake had changed Thomas, showing him the need for peace, not just with himself, but with the Father. How fitting, that a young man so in need of salvation walk through the double doors, his eyes resting on the cross, his heart creating the image of Jesus upon it.

"You ain't nailing me down," Thomas heard the memory of Maybe's voice speak. This time, he didn't laugh. This time, Thomas cried. His feet didn't feel the floor, yet, before he knew it, Thomas was standing right before Him, mesmerized by the thought of Him in a way that he couldn't recall, perhaps since Thomas had been a child.

With the weight his life riding on his back, Thomas felt for the first pew, using his hand to guide him as he sat down. Thomas felt embarrassed to be there, ashamed that he hadn't believed. Thomas wanted to. He needed to, but he couldn't. Not until that moment when he put his hands together for the first time since he was a boy, without doing it for the show of Mumma or Maybe, and prayed for forgiveness— forgiveness for not believing, forgiveness for not being better, normal, like everyone else.

"I'm sorry," Thomas told him, "I'm sorry for who I am," he softly spoke and cried profusely. "I'm broken and I need you," his voice wavered and hiccuped through the tears. "I want to be better. I don't want to be like this anymore. I can't take it," Thomas cried before Him, his heart at his feet, his soul on the cross, his redemption interrupted, by the "Ah, ah, ah, ah," echoing within the church walls.

~ ~ ~ ~

The direction of the noise was difficult to pinpoint, his enhanced hearing once again failing him as the reverberating echoes bounced off the walls in every direction. It seemed to be grunting; and sitting quietly, Thomas determined it to be coming from Pastor Carr's rectory. He gradually stood, gathering his composure as he wiped the tears from his eyes. They had been needed tears, wanted, and for the next minute, Thomas felt mended.

"Ah, ah, ah," continued to attack his ears in small, bee like buzzes. He had an idea what the noise was, and the woman who seemed to be grunting—Mary-Sue, no doubt, perhaps in another forced rendezvous with Holtzer.

Thomas's curiosity was getting the better of his feet, deliberately moving him in the direction of the noise, each "Ah," gaining volume. How stupid of her to be using her father's office with little children right down stairs. Luckily, the noise wouldn't carry that far, and the kids like Maybe, there for a routine gathering with Pastor Carr and the words of the lord, wouldn't be subject to Holtzer's new found desire for blackmail.

"Ah. Ah. Ah."

Thomas pressed his ear to the doorway. If anyone had come in, Thomas would have looked just as depraved as the two of them. For a moment, he imagined that—if caught outside the door—he would be dubbed by the whole of the congregation, "the pervert who stood there listening." Stories told would probably have Thomas touching himself, as well.

He could have walked away. What business was it of his who Mary-Sue pleasured for peace? Who was Thomas to judge Holtzer for waging a physical assault on a woman who could have let the truth be known, rather than arm his war. Something kept Thomas at the door however. Like a magnet, it pulled Thomas, leaving him unable to uncouple himself from its frame.

"Ah. Ah. Ah."

"That's right you stupid little cunt, take it all."

The voice froze Thomas. He recognized it immediately, but the language stunned him. In all the years of attending the parish, in all the countless hours of sermons and prayers, Thomas had never once heard Pastor Carr come even close to speaking like that. Why would he now? *What....what the fuck?*

Thomas waited for a moment, hoping to hear the woman's voice, and for one disgusting split second, pictured Mumma as the woman. Her infatuation with pleasing Pastor Carr, Thomas feared, may have blinded her from right and wrong—not that her marriage knew anything about the first one.

"Ah. Ah. Ah."

"You say a word about this to anyone and God himself will kill everyone you love....you hear me, bitch?"

"Ah. Ah. Ah."

Thomas was in the room before thought or caution could stop him. You don't threaten anyone with death, not in the manner Pastor Carr was implying, without deserving an intervention. Thomas broke the lock. His heart, so recently renewed and uplifted, broke seconds later when he stumbled into the small office, and the horror that came from locking eyes with his Maybe Baby.

~ ~ ~ ~

He had stormed in with a purpose so great it inflated his pounding chest with its valor, but it deflated ten-fold the moment Thomas scanned the room. Maybe and Thomas locked eyes, and where his had recently dried from a swell of tears, hers were still abundantly wet. It was pain, physical and emotional, living in her stare, the watery flow running away, each individual tear racing down her cheek in hopes of escaping. Thomas knew that pain. He had experienced it before.

Why Maybe? Why her? For a moment, Thomas wished he was back inside of his carnival nightmare, the only thing that seemed worse than his current reality.

No thoughts had entered his mind about breaking down the door. Pure adrenaline had pushed it open without a second of doubt or wonder. Yet, now, a million thoughts raced around Thomas's mind, without a speed limit to catch them, and not a single thing to keep them contained.

What had been seconds, was now an eternity of images that no success in life can erase. Pastor Carr, stunned by the young man's arrival, jumped backed, his red, blood-stained penis pointing at Thomas like an accusatory finger. Thomas could see in Pastor Carr's face that the man understood the gravity of the situation, and that he was no doubt contemplating the trouble his actions would bring upon him. He had no idea just how much trouble however, because in an instant, Thomas was on him, the young man's fists pounding Pastor Carr's head.

*Bam, bam, bam, bam, bam....*Thomas swung more times than he could count. He swung less times than Pastor Carr deserved. When the anger of hatred was replaced by the fear of possibly having killed a man, Thomas stopped, and turned his attention to Maybe. She was bent over the desk, crying inconsolably, her body still in the same position Pastor Carr had put it, with a ball attached to a leather strap wrapped around her head. Thomas removed it, fumbling with the strap, his hands red and swollen, his brain incessantly repeating the image of Pastor Carr's naked manhood in his mind. Maybe was lying there, but her mind was gone. Even with the sound of her crying, Thomas knew she was in the quiet place where people go to remove themselves from the pain of reality. He had been there, lived it—that unwanted spot where your body and mind split. But even a fork in the road has a common connection. No matter how much you forget, you always remember the pain.

He pulled up Maybe's pants, trying his best to avoid looking at the blood that had stained her backside and thighs. She tried to pull away, briefly unsure of who was touching her or why. "It's me—Thomas. I'm getting you out of here," he told her, the groan of Pastor Carr in the corner showing that the man was still alive.

Her sobbing was like a cry to hurry, but the more Thomas rushed, the more clumsily his hands reacted to pulling up her pants. Maybe was crying too hard to see Thomas, her eyes, shut tight enough to allow only the pain that was crawling inside of her out. She stumbled as she straightened her body. Her knees buckled underneath her, both unsure of the ground beneath them or whether she would have the strength to remain upright. Without any desire to make her suffer or struggle any longer than was needed, Thomas picked her up, and carried her out of Pastor Carr's office.

She was heavy for a girl her age, but that was common to her condition. What wasn't common was what Maybe had just endured. Carrying her to safety, Thomas couldn't even begin to imagine how this was going to affect Maybe. As he turned his back to open the double doors and let them out of the church, Thomas took one last look at the cross. *Had Jesus cried on the day he died?* Thomas wondered. Jesus had every right to. He had every right to cry now for what had just happened, and so did Maybe. A life can be taken without death, and we all die for the sins of others. The problem, is that we often live for those sins as well.

Pastor Carr had used his pulpit as the throne of blessings, while his sins lay hidden in the rectory. Time can show you the truth if it chooses, a luxury not always granted. Even when it skulks out of the shadows however, time still can't erase the past. Maybe was going to have to live with the memory for the rest of her life, and time, so arrogant in its late arrival, was about to show them all that Maybe was never alone.

CHAPTER THIRTEEN

August 1986:
We walk through life in moments of anguish as if we are stuck in a vivid dream. The pain, the joy, those are the emotions that stand out. The aftermath is the blur; a car speeding by with no more than tracers left for us to decipher. How relative it is to your standing, how drastically the theory changes from face to face.

It was a short ride home from the church, with Maybe doing nothing more than crying and clutching herself. Thomas tried to reach out and stroke her hair, let her know she was safe, but his hand stopped as it got closer; it stopped the moment Thomas noticed her cringe at the sight of something invading her space. Where he had once wished it had been another, had been a girl, Thomas now wished for nothing more than to have been in Maybe's place, and to take that pain she never deserved. How could he let her know she was protected, when they both knew that no one is ever truly safe. People walk around, confident, some armed, some not. What they all forget as adults, is that we are all children inside, each one of us holding out the hope that we are never reduced to what we truly are. Perhaps, if we embraced it, we would never need to feel that fear again.

After parking the car in the driveway, Thomas rushed over to open Maybe's door. In a slouched gesture, he let her know that he would pick her up, but she stood on her own this time. Unsure if she was showing him, showing herself, or showing the world her strength, Maybe made her way to the door on her own terms. She never said a word, her clothes tousled from being hastily thrown on, her hair matted down on the sides from the sweat and leather straps. Her feet, which had always been prone to dragging, scuffed along the overgrown stone pads of the walkway. She was wobbly, more so than usual, the pain clearly showing in her stride. Yet, she did it. Defiant, strong, even in the worst of times, Maybe was a warrior that wouldn't be stopped.

Thomas quickly stepped in front of her, opening the door to let her in the house. That was when she looked at him for the first time since they were in the rectory. The warrior, the defiant soldier, removed from her gaze. She was his Maybe Baby, and he could see it on her freshly watered cheeks.

~ ~ ~ ~

In an everlasting shock from the events, Thomas couldn't exactly recall how he described the incident to Mumma and Willy, but he did remember Willy reacting with a, "I'm going over there and putting a bullet in that motherfuckers head! Better yet, I'll cut his fucking balls off!"

"We already have someone over there, Willy, so just calm down," Officer Gary Axel told Willy, trying to remain clean and fresh in the middle of a shit storm, and struggling mightily to keep everyone else the same.

"Would you be calm right now, Gary, if that was your daughter Amanda?"

It had been such a long time since Thomas had seen Willy show actual compassion—if ever—and for a moment, the young man wasn't even sure if it was real or just for show.

"I'm not saying I don't blame you, but let's not make an already messy situation any worse, okay?" Officer Axel pleaded. Mumma had called the police after Maybe and Thomas had arrived at home, for once doing the right thing; and within minutes, Officer Axel, who lived only four roads down from them, was there in plain clothes.

"We have an officer down there right now getting his side of the story."

"His side of the story?" Willy asked, rightfully indignant. "What the hell do you mean, *his side of the story?* He raped a little girl!" Willy's finger pointed at Maybe, who Mumma was holding in her arms on the couch, the two of them swaying to an invisible breeze. Willy's eyes however, never left Gary's. He was, at the moment, admirable in his defense of Maybe, and even Thomas couldn't deny it. With all his faults, there was still good in Willy's heart, and he was letting it show.

"Now, that's not what I meant, Willy. They are going to take him down to the station, but we need to get the entire story, that's all. We may have to take Thomas here down with us as well. From what I understand Pastor Carr looks like he was beaten close to death."

Thomas didn't know what Officer Axel was getting at exactly, at least as far the entire story was concerned. Was the story more important to get "straight" just because Maybe was considered a crooked line in this world? Did her condition make her more vulnerable to being a victim without prosecution? Thomas wished Officer Axel had seen Pastor Carr's red dick pointed at him, then he would understand why the only satisfaction Thomas had in the world at that moment, was that he had almost sent Pastor Carr to the grave.

"He was defending his sister. Thomas stopped him. You're lucky it wasn't me, I would have killed that son of bitch, and I still just may."

The fact that Willy was not only defending, but praising Thomas, was stunning. Thomas had raised his fists to Willy only weeks ago, and now, Willy was proud of it. Pride laced with anger was what it had finally taken for Willy to value Thomas.

Listening to it all, Thomas stayed pressed against the wall. Pastor Carr's naked manhood, Maybe bent over the desk with that ball in her mouth, were all he could see; the images that bore no words or comprehension. The lightening quick rush that had overpowered his body and sent him through the rectory door was gone, leaving only the slow, constant remembrance.

Forcing it out as best he could, knowing it would hold its own time and return at will, Thomas looked at the couch. Maybe was staring into the abyss, her own memories replaying like an old school movie on a rickety reel. It was a horror movie she would spend the rest of her life reliving, too afraid to move, too attached to look away.

Willy continued to argue and claim he was going to remove Pastor Carr from this world—a hollow reaction they all knew wasn't true. Willy wouldn't give up the escapades of his life for prison. If it was any other man, he may have killed them and gotten away with it, but a man of god was shielded by tradition and forgiveness in a comfort most men weren't afforded—right or wrong.

They were living in a world full of cheating evangelists, who crying their way out of sin, walked their way into the bank with flowing donation baskets, all thanks to the honor they showed for admitting they were human. How glorious life would be if all men could admit their humanity with such luxury, but then again, who needs a road paved with gold anyhow?

Mumma had been one of the first to fill Pastor Carr's donation baskets, as well as his stomach, every chance she had. She would stop by the bank every Friday afternoon to deposit her check along with Willy's, always making sure to get the freshest five-dollar bills she could find to fill the Hayward Baptist envelopes.

Looking at Mumma now, Thomas realized she hadn't once prayed since he and Maybe had gotten home, which struck him as odd. Of all the times and things Mumma had laid on the Good Lord's feet to fix, she hadn't said a word about what had just transpired. *Was it out of respect for Maybe?* He was sure hearing the word of the Lord was the last thing Maybe wanted right now. *Or was it just coincidence?* With everything going on at that moment, most people wouldn't be focused on prayer. Yet, Mumma wasn't like most people, and Thomas knew that.

How strange it was standing there; on the same day that her baby boy had finally found Jesus, Prudence Main-Crowley had let him walk back away.

~ ~ ~ ~

February 1987:
It was a mild Northeast winter, with above average temperatures and only three real snowstorms to deal with.

Each of them dropped over ten inches of wet snow, but nothing they couldn't handle with a snow shovel or small plow. The true cold of the times was in their hearts. Pastor Carr had received two years of jail time back in the fall after confessing the sin he had committed to the police and courts, while Maybe got a life sentence in the prison of her own mind.

Pastor Carr was leniently looked down upon with his defense that Maybe, a ten-year-old girl, had actively participated in the act, and had in his words, "made advances toward me." What was most disgusting was the fact that he blatantly lied in God's name. The only thing equaling that treachery was the fact that society showed him mercy for it.

Maybe had been going to counseling since the incident. She was withdrawn, prone to crying fits. The little girl, his Maybe Baby, was gone, and Thomas was worried it was forever. *How beautiful a life we are given, only to have it taken away.* Still, each day she would smile a little more than the one before, and hope would grab Thomas out of the pining of his own heart, tightening its grip with his desire that Maybe would find the innocent peace that had made her shine so brightly before the lights had been turned off.

Mumma hadn't been back to church since the night it happened. Her faith was still with her, but the hallelujah-high-fives and apple pies were gone, leaving silence and unpleasant odors to prevail. Willy, while more compassionate towards Maybe than Thomas had ever seen him, still spent most of his time down at the bar. What was normally a night spent chasing females however, was now a nightly rant from a bar stool about all that was wrong with this world and why humankind deserved the hell it was living, a hell he was readily projecting right back with his mouth.

As for Thomas, he gave his statement and was judiciously reprimanded for taking matters into his own hands. Yet, no one really blamed Thomas for his reaction, which by all rights, was the only justice that survived in the entire mess. Thomas's jury, his executioner, was the town—their eyes and stolen looks persecuting Thomas and Maybe every time they drove or walked past the people. The stares bore through the back of their heads, tattooing the pity felt by some, and the shame felt by others.

A large number of the church congregation had looked upon Maybe as the real sinner, even before, and now, they looked at her with an even deeper intention of disdain. She was an abomination. The devil spawn who had tempted poor Pastor Carr, the widowed, lonely man, with her not-even-teenage femininity. How blessed they must have felt to see something so beautiful looking back at them through their broken mirrors.

The looks didn't just end on the streets of town, they were everywhere. Thomas knew it was going to be a long road when even shop-cop Larry Dean let Thomas walk past him, twenty minutes late every day, and not a word said. They were the outcasts, as if life hadn't already thrown them out of the ring already, it pushed them even further. Their past had caught their present. Their present was sinking their future—that blessed boat already filled with holes. Pastor Carr had raped Maybe, while they reaped the damage of what was left behind, and the unholy seed that had been left sown.

CHAPTER FOURTEEN

Present Day:
"I can't even begin to tell you how pained I was when I found out. It was like a bad memory come back to life—a nightmare really—one that can't be escaped. I was disgusted, repulsed at the thought of what that fat piece of shit had done to you. Please excuse my language, but the description of someone as disgusting as Pastor Carr is only *fit* in profanity."
Beep. Beep. Beep.

"You were different after that day, rightfully so. We are all changed by the hands of others, but no more so than by the hands of God. He had loosened his grip, only to allow his own creations to tighten their chubby, sweaty little fingers and palms around you. Not quite the plan anyone ever imagines him to have in mind; at least, that's the lie we tell ourselves to get by. He's not the one who lies to us however, we allow the voice of others to take his place, say it, say that which he never would. Those who think He would allow it, plan it, are no more than history in the books, their definition left for repetition."

"I feared how Thomas would handle it. He had become like a suffering sponge, absorbing whatever he could. Trying to protect at every corner, only to learn the lesson that broke his own father—me—that we are all vulnerable. We can protect each other, but only for a moment, and often at immeasurable cost, especially when we fail."

Beep. Beep. Beep.

"Would he bury you both with it, or would he find a new creation, good or bad. Who was he? What would your suffering make him become—better or worse? Would he finally walk away? Would he finally follow my footsteps? Questions, life is but a series of unanswerable questions. The more we know, the less we can ever be sure of anything. The only certainty is that with our heart, we create the magic that makes it all worth it. You, my dear, are the greatest magician I have ever known. But Thomas, he was still shackled. He was almost ready—I could see it in him. He was almost ready to finally break free. Without you, Thomas may never have done that. Your suffering has been my curse. Your healing has been my blessing."

~ ~ ~ ~

February 1987:
"Thomas, get the door, I'm watching the game."

It wasn't uncommon for Mumma to ask Thomas to walk past her to get the door, as she was always most comfortable on the perfect-for-sitting backside she had spent years developing. What was a new twist in the world of Prudence however, was the viewing pleasure. She had gone from a holy roller one night, to a "Jesus can find his own way home" disciple the next.

"I'm coming," Thomas half yelled at whoever was knocking. He was hoping that Mumma would feel the edge of irritation in his voice at having to answer the door. She didn't.

"Who's winning?" Thomas asked her as he made his way to the door.

"The Patriots are up by three. Let's hope they can hold a lead better than the Red Sox," Mumma bitterly grumbled.

In hindsight, if what had happened to Maybe didn't ruin Mumma's belief in Jesus, than the outcome of that past fall's World Series and the Red Sox major meltdown certainly would have.

He twisted the door handle as Mumma made her statement, opening the door to an unexpected visitor with an all too familiar face.

"Can we talk? Maybe go for a walk?" she asked, glancing uncomfortably inside—not as if looking for someone. She was clearly more concerned with being seen, and Thomas didn't blame her. After giving a quick inspection, she lowered her head, nervously inspecting her nails, before glancing back up at him.

Thomas should have said, "No." She had already tried to kill him once. What was next? Was she going to take him for a walk down a street with no outlet and give it a proper reason to be called a dead end? What did she want to talk to him about anyhow? Was this going to be some plea to show mercy on her father? *Think again, Mary-Sue.*

Still, with everything that had happened, Thomas thought about the child she was carrying—his child—which left him with a small amount of concern for her. Mary-Sue's father, her only living parent, had been a monster in hiding. What a grotesque realization to have thrown at someone, even someone with already skewed morals, like Mary-Sue.

The totality of it all was enough to keep her away from the courtroom, which had struck Thomas as odd. He had figured someone with Mary-Sue's tendency for rage would gladly be on the steps screaming her father's innocence, throwing her anger at the judge, at them, at everyone.

Perhaps her condition, which was now prominently showing, had changed her from the inside out, as well as changing how others looked at her. A woman with child is always granted a different level of compassion, and rightfully so.

"I'll be right back, Mumma," Thomas told her, grabbing his jacket from the coat rack next to the door. He stepped through the frame and out into the cold, dark night, only to face another.

The breeze on the coast is one of the worst pains of living in New England in the wintertime, with each gust like a small insect penetrating your skin and slithering right to the bone. Thomas's jacket was too thin for the wind that night, but it gave him his own nervous twitch to indulge, as he continuously pulled at the collar in an effort to protect his neck from the twenty-degree weather and buzzing ten mile per hour attacks from Mother Nature.

They walked for a minute, though it gave all the impression and awkwardness of ten, in silence. The only noises heard coming from the light slap of their shoes on the cracked pavement that mirrored their lives. The yellow of the streetlamps above gently extended their reach towards the two, illuminating the pavement in soft circles before losing their way in the darkness.

The windows of each home, some still clinging to the lights of Christmas cheer, were lit up like televisions with the volume muted, giving Thomas and Mary-Sue a glimpse of the neighbors as they continued their nightly routines, leaving them to create the words that suited the actions. *We do the same thing*, Thomas thought. *We all get a scene we can't control. The only thing we can determine is how we interpret it, and the words we choose to make it all come together.*

For a moment, Thomas was lost in the escape. Uncomfortable situations had a way of doing that to him, his mind finding another destination to make a home. For a brief second, his thoughts were one with the wind. Everything lay on the surface of the skin, yet both still burrowed to the bone.

"I've been staying with Roger's family since....." Mary-Sue trailed off, before starting again. "I'm so sorry for what happened to your sister, Thomas. I've wanted to tell you that since this all began, but....my father...."

Thomas wasn't going to chime in or help her finish her statements. She had asked to speak, so, with quiet belligerence, he was going to do his best to oblige her wishes.

He wasn't sure which one of them had failed to move their feet first, but at some point, they had stopped walking and were standing still in the middle of the street. No fear of being run over by a car came to them, as there were rarely any on the road at nine-o'clock on a Sunday evening.

"How are you feeling?" he asked, giving up his staunch stance only moments after taking it, still not wanting to talk, but afraid even more to listen.

"I get sick every morning, can't stand the smell of certain things, crave others. I told Roger's family two weeks after everything happened. I thought they would be upset considering Roger and I aren't married yet, but with everything going on, they were happy. If only they knew the truth."

Each topic was a problem with a wrong answer, or at the very least, one that appeared to be beyond a solution. She was carrying what Thomas had either been led to believe, or had assumed on his own, was his child. How could he just let it go? It was a life, a part of him. How do you walk away from that? It was the same question that haunted every corner of his world, and once again, Thomas would be no better than his own father if he let it happen. But what could Thomas do? Mary-Sue was determined to let Roger think he was the father, and Roger was a good man. What would Thomas accomplish by calling her out? He would ruin the happiness of others. Besides, what life could he give a child? If Thomas had to pick a father, he would have picked Roger over himself—the same choice Mary-Sue was making.

"He was different when my mother was alive," she returned to the original thought that Thomas had interrupted, speaking to the fingernails she was picking at again, "We were a family—trips to the park, game nights, bedtime stories. I loved him. I still do. How sick am I?" Mary-Sue asked herself, as she began to cry. "Then she passed and everything changed. He changed. I was only thirteen the first time, when…."

"When what?" Thomas asked her, afraid he already knew.

"I can talk to her—I can talk to Maybe if you want, help her." She had tightened up the ship, using her belief that she was in a position to comfort and aid another to dry her own cheeks. Survival isn't progress though, and survival, as Thomas was coming to realize, was Mary-Sue's only strong suit.

He feared what she was implying. It hit his stomach, which instantly wretched with a thought and image he tried not to conjure. Yet, as if the fact that Mary-Sue was a victim made it okay, Thomas victimized her even more by making her say it aloud. "What exactly can you help her with?"

"She just has to block it out, pretend it didn't happen. She'll get over it, even someone in her mindset."

Referring to Maybe as someone in *her mindset* infuriated Thomas. The ignorance of Mary-Sue's words quickly replaced any compassion he felt for her with anger, a disgust that once again gave his feet the ability to move.

"Is that what you did Mary-Sue? Just pretend it didn't happen?" Thomas spoke loudly over his shoulder, his disapproval apparent.

She was following behind Thomas, his pace and early start keeping her several yards behind.

"You don't know what it's like, Thomas. You don't even have a father. Don't you judge me without walking in my shoes!" she screamed.

What Mary-Sue didn't know was that Thomas understood the pain all too well. They may have had their childhoods stolen by different criminals, but the crime was the same. Thomas's father was the possession he lost upon speaking. Maybe's innocence was the jewel taken due to Mary-Sue's silence.

"You could have kept this from happening." His words pointed their long, self-righteous finger at her. "Staying silent as a child is one thing, but you're a full grown adult now. My sister will never be the same because of you!"

His stride created a distance she couldn't gap without running. Instead, she choose to stop walking, taking in the anger Thomas left her to absorb along with the cold February wind. Mary-Sue's words still carried on the breeze, however, and Thomas heard her pain and new-found tears when she yelled, "You don't know what it's like to kneel before your father. You don't know what it's like to grow up with a secret that you can't tell, living a lie because you don't want anyone to know what has happened….keeps happening. Once you accept that lie inside of you, you can't admit it was ever wrong to anyone. You don't know, Thomas. You don't know what it's like to carry that child."

The cold marrow of truth had found its way home. Mary-Sue had a reason for keeping the true father of her child's name hidden. Thomas had thought it was his name she was ashamed of; that she feared someone would find out about their night of unconstrained passion. But that is where he was wrong. Mary-Sue wasn't just sheltering herself. She was protecting the years of secrets she had been blinded with. The pain of it never-ending, never spoken, delivered with the outcome that she would give birth to the lie, and that the real truth was headed to the grave.

~ ~ ~ ~

"It kills me to see her like this."

Thomas knew exactly how Jennifer felt. The winter was mild. Maybe, however, was colder than he could ever remember seeing her. Still, Thomas held out hope. He would catch her from time to time with that slight curvature of her lips in a tried smile, though, he didn't think she knew if it was okay to be happy again, to laugh or to love. She was afraid with the worst fear of them all—of being herself.

"You think she'll ever be the same?" Thomas asked, knowing that either way he would always hold out hope. Thomas feared he already knew the answer. The young man had been wrong before however. Why should this be any different?

"I think time will tell. Her heart is so different than ours, better really. I think there's a chance. If anyone has it in them to get through this, it's Maybe."

Thomas was happy to see that Jennifer had stopped by the Hayward Heights Elementary School to see all the faces that had been a part of her summer days at the center; though a part of him suspected that seeing Maybe was her main motive. Although, in choosing her visit at the time school was letting out and Thomas would most likely be there to pick up Maybe, he also suspected she had an eye on seeing him, as well.

It had been months since she had left for Yale, and the thought of her there with Holtzer rotted in his gut, but Thomas had enough to worry about with Maybe. Yet even with all the time her recovery consumed, a memory of Jennifer always had a way of finding any free moment Thomas possessed.

"Just try to patient with her," Jennifer offered, her hand lightly touching his arm, their eyes in an embrace—until with one quick motion, she turned and walked hurriedly away.

Thomas wanted to stop her. He wanted to talk to her, about everything, about nothing. There wasn't much left to explain, yet, Thomas wanted to explain it all. No, not explain it, just tell her. She was the first person he had ever wanted to tell his entire story to, everything before, everything then, and everything that Thomas feared would and wouldn't come. It was as if telling her, talking to her, would only bring the best of life.

Being near her had a way of salvaging Thomas from the wreckage of his own heart. Her look, her touch, had a way of collecting the pieces from that which had settled. He was tormented, turned, stomach twisted, mind warped and devastated, every time he watched her walk in the opposite direction. It was time to accept it. The unlovable Thomas

Thompson, who had never given himself in full to another, had finally fallen in love.

~ ~ ~ ~

"I want to take you someplace we've never been before," Thomas told Maybe, unsure if he was doing the right thing. *How would she respond? Would it really help?* At that point, Thomas was willing to try anything.

"Where?" Maybe's voice was short, the music in the background like the sad whisper of someone crying, hurt from the fact that she hadn't sung along in quite some time. Thomas had tried long drives to beautiful counties that made up the state of Connecticut, in wonder of how many he had never seen. The winding roads where—overhung with large trees that greeted every car, every occupant—peace on earth greeted him at every turn.

What Thomas hoped would renew Maybe however, only seemed to scare her. Every cascading leaf flung to its death by the trees in fall had been like a new predator attacking, while the barren winter branches pointed at her like skeleton fingers, waiting for the right moment to close upon her and catch her in their grasp. No matter how much she tried to find the beauty, Maybe just couldn't see.

"Someplace I think you could use right now. It may help you feel better."

"Daddy took me someplace like that once. Said he was taking me for a ride to feel better. All I did was sit in the car while he cried."

"This won't be like that," Thomas told her, curious what had made Willy cry like that in front of Maybe, but not enough to ask.

"Good. I don't want to do that."

She had become quick in her speech over the past few months. In all appearances, the incident had propelled Maybe's physical development, while stunting her emotional growth.

The baby in Thomas's vision, the one Maybe had held in happiness at the lake, was real. Two months after he had carried her out of the church, Mumma and Thomas had to drag Maybe into the doctor's office. She had been bleeding and nauseous, both signs of what—at the time—Thomas thought was the only Pastor Carr pregnancy that was never wanted or expected.

It was a new life created from pain, forced anguish and suffering, yet, a life as beautiful as any that could have been a part of Maybe, no matter who shared it with her. But it was a new life that wasn't meant to be. Maybe was only a child herself, incapable of carrying a baby, not at her age. It was an added loss, the tally of Maybe's short ten years piling up on her in a most unharmonious way.

"We're almost there. Want to listen to Simon and Garfunkel the rest of the way?"

"No."

~ ~ ~ ~

The spider web of paved paths that connected Hayward were no different than those that made up most of Connecticut. They were winding old roads that had been crafted in an effort to avoid cutting through the largest of the trees and rocks, contouring to the natural shape of the land, and creating entire towns of snake like streets. River Road was no different in that aspect, but it did however hold its own unique mysteriousness, as the road had been woven on a large hill, giving the uphill incline and constantly winding path a sense of eerie mysticism. Thomas wasn't sure if his life resembled that path or if he had just chosen to see it that way, but the similarity, in all of its transient difficulty, was eerily similar.

The roads were still dry from the morning dissipation of black ice—that beautiful deceiver which had a habit of taking unsuspecting lives; the pavement, glistening, alluring, never showing the luxury of destruction it provided for those who failed to realize the slick nature of the frozen dew that rested upon it. It was still early afternoon, the road was safe for now, but still Thomas proceeded with caution, gently guiding the car to the spot he had done his best to avoid for the past eleven years; the place where his life had sidetracked, where he had become a different Thomas, no more than a mirage for the world to see.

Thomas stopped the car, took a deep breath, and stalled for a moment before opening the door. He looked at Maybe, who sensing his uneasiness, looked back at Thomas with the eyes she once held, in a moment beyond her own suffering. It was time to tell her what he feared she would never be able to understand; although somehow, Thomas knew that she was the only who would. His ten-year-old sister, with what the world had called a deficiency, was the only one Thomas could share his soul with, the only one with the ability to understand the demons that filled his room when the lights went out at night. Maybe was the only one who could see his darkness.

"Follow me," Thomas said, squeezing her hand gently as he offered a forced smile. He needed to show her as much as she needed to see. They were brother and sister. They were survivors. How they had been brought to suffer the same fate, in two worlds so different, was now, the greatest bond they shared.

The screech of their car doors echoed through the quiet grounds, the large buildings in the background returning the intrusive noise. The shutting of the car doors were like screams of displeasure on the now fully abandoned landscape. The school had been permanently shut down due to a lack of funding eight years before, the final three buildings now covered in their own set of vines.

There had been rumors of everything from amusement parks to local colleges taking it over, but nothing ever came to fruition. The Laro School was a ghost town of haunting memories, most of them living inside the walls. Thomas was the walking the apparition, and most likely wasn't alone. He knew that pain had seeped outside the walls; acts and atrocities that were lived out by evil men—the worst—with badges and authority, walked the streets, spreading the deeds to those they captured.

Kick the can. I dare ya. Go on. Kick the can.

They had parked inches from the circle of trees from his past, the rock visible through the withered branches winter had brought bare. Maybe stared at Thomas as he stood there, lost in himself, staring into the rock, unsure where to begin. It was over. It had been over, yet, standing there once again, it was as fresh as the day it happened. His mind conjured up the green on the brush, the smell of the summer growth that tickled his nose as a child, the warm sweat on his arms. It was summertime in his mind. The closer Thomas came to his own version of hell, the warmer he became.

"What are we doing here?" Maybe asked, breaking his trance.

His childhood had found him—that old memory which had held the young man back, wrought havoc on his beliefs, and at times, even threatened to kill him. He had dark shadows that had shaped him, shadows that came to life at night when everyone else in the house was sleeping. Every night, Thomas would tuck Maybe into bed, wishing her sweet dreams, only to go to his own room, silent in his nightmares.

Unable to think of just how to tell her, Thomas left thought behind, and instead allowed his uncontrolled heart to speak. *Will it help her? Am I doing the right thing? Will I only scare her more?* All these questions continued to flood his mind, which was now nothing more than an onlooker in the story, one left only to hide in the corner and take document of his shame.

"This school, the Laro School, was built in the early 20's as a sort of housing for people with different kinds of disabilities, many of them just like you, Maybe; though, everyone in the town knew it was really a hideaway, a place of torture—doctors conducting experiments, unspeakable conditions that society quietly ignored and funded. Many of the people in Hayward were the workers, the caregivers, and in some cases, the abusers. Two boys who had been abused themselves found me walking past here one day. They showed me the world I never wanted to see. A world I thought you would never know."

Maybe was looking at Thomas, stone faced, leaving him to wonder how much she was absorbing. But much like that day years ago, it was too late to change. He had started the story. Now it was time to follow it.

"Most of the disabled adults were free to wander the street, most of them harmless. I had seen what I thought was all of them walking the streets in the neighborhood. We had stupid little nicknames for them. There was Jimmy Stilts, a tall kid who walked the streets with a shower cap on his head, rain or shine. Walter Flashback, who twitched constantly as he walked—everyone assumed he was stuck in a never-ending acid trip. I had never seen the two boys who grabbed me though, and the first time I did, it was too late."

"I tried to stop them, but I couldn't. They were strong, too strong. The boy holding me had....it was the first time I had ever been that close to anyone with down-syndrome. The boy who...did it, had something else, I'm not sure what. All I know is that I prayed for mercy from God while it happened. I wanted to know why it was happening to me—a boy. 'I'm a boy,' was all I could say while it happened. I thought things like that only happened to girls."

The anguish, as if back from the dead, was fresh on Thomas's face. With the story came the buried tears, like a broken dam of words and water combined. *What have I done by telling her? Am I just violating her more?*

He took a moment to dry his eyes. Afraid to look at Maybe, Thomas kept his focus on the rock. There was no going back. Whether he had said too much or gone too far— right or wrong—she would know.

"I thought about all the girls who had walked this same road almost every day of their lives, and as..." his lips had begun to quiver again, his eyes in a battle to keep the tears contained. "While it happened, I, I wished it was them. I wished they had been the ones. I asked God why. I asked him what I had done to deserve it. I was a boy, it wasn't supposed to happen to me, but I was wrong. Asking him was wrong, yet, here I am now, all these years later, a part of me asking 'why?' to someone I fought believing in, talking to a myth I swore I would never utter a word to again."

"I've never told anyone except Mumma and my father. Can you believe it?" Thomas awkwardly, nervously laughed. "Not even Ralph. I've kept it buried. But I feel it, the longer it stays in here," Thomas pointed hard at his chest, "killing me more than the memory of it alone. Who would want to know anyway? That's what I say to myself. Life violates us all at some point anyhow. What makes my story any different? Who would really care? I would just be a freak."

Thomas stopped and took a moment to regain what little composure he had. Still, he couldn't look at her.

"Mumma didn't know exactly what had happened, but she was the first to notice that something was wrong. By the time I got home my clothes were dirty, which in itself was normal. I was an active little kid. Even on a rainy day, I always found a way to keep myself entertained outside. This was a different kind of dirty though, and she knew it. This wasn't the usual dirt and mud or occasional tear on the knee of a pair of pants, requiring a patch. She saw that my clothes looked torn, that I looked torn, but it wasn't until she turned me around and saw the blood on the seat of my pants that she feared the worst."

"Mumma asked me what happened, though a part of her already knew. Her normally talkative, unable to sit still child, was standing in front of her, unable to move," Thomas told Maybe, trying to speak about it with a straightforwardness that he hoped would help separate him from the crime. "Willy doesn't even know about it. No one knows except Mumma, my father, and now, you. We only spoke about it that day—the day I told them. From that day on we hid what had happened. It was the pain we never spoke about. The pain we could keep silent on our lips, yet never keep from the voices in our head. It was—I was—our dirty little family secret."

The memory of his parents was alive again as Thomas stood there; and for that moment, he was the eight-year-old boy standing at the table with blood stained pants.

"We need to go to the police," his mother had pleaded with his father, but his father wouldn't listen.

"For what, to tell 'em our son took it in the ass like a little girl? No, No! We don't talk about it! We won't talk about it," his father had yelled back at her, pounding his fists on the table. His voice, like his anger, had started out sharply, loudly, but it slowly reduced in volume as the idea of forgetting steadily grew traction. "We won't talk about it," he issued with a false confidence the next moment, using each second that passed like an eraser, wiping away the truth. But some things could never be taken away, and the clear chalkboard that made up Thomas's mind would forever show the blur of memories once written upon it. His father, who had prided himself on being a Man's Man, couldn't look at his own son the same. Deep down, a part of him blamed Thomas for what had happened, and Thomas knew it even then. "He's a boy, this shouldn't have happened," Thomas had heard him muttering. His father had chosen denial, the first instinct of dysfunction, and where the man had readily walked on the border, that was the day which easily pushed him over the line.

"I'm going to kill those fucking boys. You mark my words they're as good as dead."

"My father's first inclination was a lot like Willy's, he wanted to kill the boys that had done it." Thomas was back with Maybe, though a part of the young man would always be back standing at the table, that little boy unable to sit down.

"Mumma talked him out of it, at least we thought she
had—Mumma was different back then. She hadn't found God
yet, but she was stronger. My father couldn't reach her
strength however, he needed payback for the way those boys
had changed me; and retribution at a place like this, well, it
had a way of coming without the flashing lights of red and
blue."

Thomas heard a scream from the past ring in his ear,
the criminals who had committed the act against him, victims
of time, tortured by circumstance. The quiet punishment that
society would never see, echoing in the field behind them, for
only those with closed lips and deafened ears to hear. The
unspoken crime hidden when those boys went to the grave,
thankful to be removed from a life of suffering.

"This is where he worked—my father. I'm sure he
wasn't totally innocent in how the patients here were treated,
but I don't think he ever did the things those boys did to me.
At least, I can't bring myself to believe he would. Working in
this nightmare is how he had connections; friends in low
places that could help quiet the storm, though he himself was
no more than a janitor, cleaning the messes and sins of those
above him. As quietly as those boys had stepped out of the
bushes, the events of that day—my rape, their murder—slunk
back in. What started out as a one-victim crime, threatened to
become an evening newsroom delight if I told anyone what
happened here. So following what I was told, I never did."

*"You can't say a word about this, either of you!" His
father's voice rang from the past, warning Thomas and his
mother.*

"If I spoke, evidence threatened to come clear that
many of the boys were victims themselves, a devastating circle
of abuse that would have encompassed thirty to forty people,

my father included, for his part as the cleanup man. I was just part of the line, the unknown victim, my father, another member of the unholy avengers."

"He was never directly cruel, but I could tell that he didn't know how to come near me anymore. He couldn't look at me the same. I can't really blame him. I've never looked at myself the same either. I suppose a part of him couldn't stand the thought of going back to this building every day; a place like this stays with a person. You can see it in the people who used to work here. There's a grey spot in their heart. Whether they aided the pain or just observed it, they carry a piece of it with them, even when life goes on. He left Mumma and I two days after it happened. After his threats and warnings had been planted, he left without a goodbye, and no more than a note that read,"

Thomas,

Those boys will never hurt anyone again. Never doubt it.

If only the truth came as easy as believing a simple set of words written on a piece of paper.

"Whatever he wanted me to believe, a part of me knows that those two boys have followed me every day since."

Maybe almost knocked Thomas over with her hug, her wet eyes letting go with a force he hadn't seen since the day he carried her from the church.

"I love you, Thomas," Maybe loudly cried.

"I love you too, Maybe Baby," Thomas told her, unable to keep it in any longer. With the ghosts of their pasts standing with them, forever inside of them, Thomas knew right then that memories, no matter how bad we feel them, are relived to be forgiven.

Maybe was going to be okay; Thomas was going to be okay. Their pain and suffering were their bond at that moment, but their laughter and perseverance were their true strength.

Thomas had forgiven the boys years ago, when Maybe was born. But standing there, holding Maybe, he forgave himself for holding on to it. He forgave his father for walking away. For the first time since Thomas was that little boy, he felt innocent wonder. All he could hope was that, with time, Maybe could do the same.

They stood there for a minute or two, when Thomas asked, "You want to go get a hot chocolate down at Bee-Bee Dairy's?"

"Yes," she said, jumping at the chance to have her favorite wintertime drink.

"Alright, well let's go," Thomas told her, letting go of their hug, taking a step towards the car, and falling flat on his ass due to the slick pavement. *So much for the roads being ice free*, Thomas thought, groaning from a very "less than Mary-Lou Retton" style landing.

In his pain and what was undoubtedly going to be his black and blue backside, the most wonderful thing happened—Maybe, for the first time in months, laughed. She laughed hard. While the pain Thomas felt wasn't going to go away anytime soon, the pain he felt for Maybe flew away faster than his feet.

"Ha, ha, ha, ha."

"Oh, you think that was funny, do you?" Thomas asked, smiling at her as he picked himself up, the pain fading away with each inch that Maybe's smile grew.

I'm sorry, I'm sorry," she continued to laugh.

"Yeah, yeah," Thomas said, smiling at her enjoyment. "Just get in the car, *Silly*."

Thomas would never forget the day he told her about their unwanted connection, though they never spoke of it again. Perhaps they would have, had they been granted more time. But there wasn't any need to. He would never forget the tears that were followed by the laughter, or the one final look Thomas gave the Laro School. Looking up, he saw his father in the window. The man he knew only in memories, looking down; his dull green work uniform as fresh as the day Thomas limped home.

Looking at the apparition, Thomas knew right then from the tear in his father's eye what he had always wondered, *that Daddy never left him, and that somehow, someway, ghosts cry too.*

CHAPTER FIFTEEN

April 1987:

Maybe melted the winter snow. Each day she grew warmer, and so too did the weather. Before they knew it, she was back to normal—well, as normal as you can ever feel after what she had been through. Memories are always a danger after a tragedy, and Thomas knew Maybe would have those moments of caution. Just as long as she didn't let them stop her, she would be okay.

The new puppy helped. She had begged Willy to the point where he finally gave in; though Thomas thought Willy was just happy to see her smiling again. With Maybe's return to smiling came Mumma's return to Jesus, her church of choice now one town over in Cawley, CT. While Willy was a somewhat religious man himself, Thomas was sure that there was a part of the man which was hoping Mumma's love for God would never return.

"Honey, can you grab some blueberries down at the farm stand on your way home? They just opened back up last week," Mumma asked Willy, who was far from excited about it.

"What in the world are you baking now? And for who?" Willy asked, whining like a little kid.

"I'm making a pie for the wake tonight. You know, I only told you it was *tonight* about twenty times, or have you been too drunk to remember?"

She was feisty, like the woman she had been before Joseph had left, leaving Thomas to wonder if everything that had happened had finally led her to the balance between religion and reality she desperately needed.

Willy, who clearly by the look on his face did not remember, answered in a deeper, but still whiny, "Yeees, of course I remember."

She looked at him, for the first time in a long time, as Willy deserved to be viewed—like an idiot. They were family however, and even if Willy was an idiot, he was theirs, and they loved his stupid ass. He had finally been staying home at night, and even if that meant he got drunk and forgetful, they were all still glad to be together.

"I'll stop and get them on my way home," Thomas told them, trying out of the kindness of his heart to ease Willy's burden. Willy was trying, *why shouldn't I?* Thomas thought.

"Thank you, Thomas," Mumma said, grabbing the young man's cheek and giving him a kiss, her expression still the same when she looked at Willy.

"You think she's ready for tonight?" Willy asked, changing the subject as the memory of entering the lion's den reemerged from the haze of alcohol.

"She said she wants to go. I asked her a million times if she was sure," Mumma said.

They all looked at Maybe. She was oblivious to them as she sat playing with the newest member of the family, Goliath, who she had named after the Sunday morning cartoon.

"Oh Maybe, Oh Maybe," Maybe kept saying over and over, scrunching her face and pretending he was the one talking.

"I think she'll be alright," Thomas told them confidently. "Besides, we'll all be there for her."

Thomas meant what he said. They had all been bonding in their own strange way; and while they weren't a regular family, at least, nothing like you would see on TV, things were looking better. He had faith that they could handle the situation and help Maybe do the same. Little did Thomas know however, that death was lurking in the shadows beyond the funeral home—waiting, wanting—and that by the end of the night it would wrap its hands around the throat of another, taking the breath of life with it, and leaving more than one left to grieve.

~ ~ ~ ~

"Shouldn't you be at school, Ma'am?" Thomas asked her, finally feeling the nerve to be himself.

"Shouldn't you be working or spending time with your sister?" She volleyed without turning around to speak directly to Thomas, continuing her search for the right peaches.

He could see a slight change in her stature upon hearing his voice. There was a smile that came to her face, as well. She was trying to suppress it, hide it from him with her hair, yet, Thomas saw it even when she wanted it to be gone. He wasn't alone in how he felt. The more Thomas knew it, the more he became the man he could be, should have been all along.

Thomas could see how women looked at him, and while he never thought of himself as attractive, there was something about him that seemed to garner attention. *Have I always been oblivious to it? Did the past, like a set of blinds, conceal the world to me*? His perception of who he was had changed, taking his view of the world with it.

"Nope, that one's no good," Thomas told her. She had grabbed a peach to put in her bag, but he stopped her, gently grabbing a hold of the hand she held it with.

"What are you an expert on peaches?" She said, teasing Thomas.

Tuttle's farm stand was no more than a small shed next to a large apple orchard. It had been there since Thomas was a child, and from the looks of it, lifetimes before that. He hadn't expected to see her—certainly not there—yet, how fitting Thomas thought, to find a woman so ripe, in a place so swollen with fresh fruit.

"Oh, you'd be surprised at all the things I'm an expert at," Thomas told her, gently removing the peach from her hand, replacing it with another, without a clue in the world if the one he had picked was any better.

Thomas Thompson was as smooth as that fuzzy peach. "How are you?"

She had fully turned around to ask him, her face, mere inches away. Looking into her blue eyes, it dawned on Thomas—this was the first time Jennifer had ever asked about him before asking about Maybe.

Even more rejuvenated by her action, Thomas raised the bar and told her, "Better, now that I see you."

"You're so weird," Jennifer spoke gently, her hand smacking his arm. Thomas would have felt awkward, as if he had said the wrong thing, if it wasn't for the smile and faint rush of blood that had settled on Jennifer's cheek.

"How's school going, almost over?" He asked her, pleased to keep the conversation away from Maybe—not that

Thomas couldn't talk all day long about his sister, but he and Jennifer needed more. Perhaps, Thomas just wanted more.

Jennifer continued to fill her basket again, this time, without his expertise. "Well, the drive has been tough, the classes are even tougher, but I've spent my entire life beating the smart kids. That won't stop."

Thomas had raised his level of confidence, and equal, if not greater to the challenge, Jennifer had lifted hers as well.

"I see Holtzer quite a bit. I think he's been doing his fair share of partying, has a bad case of the sniffles all the time if you know what I mean," she continued, a light frown appearing on her soft face, the unusual lines distorting her beauty, as if they were an intruder that didn't belong. "He isn't alone. All the boys are caught up in it, especially the Frat Brats like him. He follows me around campus, still wants us to be together, not that we ever truly were. How could we be together after knowing how he is and what he does?" Jennifer asked Thomas. Unfortunately for Thomas, she was also asking herself, contemplating a question Thomas wanted no part in hearing, a question his heart wished she would never even ask.

Thomas could see in her far-away look that it was a consideration in the running, and that the thought of her being with Holtzer held a chance in the election. Any confidence Thomas had mustered, any feeling that she wanted him or that they could get past their differences, was gone. Thomas and Jennifer were different—very different. The same way Thomas would always be different from Holtzer. The same way his family would always be different. Thomas was the son of an absentee who ran away instead of running for votes and community standing. He couldn't compete with the men like Holtzer that dominated Jennifer's world. How foolish he was to ever think he had a chance.

"I don't suppose you're going to the wake tonight?" Jennifer asked, directing her inquiry only to Thomas this time.

"Yes, we are," Thomas answered, politely, but short. Why indulge flirtation with someone who could so easily indulge a man like Holtzer. It was one thing not to know how Holtzer was, like so many girls who had fallen prey. It was another to know exactly what he was like, and still go back. That, to Thomas and his jaded mind, made Jennifer no different than Holtzer himself.

"Does Maybe want company at home while you go?"

"No," Thomas replied, dumbfounded by her offer. "She insists on going."

"She can't go," Jennifer instructed Thomas, her voice in a scolding tone that he neither cared for nor appreciated. If Jennifer wanted to tell Holtzer what was best, than that's what she should do. She could leave Thomas and his choices to the person who had to live them, and last Thomas had checked, that was him.

"Well, she's going. If she can't handle it and wants to leave we'll take her home." His irritation was precise in its target, Jennifer's ears as well as her blood pressure rising with his tone.

"What about all the people who are going to be there? Have you thought about that? How are they going to treat her when half of this town blames her for his sickness?" She jabbed back, hitting a spot that was already sore.

"You know what? I've spent my whole life walking the streets of this town with Maybe. I've *seen* every look, I've *felt* every stare, and I've *heard* every single little word spoken under the breath of the people of this town. You know what it is? Bullshit! People can pretend to think they know the truth, or what's better or who's better, but they don't have any more of a clue about life than Maybe. If anything, she's the only one who does! I learned something a long time ago, Jennifer. When the ignorant people who would rather have the show of normalcy, look down as she walks by, she still smiles. She doesn't need their approval to be happy. She doesn't need some frat boy from Yale. Maybe can see a good person when they're standing right in front of her and so can I. So I don't need *you* to tell me what to do with *my* sister."

There it was. The emotion of feeling like a secondhand object, coupled with Jennifer's dismay at their decision, spewed out in a nonsensical display of anger for everyone at the farm stand to witness.

"Now if you'll excuse me, I have to pick up *my* sister. Or does anyone here have a problem with that," Thomas daringly asked anyone who felt like joining the conversation they had all just become a part of on account of his volume.

Jennifer, looking as if Thomas was the Cyclops at the local freak show, stared at him, unsure of what to say. He had started out with a passionate confidence for love, yet here he was, walking away with a newly found passion for anger. It was an anger that stayed with Thomas, perhaps because he needed it to get through the night. Jennifer was right to worry about Maybe, but she wasn't the one Thomas wanted to hear it from, at least, not after seeing her contemplate a relationship renewal with Holtzer. Anyone, except for Jennifer, could have asked Thomas the same questions, in the same tone, and most certainly would *not* have gotten the same reaction. Young love was what Thomas had hoped to embrace, but is was ageless hate that he held, a hate that had spent a lifetime more than happy to hold him back.

~ ~ ~ ~

What are we doing? The question had been bouncing around in his mind long before Thomas had run into Jennifer. After seeing her however, and hearing her ask the same thing, it became even louder, the thought of how uncomfortable it would be wrestling in his gut. It was already dark by the time the calling hours began, the slow creeping of a sleeping sun giving way to an awakening moon. Perhaps it would be full and they would be walking into a den of werewolves, which for the moment, seemed a more pleasant scenario.

Thomas worried about Maybe. He wasn't sure if she understood what they were most likely going to walk into. They were the people who should have stopped her. Yet, here they were, the idiots accompanying her.

He saw Willy take a deep breath after putting the car in park, its tires safely resting on the dirt parking lot of the funeral home. Willy looked at Mumma and smiled in an uncommon act of comforting. In all of his shortcomings, Willy was strong for them that night. He proved it when he looked at them before exiting the car, and told Maybe, "You haven't done anything wrong. You are the one who is now, and has always been, with the lord. You hold your head high. It takes a lot of courage to show compassion for someone who has done what Pastor Carr did, certainly more than I have— I'm glad he's dead. But that's what makes you and I different, Maybe. You still care about him going to Jesus, and that's why you're better than me, than all of these people here, and don't you forget it."

They could have stayed home. They could have said their goodbyes from the comfort of their living room; although, they probably would have said good riddance instead. It definitely would have been a whole hell of a lot more comfortable for everyone, them included. Yet, they weren't just there to say goodbye to Pastor Carr. They weren't showing up for sympathy or respect. They were there to make a stand, right or wrong, for the justice of salvation and the love of redemption; and it was all because of Maybe. It took Thomas eleven years to let go of what Maybe was willing to forgive in one winter. Eleven years he had spent holding back, holding on, afraid to forgive himself or others. Maybe, as if she was Jesus herself, forgave without having to forget. The school system may have counted Thomas' IQ twice as high as Maybe's, but the fact remained, he was no smarter for it. Inside of Maybe's heart, was the key to a better world; Outside of her body, was a life full of bounds.

~ ~ ~ ~

They passed the fellow mourners as they made their way to the door. Sticking together, they all saw the gasps and shock of having brought Maybe to the wake of a man who had raped and tortured her so inhumanely. Their looks were like accusations, pointing fingers labeling them no better than Pastor Carr. Everyone thought they understood forgiveness, but not a single member of the congregation ever thought Maybe could achieve what they couldn't even fathom. Thomas wanted to point a finger back—the middle one. Yet, he couldn't judge them for something that he hadn't understood at first either.

The family had received word from Officer Axel that Pastor Carr—while sleeping peacefully—had died in his cell from a heart attack. Mumma's pies, undoubtedly, exacting the revenge that the justice system had never allowed. The news that it was going to be a full wake and ceremony surprised them, as they were expecting a private affair for family only. Much to their amazement, upon hearing of his death and the calling hours to ensue, it was Maybe who insisted they attend. Stuck on her opinion, one they didn't agree with at first, Maybe remained steadfast in her belief of saying a proper goodbye, no matter what or who may try to stop them.

They hadn't been through the door more than a minute when, what Thomas was sure must have been a relative of Pastor Carr, came storming in their direction from a huddle of family that was glaring at them, the victims of their false accusations.

"I would kindly ask you all to leave," she said, an air of superiority wafting through the funeral home. *Must be nice up there on that high horse*, Thomas thought, *probably helps to skew the view of what a family member like Pastor Carr really was.*

"We are here to pay our respects. Pastor Carr, no matter what has happened, was once a man who held a great standing in our hearts, and that is how we choose to remember him," Mumma said. In an instant—that instant—Mumma was more beautiful to Thomas than he could ever remember. But it wasn't Mumma's looks that had caused the enlightenment, it was her heart that shone brighter than the moon above the steeple.

"Well, you have some nerve considering it was your idi...."

"That will be enough, Aunt Joline," Mary-Sue, the rotund and unexpected savior interrupted, showing the force of will Thomas knew all too well that she had within her.

"They have every right to pay their respects. They spent every Sunday of their lives listening to Daddy and supporting our church. It isn't Maybe's fault what happened, and I think it's time people realized that and started treating her with some respect, rather than the whispers and name calling she doesn't deserve."

Mary-Sue had spoken it all loud enough for others to hear, making her point very clear, and Thomas was grateful for it. Even if Mary-Sue couldn't admit her own grief and misfortunes, he was glad she was standing up for Maybe's.

"Well, just pay your respects and get out of here." As strident as that, Mary-Sue's aunt turned and walked back to the circle of humanitarian bliss she came from.

"Don't listen to her. Aunt Joline's just a bitter old woman. Daddy had been sending her money every week to help her get by. Why? I have no idea. That old bitch has more money than all of us combined. She can use her ass as a vault for all I care. She ain't never been very nice to me." Mary-Sue was calm in speaking her unflattering description, leading Thomas to believe she was telling the entire truth, as she saw it.

"You want me to walk up with you guys?" Mary-Sue asked with a consideration Thomas hadn't expected, and a will to be the better person that stunned him, for no other reason than it was coming from her. Thomas didn't think she would be rude to them, at least, not belligerently. The last encounter between the two hadn't exactly been a joyful occasion. Still, he hadn't had any idea that Mary-Sue would be their protector in that room and that without her, they may have left only seconds after the door shut from their arrival.

"That would be very nice Mary-Sue, thank you for asking," Mumma answered, while Maybe, Willy, and Thomas were all glad to let them lead the way. "How are you holding up with?....well, everything?" Mumma asked Mary-Sue, alluding to more than anyone cared to speak aloud—not just on the day of a wake—but on any day, at any occasion.

Mumma's question came with care, her eyes focused on Mary-Sue's protruding belly that was ready to pop. She was doing it in hopes that Mary-Sue would respond to only the positive in her life. *If Mumma only knew,* Thomas thought.

When Mary-Sue didn't answer right away, and Mumma feared the young woman was only focusing on the negative, or what Mumma saw as the negative, she added, "Roger must be thrilled about becoming a father. You two will make great parents."

Mumma was trying to be kind with her questions, yet, not knowing the depth of severity in the situation, was only making Mary-Sue more uncomfortable. Still, Mary-Sue, as if she was born to rise to her own height of greatness in that moment, pushed forward with a smile and satisfied Mumma with a, "Yes, we are both very excited, thank you for asking."

The odd group of mourners arrived at the back of the line for the open casket, with both Mary-Sue and the eyes of every member of the church guiding and prodding them on their way. Maybe had been quiet, too quiet, and the fear that wouldn't go away came back as Thomas thought of the images her mind might have been creating. Thomas knew why they had come. He knew it was a noble cause that Maybe had led, but nobility has a great way of looking like stupidity at times. Every time Thomas convinced himself that they were right to allow Maybe to pay her respects, he looked at her, and it felt wrong all over again.

"I'll be right over there," Mary-Sue pointed to a row of seats where Roger and his family sat looking off into their own distance, the same discomfort showing in each of their far away stares. "You guys are more than welcome to sit with us if you care to stay." She smiled at my mother, looked at us with remorse, perhaps mirroring our own expressions, and left us waiting to see her dead father—the father of her child.

Thinking back on it as he waited in line, Thomas began to believe that a piece of Mary-Sue—a large one—was most likely happy her father was gone. Pastor Carr was like a rock that could have shattered the one window through which Mary-Sue had finally envisioned a happier world, and now that he was to be buried in the soil, he was unable to throw his own stone. There were only four people left that knew Roger wasn't the father of her child, and only two, as far as Thomas knew, who knew the true supplier of the seed. Mary-Sue and Thomas had had their share of good moments—and they had their share of bad. Yet, Mary-Sue knew that Thomas would never tell, not if it wasn't his; and he knew that Jennifer wouldn't say a word—why would she? What Holtzer might let out of the bag, however, well, that was a different story.

Mumma went first with Maybe, kneeling on the pedestal, the focus of every soul in the room. Silently, the two prayed, Maybe continuing to steal glances of Pastor Carr over her clasped hands. She amazed Thomas, amazed everyone, with her respectful behavior. Most people probably looked at it as a sign of her disability. *She's too dumb to be angry*. That is what Thomas pictured them saying, but he saw the truth and the pain in the slow rolling tears on her face as she went with Mumma to sit down. In a world where most people couldn't even face their ex who cheated on them, or couldn't stand others just for something as trivial as the color of their skin or the fact that they were attracted to people of the same sex, Maybe stood and knelt for love and forgiveness. Everyone but Mary-Sue had looked down at her from their own pedestals, or even worse, from the crosses they had nailed themselves too. When truth be told, there was only one person in that room equal to the words of Jesus Christ. There was only one person who could bear a cross that not another soul in that room could even imagine carrying, and that person was his sister, the greatest soul Thomas had ever known. Maybe Baby was truly God's child, and as the next hour progressed, his greatest entertainer, as well.

~ ~ ~ ~

"It's a little more than just a nervous reaction, it's kind of a healing habit," Mumma told Roger's mother, describing why Maybe spent every minute or so walking up to the casket, peeking over at Pastor Carr's lifeless body. Most people probably thought she was checking to make sure he was dead, but it was just Maybe. She had done the same thing when Pastor Carr's wife, Mary-Sue's mother, had died.

Roger's family was extremely uncomfortable, even more so than Thomas's family, and that was saying something. Maybe's continuous trips to the casket weren't making it any better for them, either. Thomas didn't think anyone was quite happy they were there, and letting Maybe walk freely was challenging everyone's belief on acceptable freedom.

Thomas had done his best to offer condolences to Roger, who was sitting alone in a back aisle of folding chairs, one second leaning casually against the wall, the next sitting anxiously forward. Thomas told Roger he was sorry for the loss of his father-in-law, and how happy he was for the soon to be fatherhood Roger was facing. Roger was grateful for Thomas's kindness, and oblivious to everything else. Perhaps, it was just better that way.

Thomas listened to Roger talk about the army, though, he couldn't help but notice that Roger was no longer talking about it to be boastful. Roger wasn't painting himself to be the hero he once seemed so eager to frame with greatness. The young private was nervous. Nervous about the thought of going somewhere dangerous, nervous about his life with a wife and child, nervous about damn near everything they discussed.

"I just hope we can make it all work. I don't make a lot of money in the army, and what if I can't even make it through my time without going crazy thinking of a wife and baby at home alone." Roger looked down, and never directly at Thomas.

"Well, your family is here for you now, I'm sure they'll be there for you if that happens," Thomas said with a smile, which he truly hoped would pick Roger up. If Roger couldn't handle regular problems, how in the world would he ever handle finding out, as Paul Harvey would say, "The rest of the story," if Mary-Sue ever chose to tell him—though Thomas highly doubted she would.

Thomas hadn't noticed their entrance into the funeral home due his new found occupation as Roger's therapist. It was fairly crowded for a man who had committed the sins that Pastor Carr had devoted his time to engaging in. Yet, if Thomas and his family was there, how could he really be surprised that anyone else was?

Jennifer had insinuated that she would be there. What Thomas didn't expect, even while she had alluded to potential feelings that remained, was Holtzer to be accompanying her.

Holtzer caught Thomas's stare as he and Jennifer walked to the deceased. Mildly smiling, Holtzer's facial expression was dripping with a reserved sadness; his manner befitting a politician who was more concerned with the appearance of sadness rather than actual grief itself. Thomas watched them, kneeling together, the picture of life in a background of death. *How beautifully deserving they are of each other*, Thomas thought, disgruntled.

"You like her, don't you?" Roger asked, turning from the patient to the prier.

"No," Thomas said, on the verge of stumbling over his own tongue. "It's complicated."

"I can see it. Just be careful, because if I can see it that means Holtzer definitely will," Roger told Thomas before turning his focus to Mary-Sue, who had been making her way around the funeral home, thanking everyone with a grace Thomas had never seen in her before. Her father was gone, and while there were always shackles in life to be avoided, Mary-Sue was finally free.

Jennifer spotted Maybe as soon as she stood and instantly reached out to embrace her. Thomas watched Jennifer, holding Maybe like a sister, a mother, while Holtzer stood behind them, watching Thomas. Maybe led Jennifer in Thomas's direction, ignoring Jennifer's companion as she pulled on her hand. It was clear Jennifer didn't want to see Thomas, her effort to pull away from Maybe, however, was flawed by a lack of desire to hurt Maybe's feelings on a night she was showing so much strength.

"Thomas, look who I found," Maybe said, alluding to Jennifer like a child who had been hiding—another child of God lost in the world, another child in need of being found.

"She found us, alright," Holtzer slid in, slyly trying to make Maybe aware of his presence behind her, as well as his joint arrival with Jennifer.

Maybe looked at Holtzer for a second, quizzically, as if she thought she saw something beyond his crisp suit, good looks, and aromatic pleasantry. Holtzer was unsure, and for a moment, uncomfortable with Maybe's depth of perception, causing him to squirm uneasily. It was the first time Thomas had ever seen Holtzer like that, where, for a moment, he wasn't the one in control. His charm, his standing, was lost on Maybe. Even though it was wrong, Thomas loved every second of it. He loved the look on Holtzer's face, the look of being less than he hoped to ever appear. Thomas enjoyed it, because Holtzer finally knew how it felt to be the other person in the room with him.

As quickly as she had turned Holtzer into a pile of muck, Maybe was gone and back at the casket.

"Well, what are you doing here, rustling the feathers in the coop?" Holtzer asked, regaining his air of dominance that would not work on Maybe, but he knew all too well worked on Thomas.

"We're just here to pay our respects, Maybe insisted on it," Thomas told him. He didn't need to defend himself, or Maybe's decision. Yet still, he did.

"Seems a bit perplexing for her to take in, isn't it? Especially with everything that happened. Why in the world would she wish to say goodbye to a man who would do such monstrous things?" Holtzer scoffed, his arrogance reaching a new level.

Thomas had always felt like less of a person than Holtzer, but it had always been his own doing, or so Thomas thought. Perhaps, Holtzer's time away at a school full of equals had emboldened him to realize just how much better off the two young men both saw his life. For whatever reason, Holtzer was speaking to Thomas in a way he had never indulged before, with the purpose of making Thomas feel how he normally felt without Holtzer's aid. Jennifer, who Thomas could tell was distressed by Holtzer's behavior, stayed quiet, and in that silence, screamed volumes.

"Maybe has a good heart. Better than most people I..." Thomas was interrupted, as was everyone in the funeral home, by Maybe, who had given up her pacing beside the casket for a pulpit right in front of it. Standing there in front of the light blue shaded coffin, in a surreal attempt of preaching the Lord's word, Maybe directed her belief at the continuously crying congregation.

"People, listen. Pastor Carr did bad things to me. But he loved Jesus, and I love Jesus. You all need to love Jesus, too." With that came the gasps and gawking, followed by Mumma on her feet and at the casket, gathering Maybe before she began rambling her thoughts like Pastor Carr on a Sunday morning. Mumma quickly led Maybe out of the funeral home, with Willy following right behind, issuing an unfelt, "Sorry," and gladly felt, "Goodbye."

It wasn't God who had raped Maybe. It wasn't religion, or the idea of it that hurt her, though, it has had its own share of indiscretions throughout the course of time. It was love that Maybe stood up for. Love for Pastor Carr—the right kind. Love for Jesus, who Maybe saw in every cloud in the sky and every eye that looked upon it with wonder. It was love, pure and simple, for herself first, and for all of all as well.

Thomas looked at Holtzer and Jennifer one last time, a look of "I told you so" smeared on Holtzer's face, an incredulous look on Jennifer's, and said, "Looks like it's time to go. Take care," before following his familial precession to the car.

CHAPTER SIXTEEN

Present Day:
"*They brought her to the wake, can you believe it?* I heard them say. It was priceless, watching them, their disbelief glowing through the glass cage they were living in. One woman almost fainted. Had her husband not caught her, she may have hit the ground. They did good bringing you. You did good, my dear. I could only imagine what you thought looking at him, but you were far more composed than most. I was proud of you, as if you were my own; though, perhaps you are, in a way. It was my failure that brought about the circumstances of your life, but I know you've wanted me to forgive myself, while your life is my forgiveness. Everyone speaks of forgiveness and redemption, but only a few actually hold it by the hand. You even stood up and told them that they need to love Jesus. With him rotting there, you prophesied in peace. Good for you. It was good. You did good."

He was in between the heavens again, interjecting his own life into the story. He was right to do it. Without his actions, his failures, the story would have been another, and her part may never have even existed.

Beep. Beep. Beep.

It was the end that hurt him—that had hurt her—the most. Still, he needs to speak of it one last time to her, to himself. He needs to listen to the voices in the memory, those lasting sounds that forever whisper in his ears. He needs to tell it for him, for Thomas.

Picking up the book, he asks aloud, "Now, where was I?"

~ ~ ~ ~

April 1987:

It was a cleansing rain. The vibrant nighttime sky, now crisp in its glow, appeared as if the moon had been washed and waxed. The white beams reaching down—fresh and reborn— lit up the houses on the street as they zoomed passed them in the car. They were ready for a new beginning—deserved it really. Who amongst us doesn't warrant that breath of pure air and enlightening shine? They had found it. No one had shown it to them, and they were better for it, at least, better than most.

Maybe was happy with her performance, even if it was only short lived. In her mind, the people at the funeral home needed to know that Jesus loved them. They needed to hear that Jesus loves all of them, no matter how they acted. In the past, Thomas would have felt better telling them all to go to hell, but even he wasn't in the mood to berate them. He wasn't sure if there was a heaven like the bible spoke of, but Thomas was pretty sure there wasn't a hell at all, and if there was, this world alone was it. Perhaps, Thomas was just preparing himself for a warm afterlife without Maybe, but one with lots of friends and family to keep him company.

"You done good Maybe," Willy broke the silence of the ride. "Those people—I mean, how have we put up with them? All those years we've been going to their church, what have we been listening for, the word of only Pastor Carr? Cause I always thought church was for listening to God and Jesus above the people."

Willy was ranting in a calm but perturbed state of new-found integrity, to no one more than himself. Mumma, however, feeling the need to join in, said, "Maybe, you taught me something tonight. You know what that was?"

"Love Jesus," Maybe said, quickly, upset with the fact that she had been pulled from her moonlight reverie.

"Yes, that too, but you taught me that my belief is different than other people's at times, and that's okay. I don't need to treat my faith like a competition. I'm a good person, I'm forgiving, though, I don't think I will ever totally be able to forgive Pastor Carr for....well, that's behind us. I just hope I can have your strength someday," Mumma, reaching in the back seat, patted Maybe's leg while offering the most normal smile Thomas had seen on her face since he was a small child.

"I'm very strong," Maybe said, causing a slight chuckle from the rest of them. They weren't sure if she was paying enough attention to tell the difference between the emotional strength that Mumma was currently talking about, and physical strength. It didn't matter if Maybe had heard them, others were meant to learn more from her than she was ever meant to learn from herself, and Thomas knew that, now more than ever.

Maybe could lift more weight than most men Thomas had seen in the shop. She could also forgive a man who did something horrible, even when she would never forget. The nightmares she would forever live with showed them that, but even when darkness crept into Maybe's bed, the light inside of her was always bright enough to chase it away.

~ ~ ~ ~

They pulled into the driveway, exhausted from the eventful evening. Willy put the old Dodge Datsun in park, the car giving one last slight movement back as it rested on the brakes. "I need a beer......" He stopped. His repetitive nature of opening the fridge for a Schlitz had led him to see, like the light that instantly appears, something different. Willy looked both perplexed and surprised. It was that different type of surprise for Willy, the one that only comes when you have surprised yourself. Willy, though Thomas would have doubted that the man could even spell it, had been blessed with an epiphany.

"You want to go get a cup of coffee down at Rosie's?" Willy asked Mumma, looking at her like it was the first time he had ever seen her.

Somewhat shocked, Mumma looked at Willy in her new fashion of believing he had two heads, only this time, Mumma found them both pleasantly engaging. The slight blush on her cheeks gave her enjoyment away. How lucky they were, all those years later, all the good and the bad, to finally be falling love.

"Yes. I would," Mumma said, before directing her attention to the backseat where Maybe and Thomas were still idling. "Thomas, you have your house key on you?"

"Yeah, I got it," Thomas said, pulling the handle where his hand had been resting, and using his elbow to push open the door. "Come on Maybe, I'll help you get ready for bed."

Thomas held the door open while Maybe scooted over in the seat, stopping to give her father and mother a goodbye kiss near the middle console before exiting the car.

Maybe was going to close the door, when a thought came to her, and before closing it, she stuck her head back in the car, and said, "Love you both, with all my heart."

"We love you, too," Mumma and Willy said back in unison, the closing door muffling the last word.

What Thomas heard next, were words that touched him, hit him really. They weren't something he was used too, or extremely comfortable with, yet, when Thomas heard Willy say, "We love you too, Thomas," the young man felt it, and it was like being reborn all over again.

Thomas and Maybe watched the car pull out of the driveway, Mumma and Willy's waving hands following the headlights on the car.

A part of Thomas needed that moment, needed to hear what Willy had said. It would take a lifetime to undo the man Willy had become, but that could probably be said about them all. All Thomas knew, was that Willy was different that day. Willy had been a good man who appreciated his family, who appreciated Thomas, and the young man was thankful for it. Thomas needed that feeling of acceptance, especially when in the next hour his life would flash before his eyes, in that one strange moment we all face before death.

~ ~ ~ ~

The rain picked up again after Mumma and Willy had left for coffee. Rushing, hoping to avoid a possible lightning storm, Thomas coaxed Maybe into taking a quick shower, which was no small feat. She had always preferred baths, and while the pelting of rain outside never bothered her, the stream of it in the confined bathtub scared Maybe, right to the point where Thomas contemplated taking her outside with a bar of soap instead. Maybe got through it however, sparing their neighbors the scene.

It was a good thing they had hurried, no sooner had Maybe stepped outside of the shower, then the booming flash and crackle of thunder and lightning came. If the shower hadn't scared her enough, standing naked in the bathroom while the lights flickered did the job.

"Ah, Thomas help me!" She screamed, as he wrapped the towel around her.

"It's just a flicker, we still have power. Let's get you dressed quick, though, just in case," Thomas told her, trying to remember if he knew where the flashlights were stored.

"Okay," Maybe agreed, happy to be rid of the feeling of vulnerability that comes with a naked body.

The storm was deafeningly loud and bright as the lightning charged from the sky to the ground, but they never fully lost power. Thomas was glad they didn't. The last thing he needed while trying to keep Maybe calm was the feeling that he was stuck in a scene from a cheesy horror movie. In reality however, horror often strikes when the lights are on. All it takes is for somebody at home to answer the door. Maybe and Thomas, were that somebody.
Knock, knock, knock.

They had been raised to fear two things during a lightning storm, one, was the phone, and two, was the television. You never turned on the TV, and you never answered or used the phone. Willy had drilled into their heads the story of his mother, who in an act of defiance, picked up the telephone to call his father at the bar one night during a storm, only to be thrown against the wall by the shock she received.

"The lightning got to her before Dad had a chance," Willy would say, joking away an all too unfortunate reality he had lived, one of watching his abusive father "handle" his mother. In all his shortcomings, and even though he had once crossed that line with Thomas, Willy had never laid a hand on either Mumma or Maybe. Thomas believed that Willy had made a choice in his childhood to keep himself from being that same man his father was—certainly one different than his brother—and even if the man Willy had become wasn't much better, it was still a hell of a lot better than that.

Knock. Knock. Knock. It came again.

"It's the Boogetyman," Maybe cried instantly, yet in a much softer voice than her usual, which showed Thomas that she was actually afraid.

Maybe had been sitting quietly on the couch, combing the hair of one of her dolls, while occasionally petting Goliath. Thomas, sitting at the kitchen table, was reading one of the only books he had ever seen Mumma pick up besides the bible, a book Mumma conveniently kept tucked away inside of the pantry closet—*The Happy Hooker: My Own Story*, by Xaviera Hollander.

"It's probably just Nadine," Thomas told Maybe, trying to ease her worry. In all honesty, Thomas couldn't imagine who it was knocking on the door. For a second, he even contemplated not answering it, but what if it was a neighbor in need? Whether they had been worthy or not, whether they had taken more sticks of butter than they had given back, they could still be good people and try to help.

He tried to see who it was by peeking through the living room window. The Boogeyman—or the Boogetyman—as Maybe had named him, was not real. Yet, the human mind has a way of conjuring up images. As soon as Maybe spoke his name, the Boogetyman became a possibility. It was foolish, childish, but as Thomas parted the curtains with careful deliberation, so as not to alert the Boogetyman of his presence, Thomas felt fear, as if death itself were knocking at his door. Unable to see through the rain-smeared glass, or even catch a glimpse of the man who Thomas was now certain would bring his demise, Thomas walked over to the door; and with a macho stance for Maybe, and partially for his own mind, opened the gateway to the afterlife.

Their Boogetyman, their darkness, wasn't a man at all. It was, however, another unexpected female standing on his doorstep. She looked like she had walked a mile in the rain, her hair drenched from the downpour. Her car was behind her however, pulled along the edge of the road.

"I've been standing here for a few minutes. I almost didn't knock," she shivered as she spoke, still as unsure if she had done the right thing by knocking as they had felt about taking Maybe to Pastor Carr's funeral.

Thomas didn't want to see her, but he drank her in as if her soaked body was the only thing that could quench a thirst he had been dying from.

He should have asked her if she wanted to come in. It wasn't polite to leave a girl out in the rain like that. Good men were supposed to do great things for the woman they cared for, and he had certainly seen enough old movies full of those great men. Thomas, however, wasn't feeling very much in the chivalrous mood, at least not when it came to Jennifer.

"Who is it?" Maybe asked nervously from the couch, the spot where she was poorly hiding, her cover a see-thru knit blanket that Mumma had taken from Grandma Main's house when she had died. The blanket had held up well over the years, which Mumma was grateful for, especially seeing how it was, as Mumma often described with a sour expression while folding it over the couch, "The bulk of my inheritance."

Thomas knew that if he told Maybe who it was, that Maybe would have dragged the soaked young woman in, and Thomas wasn't much in the mood for Jennifer's water-logged company. Besides, why would someone of Jennifer's standing want to slum it with them. They could get over the smell of imperfection that people like her so perfectly and often admonished, but could she? Thomas knew deep down that she had a good heart, but he knew some assholes that did, as well.

"Just a salesman," Thomas yelled back in the house to Maybe, his voice louder than the rain.

"What are they selling in this weather, sunshine?" Maybe asked in a sarcastically straightforward manner.

"No, smart ass, they're selling Ginsu Knives," Thomas told her, picking the first and worst lie that came to the top of his head. "Just go back to playing. I'll be right here on the porch."

"Okay, but we already have knives in the drawer," Maybe whined, still scared and clearly unhappy that Thomas wouldn't be in the living room with her.

"Where's Holtzer?" Thomas asked, lacing his question with disgust.

"Holtzer's not here. I came on my own. God, why do I even bother trying to talk to you, Thomas. You clearly haven't gotten a clue when it comes to people."

"Funny, I think I could say the same thing about you," Thomas retorted.

Jennifer was frustrated and the steady stream of rain wasn't helping, though the overhang from the porch blocked most of it. Looking at her, Thomas didn't think there was a possibility she could collect any more rain. She was an overflowing drain, with her moist clothes clinging to her body, her shirt accentuating her perfectly rounded breasts, making it extremely difficult for Thomas to stay upset with her. He had to though. He had to stick to his guns, his beliefs. Jennifer had chosen Holtzer, so why the hell was she here?

"Why don't you give me a clue, Jennifer," Thomas emphasized her name, like a parent scolding a child. "Why do you bother trying to talk to me when you're obviously with another man?"

"I'm not with him. I only went to the funeral to keep him away from Mary-Sue. I don't know her, and frankly, what I do know of her I definitely don't like, certainly not as much as you do, *Dad*, but she's been through enough." She was struggling to look at Thomas, the raindrops trickling on her forehead, impeding her vision. "Holtzer doesn't see things like that. He just sees where he can flaunt any ounce of power he has for his own self-serving desires. He plays with people like toys, and might I remind you, you were friends with him long before I ever knew him. You're no better than I am."

She was right about everything except for the "Dad" part—certainly about Holtzer. Thomas didn't want to admit it, but she was right. He had been looking at Jennifer, doing his best to look down on her for every reason he could exploit in his own mind, when the entire time, Thomas was judging her in the same thoughtless way. In an instant, he felt like the ass she was basically calling him. Still, Thomas wasn't going to admit it.

"He's been different lately. I don't know exactly what's changed, he just is," Thomas told her, repeating what she had tried to tell him earlier that day at the stand. He had failed to listen to her however, and now, Thomas was trying to think back on a specific incident or time that had brought about Holtzer's new personality, wondering if there even was one.

Perhaps it had been such a gradual change, that Thomas was blind to it. Even more sobering, was the thought that Holtzer had always been that way, and that Thomas had chosen not to see it.

"I wanted to make it easier for everyone else tonight. He took it the wrong way. Thought it meant I wanted to be with him. He tried to...." She collected herself, on the verge of tears, "I don't know how I got out of the car, but I ran. I told him I had feelings for you. He didn't take it well, told me I was 'his'. He isn't right, Thomas. I don't know what he's on, but he isn't right."

She was clearly frightened. What exactly had Holtzer tried to do? Thomas didn't want to press her with questions. For now, all he knew was that Jennifer had shown up on his door looking for empathy, only for Thomas to greet her with disdain. In that instant, his contempt altered its focus, and Thomas wanted to kill Holtzer. Whatever had happened, whatever had or hadn't been done, Jennifer was frightened, and he didn't like it. Thomas didn't like it one bit.

It wasn't intended, yet, suddenly they found themselves standing on the porch with the rain surrounding them, locked in an embrace. Thomas stood there for a moment, her head against his chest. In the pain and fear, Thomas knew what he had always known—he loved her. He knew that a piece of his heart always would. It was a love that you crave with such passion, and need with such want, that a part of you instantly despises its very existence.

Removing Jennifer's head from his chest, Thomas looked at her, into her, before kissing her, passionately. They only kissed for a minute, the blood-raised desire turning that minute into an infinite eternity. *Never end. Love me, the man I am today, because I can't promise that I'll be this same man tomorrow,* his lips were trying to tell her. All Thomas wanted was for that moment to *never end.*

Before he could say a word or even finish kissing her properly—knowing he needed an amount of time that could never be satisfied—Thomas saw the curtain that he had peered through moments before move out of the corner of his eye, the tell-tale sign of a spy. Maybe, no doubt, was wondering what Thomas was doing and who he was with. Most likely, she was growing nervous with every second that passed.

"Come inside," Thomas said with gentle strength, now unafraid to show Jennifer his reality, as imperfect as it may be. If she could see Maybe and Thomas for who they truly were, than she could see the space, good or bad, elegant or unsettling, that had helped shape them.

"I can't," Jennifer said, her answer surprising Thomas. Her facial expression, turned nervous again as she glanced at the window that Maybe had just been peeking through.

"She'll be happy to see you," Thomas told her, not wanting to let go. She was close, body-to-body close, and Thomas didn't want that to change.

Jennifer did, however, and with one quick push separated herself from Thomas, and walked quickly, nervously, to her car.

Thomas had a fear of his own at that moment. He feared that he had rushed her with a kiss she wasn't ready for, at a time when intimacy may have been the last emotion she could handle. Whatever had occurred with Jennifer and Holtzer, Thomas may have just made it worse.

"I'm sorry. Jennifer, wait," Thomas shouted in the rain. He wanted to run to her, close her car door and tell her how he felt; that as stupid as he was, he always had and always would love her. In that one great moment, Thomas needed wings to fly, but his shoes were made of cement, his feet, unwilling, unable to move. All Thomas wanted to do, needed to do, was now destined to be left unspoken.

Jennifer looked at Thomas, registering whatever her mind had been collecting, before getting in her car, starting the engine, and driving away from him.

Standing there alone, the memory of her parked car on the side of the lawn, as fresh in Thomas's mind as if it was still there, surreal enough to make him wonder if it ever truly existed. Thomas had opened the door to what he expected to be the Boogetyman, only to find the one woman who his heart always seemed to be yearning for, and could never have.

What Thomas failed to realize in it all, was that the Boogetyman hadn't rung the doorbell. The Boogetyman was already inside, alone with Maybe. While Thomas stood on the front porch kissing an angel, a demon had snuck in the back door, and Maybe was the one who greeted his arrival.

CHAPTER SEVENTEEN

April 1987:
"You should have stayed away from what's mine."

In that house, there was only one person who deserved to have a line like that spoken to them. Willy wasn't the person he was speaking too, however. This time, Willy wasn't the one with a gun pointed at his chest.

He was holding his hand over Maybe's mouth, her fear looking out over his fingers. Thomas could feel the breeze coming in through the back door that seldom saw use. *Had he broken in?* Thomas was sure he would have heard him; but he was quiet in his entry, and the rain outside, along with the strong beat in Thomas's heart that had crept up to his ears after looking at Jennifer, could have easily muffled the sound. The lock was always more of a comfort anyhow, and Thomas knew it. Where there was a will there was a way, and all it would take was a strong enough card to slide the bolt of the lock back.

Thomas's mind had trouble processing what he was seeing. As he shut the door, all Thomas expected was to see Maybe, pretending she hadn't been peeking through the window, but he knew right then that Maybe wasn't the one who had been looking.

"Just put the gun down and let her go," Thomas said, standing still, afraid any movement may startle him and create a reaction with dire results.

"Is that what you want, dear? You want me to let you go?" He asked her mockingly, never removing his hand from her face.

"Come on. This is between you and me. Let her go. My parents are going to be home any minute now. Let her go and we can pretend this didn't happen."

Thomas was pleading without begging, trying to stay calm like one of those cops on *Hill Street Blues*, but Holtzer knew Thomas too well. In fact, Holtzer was about to show that he knew Thomas better than the young man had ever imagined, and that Thomas had been right in thinking that he didn't know Holtzer at all.

~ ~ ~ ~

Present Day:
"I knew that boy was trouble. He was no different than his father, lost in the lust of power, at his truest form when he was wielding it. I always hated that man, and because of it, hated his little brat, too. People like that get away with things, but worst of all, they walk away with satisfaction instead of pain. While men like myself cry, hide, they laugh out in the open with handshakes and bank accounts, reaping the rewards of misery that were paid for in the hearts of others. Fallen angels don't drop from the sky, but you can be damn sure that there are ones walking in comfortable shoes on the ground."

~ ~ ~ ~

April 1987:

"Listen to you, Mr. Calm, Cool, and Collected. You don't fool me, Thomas, and I don't care if your parents do walk in here. I have plenty of bullets for all of you," Holtzer said, eerily confident, like a man who knows he has what it takes to kill.

"It's ironic, truly it is," Holtzer began again, the gun no longer pointed at Thomas, but now digging deeper into Maybe's head with each finished sentence, causing her to squirm in pain, her muffled cries seeping through his fingers.

"See, I know all about you. I have always known about you. Your dirty little secret, always right here on the tip of my tongue," Holtzer prodded, licking Maybe seductively, sadistically with the tip of his tongue.

"I know what happened to you when you were a young boy, Thomas, how fitting that the same exact thing happened to Maybe here," he said, a cruel laugh escaping Holtzer's throat. "I guess some people were just meant for a life of being fucked up the ass—literally, nonetheless. Oh wait, I'm sorry, Maybe, I guess life fucked you right were you wanted it, or was Pastor Carr the first back door man to ever get hold of you?"

"Leave her alone," Thomas growled this time, contemplating whether or not to charge at Holtzer. How Holtzer knew about Thomas's past was a mystery. If Holtzer wanted to try to hurt Thomas with words however, let him. But there was no reason for him to involve Maybe.

"How is it you think I know about your rough childhood, Thomas?" Holtzer was using Thomas's name like a set of nails on the chalkboard, scratching, irritating Thomas with every instance.

"I don't care. Just let her go."

"Maybe Baby," Holtzer teased with her name this time, "I'll show you the good time your former Pastor wasn't able to finish, thanks to your brother here. I'll show you things Pastor Carr never even *dreamed* of trying with you."

He was colder than the winter wind, each word, each sentence, digging to the marrow of Thomas' bones. He was teasing Maybe, while torturing Thomas. *Why? Was it all because he knew a secret, or only because he saw me as a love combatant?* Neither one added up.

"What was it like, Thomas. Was it as good for you to have a boy inside of you as it was for our girl Maybe here to have a man inside of her? What do you think happened to those boys, Thomas, after they were done with you?"

Holtzer was staring right at Thomas, his eyes, which had been back and forth from Thomas's face to Maybe's, fixed on Thomas, and he yelled, "Answer me!" only to fade into a psychotic calm and mutter, "What do you think happened to them?"

~ ~ ~ ~

Present Day:
"I had left for work that night, as changed in my heart as Thomas, accepting that my destiny was to kill them, but first I had to find them. As luck would have it, finding them was the easy part. It was the act of killing them where I struggled."
Beep. Beep. Beep.

"I had a list of boys who could have been the rapists. Using the guise that I was removing the trash, I took the names of those who had signed in and out from the clipboard that hung inside of the nurses' station. I made a quick list—careful not to be seen—of the boys that had been outside that afternoon and their room numbers. I was hoping that, perhaps, I would hear something, maybe even know through some mental connection of anguish, which ones they were."

"*We don't talk about it!* I had yelled at your brother and mother. But in the end, I was the weak link, the one who broke the silence. I was the one who opened his mouth and set this all in motion. It all started when I stopped with my bucket outside of room one-forty-two, and the sight of the hat I had bought Thomas, the circles of the Boston B staring at me like a set of eyes perched on the bed."

~ ~ ~ ~

April 1987:
"Answer me!"

Holtzer had yelled it, but still, Thomas knew he didn't want him to answer. Nothing Thomas said would have been good enough to quell Holtzer's anger, an anger Thomas didn't understand at first. Thomas was the one who had been raped. Thomas was the one who had been traumatized. Why was Holtzer acting like a victim?

Speaking again to Maybe, Holtzer showed the creator of his demons when he said to her, "Joseph Andrew Holtzer, died July 28th 1976, in the darkest hours of the night, from a massive heart attack that some say was caused by electric shock therapy. Amazingly, his closest friend at the Laro School, Daniel Gregory Brown, died that same exact evening. Both deaths occurred less than twenty-four hours after young Thomas here came home with a crooked walk and a new outlook on life. What an uncanny coincidence," Holtzer said, while his face, wore a mock smile that would have made the Joker himself envious.

"My father knew what had happened. The Laro School is where his political career began—the Head Administrator, making his way up from the lowest dregs of society—not that the top is any better. He made a name for himself through cover-ups and quiet goodbyes. If the public could only hear what's said in private, Maybe. I heard him telling my mother the night he came home. He even knew it was your father that had killed them. I was just a young boy, eight-years-old, listening to the death of a brother I hardly even knew. I heard him telling my mother why your father did it, and that's when I learned your secrets, Thomas. While my father never pursued it, I waited, watched. I didn't expect it would take this long, yet, I never wanted it to happen so soon, either. Besides, my father was more than happy to have the family blemish gone. It was easier for him to let my little down-syndrome brother die quietly than it was to admit he had ever put him in that place to begin with. But I'm not my father, Thomas. I'm my own animal, and I say an eye for eye—just like in the good book that your sister here is so fond of. They told me that Joey had died in his sleep, but I had already heard the truth. I already knew." Holtzer was stoking his inner flame, the fire that lived within him, ready to rage upon whim.

~ ~ ~ ~

Present Day:
"There I was, standing at the door to the room, frozen by the sight of his hat; it had only been a week before that I had bought it for Thomas at the Hayward Sporting Goods store. I remember driving through downtown Hayward with the hat on the seat next me, the dream of all the things Thomas

would accomplish in that hat, riding right there with me, the nightmares, now, the only passengers remaining in the seat."
Beep. Beep. Beep.

"Looking past the bed, and the hat with eyes, I saw them, both of them, sitting in the corner of the room, their legs folded Indian-style. They were rocking back and forth, whispering, oblivious to the sight of me in the doorway. Joey A. Hostler, and Danny G. Brown: the first, a boy with down-syndrome, the second, a supposed case of lost oxygen during birth. In other words—words spoken under the breath of the doctor's when no one was around to hear them—he was fucked up, and no one could figure out exactly why. All I knew was he had a criminal's heart. Every time something went missing in that damn place, all I had to do was check room one-forty-two, and nine times out of ten it was found."
Beep. Beep. Beep.

"Mentally, they were children, with all the lust and power of teenage desire. They were victims of abuse themselves—abuses I had walked away from, put out of my mind, at times, cleaned the mess that remained, and still, I hated them. I wanted to drop my mop, rush in the room and choke them both to death. I imagined my hands around their necks, choking the life out of them, but something stopped me, held me, and to this day, I don't know what or who it was. Unable to crease the door, be the killer that lived in my heart. I went to the administrator's office instead, and where I had told Thomas and your mother not to say a word, I talked, and I killed them all by doing it."
Beep. Beep. Beep.

"What was I supposed to do, let them go? Leave them free to hurt more kids? If I talked, I ruined the lives of every man and woman that worked at the Laro School. If I stayed silent, how many more children would be pulled from the streets like Thomas, left with a life of suffering. Either way, I murdered those boys. Nobody cares what a lowly janitor thinks. It was Holtzer—the old man, who took matters into his own hands, and it wasn't until that night when his son held a gun to your head that I knew exactly why. He wasn't keeping the streets safe from monsters. He was covering up his own loose ends. The last thing he wanted on his watch, with his ambitions, was the scandal that was sure to follow; and the trail of genes led right to his office—up until I heard his son say it to Thomas, I had no idea. He ordered "aggressive therapy" for the patients, made me watch what he watched—the death of his son. We both killed our children that night, but only one of us cried. We were both murderers, but perhaps, one way or another, we all kill to survive."

~ ~ ~ ~

April 1987:
"It's a shame you weren't born back then, Maybe," he spoke with a deliberate, sickening focus on her. "From everything I've learned over the years, you would have been a big hit at the Laro School. If you had been around, they may never have even looked twice at your brother here." Holtzer's eyes moved, his lips, kissing her ear. "You're so sweet Maybe, it's a shame I'm going to have to kill you. You want me to kiss you the way your brother just kissed my girlfriend out on the front porch, or do you want me to kill you the way Thomas' father killed mine? I could do both if you prefer."

Had this Holtzer been lurking underneath the skin his entire life? If so, he was a magician. Every conversation, every word he had ever spoken to Thomas, was an illusion.

"You know what?" Holtzer snapped, "There ain't a chance in hell I'm going to fuck you, you stupid little bitch." With that statement, Holtzer let Maybe go, pushing her in Thomas' direction.

Placing Maybe behind him, glad she was away from Holtzer, Thomas knew that they were still far from safety, far from getting out alive; but Thomas was grateful that if they did go, that he and Maybe would go together.

Holtzer raised his gun, causing Maybe to scream when, as if possessed by the ghost of Brew, Goliath (who had been casually chewing on his toy and unaffected by the commotion) jumped towards Holtzer. Knowing the dog couldn't stop him, Holtzer gave the puppy a boot to the stomach that sent little Goliath yelping away. But the damage of the insignificant attack had already been done. Holtzer's hand, the first victim of his reflexes, reacted to his own sudden movement when, without intention, he squeezed the trigger, and in an instant, Thomas and Maybe were covered in blood.

Chapter Eighteen

I am the ghost in the corner, a shadow within a shadow, unseen. Blended by shyness into invisibility, my true personality lives inside of my own mind—alone, afraid of failure, afraid of success, fearing the thought of being looked upon. Even to myself, I am often a mirage in the distance, never meant to be held, never there to be touched.
A Heart Called Joseph

April 1987:
The force of the bullet hit Thomas like a sledgehammer, pushing him backwards, and dropping him on top of Maybe. It had ripped below his right shoulder, though it would take him a minute to realize, as the shock of hearing the second shot had won the battle for his attention.

One shot for Me. One shot for Maybe, Thomas thought. Spinning over on top of her, the burning pain removing his ability to lean on his right side, Thomas saw her closed eyes and limp body on the floor, blood soaking both of their shirts.

With tears filling his eyes, Thomas wobbled as he pulled himself up to his knees. Looking at Maybe, he felt a searing pain in the back of his head, along with the sudden realization that the worst damage Holtzer could ever inflict on Thomas, was leaving him alone, alive without her.

Thomas' vision was blurred from the salty permeations and radiating agony of his wound. In a sudden panic, he scanned the spot where Holtzer had been standing, only to see empty space. Holtzer was nowhere to be found. Still, Thomas knew he wasn't alone. In the doorway leading to the kitchen, stood a man dressed in black, his long overcoat accentuating the sight of his pale hand and the gun in its grasp. He looked bothered, but calm.

It had been a long time, yet Thomas recognized him in an instant. The dark hat covering the man's head had kept his features hidden, like a shadow in the midst of man, but as the light of the living room slowly worked its way past the obstruction, Thomas could see.

Looking at the man over his own blood stained, outstretched hand, Thomas whispered without hesitation, "Daddy."

~ ~ ~ ~

Present Day:
"I saw the bullet hit Thomas. I was hoping that it wouldn't come to that, but the crude nature of circumstance had other plans. I couldn't tell if you had been shot as well, so I began to react, but there was only one problem, perhaps the only solution—she reacted first."
Beep. Beep. Beep.

"She was better prepared anyway. Once again, I was the harbinger of death. Once again, I was standing there, the silent witness. Only this time, I took the fall I deserved. This time, I stepped into the light."

~ ~ ~ ~

April 1987:

She had never killed before, and she would go a lifetime never killing again. He had hurt her that night, gone too far. She had thought the cocaine had changed him, but now she knew it was only amplifying who he really was on the inside. Bradley Holtzer was sick, and when she passed his abandoned car only one street up the road from Thomas' house, Jennifer knew the silhouette she had just seen in the window was more than a conjured image created by a frightened mind.

Standing outside of his car, another woman with a rock in her hand, Jennifer thought about the two things she had learned that night about Holtzer's addiction. It came with two major flaws. One, was that Bradley Holtzer had difficulty getting an erection when he was coked up—which when you don't want it, like Jennifer hadn't that night, is a good thing. And two, was that in his new state of paranoia, Holtzer carried more than one gun. Wielding the rock with a force that would have made even Mary-Sue jealous, Jennifer smashed in the passenger side window, opened the glove box, thanked God that there was still a gun to grab, then prayed to God that Holtzer wasn't planning on using the other one.

~ ~ ~ ~

The ghost with a tear stood in the doorway, looking at the blood on his son's hand. At that moment, they were his hands. He had a played a major part in causing this, all of it, and it was time for him to finish it. It was time to leave the darkness.

It was her face that Thomas now saw, as if they were coming to life out of the nothingness, appearing from where they never were. Her look was like a kiss of death, yet, it was her gun that had done it—brought an end to Holtzer. The old man, his father, "Daddy," stopped to look at her. She had snuck in the same backdoor, the third and final set of feet to break the plane. The last one to enter, she was the first one to end it. The old man had been lost in the story, too worried about making a noise. Lost in Holtzer's revelations, he hadn't even heard her enter. He was no different than Thomas on the dock with her—deaf to the world. Like son, like father.

He could see her shaking, the gun in her hand, trembling with her entire body. *Another soul in shock,* Joseph thought. He didn't know how much she had heard, or how long she had been there, but however long it was, it was already more than needed.

"You did what was necessary. Be at peace with it," the old man said to Jennifer—kind words, from a man who knew nothing of peace. The old man was just another hypocrite, another beautiful, broken hypocrite, with a heart in all the right places, and a mind that never could find its way.

"Who are you?" Jennifer asked, though she knew who she was looking at. Their eyes were different, yet their eyes were the same.

"I'm the reason we are all here, the reason that you can't stay," The old man told her.

"Where did you get that?" Joseph asked her, his mind already spinning the tale.

"It's his," Jennifer pointed to the mound on the floor. "I smashed his window and took it out of the car."

"Give it to me," the old man instructed, "It's time for me to take my blame. Give it to me, then go. Never speak about this. As far the story goes, you were never here."

Time stood silent while the two of them talked. His father had left her with a decision—a choice to never speak— the same decision he had chosen for Thomas years before.

This time, Thomas was thankful. He could bear the silence, he could bear the loneliness that came with suffering, but Thomas could never bear to see her fall.

Whatever she chose, they all knew that Jennifer would never forget that night. Memories would make sure of it, and sanity would forever ask the question, "Can you survive?" But Jennifer had a future, a life. All Joseph had was a life of following. The old man's eyes spoke to her, while his fingers gently removed the gun from her hands. She wanted to run to Thomas, hold him, hold Maybe, but something told her to listen to the old man; and with one quick sob, and one final image she would never erase, Jennifer left the house. This time, Jennifer Lynne never returned.

~ ~ ~ ~

Thomas saw her walk away—again. He wanted to get up, go to her, stop her, but he knew why he couldn't move. He knew why she had to.

Thomas wanted to yell to her, but his tongue, as if held hostage, was only free enough to repeat, "Daddy, Dad...."

The more times Thomas gave voice to the title, the less audible he became. The loss of blood was making the young man woozy. Thomas's body wished for him to go to sleep, the vision of his father, the only thing keeping him awake.

"Wake up now," Thomas' father barked at him, forcing a quick startle in the young man. He had lost a lot of blood, the pain causing a confusion Thomas couldn't seem to shake.

Is it all a dream, Thomas wondered, *has it all just been a bad dream? Maybe.*

"Maybe," Thomas lightly cried, freedom creasing his lips, the young man's focus leaving his father, "Maybe?"

"I don't think she was hit, but I do think you knocked her unconscious when you fell back. She has a pretty good knot on her forehead," Joseph told him, trying to remain calm for his son.

Thomas thought of the pain he had felt in the back of his head, yet, he still couldn't make sense of it.

"All this blood on her is yours, Thomas. Here, put this on your shoulder and press down on it," Joseph said, removing his black shirt and placing it on Thomas' wound. "You hear me? Press hard," his father commanded.

The old man could see in Thomas's expression and state of shock that the young man feared his father was only an apparition. Thomas was afraid to take his eyes away from his father, yet, with what little strength he had, Thomas glanced over once again to the floor where his so-called "friend" had been standing.

"I don't think he's going to be getting up anytime soon," his father told him, nodding his head to what had once been Holtzer's position. Looking further down than his eyes had allowed before, Thomas saw what was left of Holtzer, the former friend's feet protruding from behind the couch, the rest of his body swimming in the pool of blood that had been expanding on the floor. In a moment, Thomas feared, their blood would merge.

Little Goliath had begun barking at the dead body, as if he wished for Holtzer to get up. The feisty little dog was looking for another piece of the Ivy League idol, but Holtzer was dead, leaving nothing more to be had.

The blue and red lights startled Joseph as they swept through the creases in the curtain windows. He knew Thomas had to get to a hospital though, and he was thankful to hear the sirens as they pulled into the driveway. Apparently, murder didn't go as quietly into the night as Thomas had once believed. Someone had called the police, perhaps Jennifer, or perhaps even the neighbors couldn't look past the sound of gunshots. None of it mattered however, the damage was already done.

"Goodbye Thomas," his father told him, a tear running down his face. "I love you, son," he said, his voice shaken.

"Don't go," Thomas attempted to plead, knowing the man had to.

"I'm never gone, Thomas. Even when you can't see me, I am always here," Joseph told Thomas, his hand on his son's heart.

In what seemed like an instant, Thomas's father walked out the front door, the gun tucked visibly in the waist of his pants, and his arms raised skyward in surrender.

"Maybe. Maybe. Maybe?"

Thomas's voice ran home.

~ ~ ~ ~

Present Day:
"I took one last glance in Thomas' direction before heading out the door. I wondered if it would be the last that I would ever take of him. Would I spend the rest of my days in jail? Would he come see me? Would I want him too? I never once questioned whether he would survive. Even then, I was still thinking of myself. Watching him had been like reading a book. I was always there, yet never seen. Suddenly—that night—I found myself walking in the story once again, alive, breathing in between the pages."
Beep. Beep. Beep.

246
The Light of a Bright Sun

"I had killed the Holtzer boy in defense, or so I claimed, though never vehemently. Explaining that I was there stalking my son's existence wasn't exactly winning me any support, but so be it. I knew why I was there. It was the closest I had gotten to Thomas in eleven years, my location born from the circumstance of seeing that dirt-bag sneaking around the back of the house in the rain, and that was all that mattered to me."

Beep. Beep. Beep.

"I was up against a son of power however, and power demands vengeance—the exact reason I took the gun and made her leave, though she may have had the power to fight back. Why risk it? I figured. Yet, vengeance never came. The older Holtzer looked at me like a ghost, one that could spend a lifetime haunting his future. I had no desire to talk about the past, and he was content, even in his mourning, to keep it that way. Some things are better off left as dirt, and neither one of us had any desire to pave that road for the public."

Beep. Beep. Beep.

"Fifteen years for Manslaughter One. I was impressed, actually. I thought I would get more, but it turns out young Bradley had quite a stash of weapons and cocaine in his car. He was as much a victim of time as any. Please excuse my language, but it *was* the fucking eighties; when every feather-haired Yuppie with a bag of cocaine and a gun thought they were the next Don Johnson."

Beep. Beep. Beep.

"His lawyers tried to pin it on me, say that I had broken the window and planted the drugs. That defense didn't work however. There were already too many people who knew which way the wind blew with young Bradley, and that most of the time, it blew right up his nose, creating more than his fair share of seedy associations. I spent the fifteen years in prison reading in solitude, the last thirteen years outside of prison doing the same. All the while his father spent it in the spotlight—the martyr on the stage, with another son's life used as a steppingstone. The tragedy became old Holtzer's triumph. I would hate to be his wife. Without any sons left, who is there to sacrifice next?"

Beep. Beep. Beep.

"I think of her often—Jennifer. Where would we all be without her? Would either of us be sitting here today? She did nothing wrong, she walked away—ran really, the rain washing away all it could. Only she can wash away the rest. In all that has scrambled my mind, I know that much is true."

~ ~ ~ ~

August 1998:

"It looks pretty out there."

Maybe has grown to love the feeling of the water; though, outside of a constricted shower, she always had. Sitting in her room, her eyes looking out the window, she can still feel the rain in her hair, the drops of water that would make their way down the side of her face like fingertips caressing her cheeks, and always evoking the sensation of love.

"Don't you just love the rain, Thomas?" She asks him, knowing.

"I do," Thomas answers her. "I always have."

"What did you do today?" She continues, keeping her focus out the window. It's the same question she has asked Thomas every day, but she never gets bored of the repetition; Maybe loves to hear about how Thomas has spent his day. His life, to Maybe, is like the sunny breeze you think of on a cloudy day, always relaxing, comforting—free—which has always made her feel better about it, about everything.

"I saw Ralph today, sat with him. He reads—all the time. I like to listen to him read. He has learned so much in books, yet, he does nothing with it, just hoards all those worlds to himself. He is happy, especially when he's had a few, but I wish he would do something more with all he's learned. Although, he does at least spread it to his children. They love to read, as well. For all the 'go to work and pay the bills,' he's reached a level of general happiness that keeps him content, and for that, I'm grateful. He has always been a good person. But I can't help but wish that he would do more."

"How is Jennifer?" Maybe asks, knowing that Thomas spends every day in her mind with Jennifer.

"Beautiful."

"Oh Thomas, you two are so lucky to have one another," Maybe tells him, her heart, in love with the thought of them.

Looking back from the window, her focus directly on Thomas, she knows reality has crept in the window while she was basking in the rain.

"Daddy said Goliath's going to die soon, that he's sick."

"I know. He's been a good dog, Maybe Baby, but he's hurting. No one should ever have to suffer."

"We all suffer, Thomas," Maybe tells him, knowing Thomas can't argue with that. "Why does everything have to die?"

"I don't know, Maybe Baby, perhaps it's for the best. Maybe the world just can't handle all that love at one time."

"You'll never leave me, will you Thomas?" She's crying, the hurt from losing Goliath, from Thomas, sitting on her chest like a dead man's coffin.

"If I haven't left you yet, what makes you think I ever will?"

Maybe looks at him, mirrors his smile, the one emanating from his old My Buddy doll, and asks him the same question she has repeated for the past eleven years, "Thomas, what's it like to be dead?"

CHAPTER NINETEEN

Do not stay in the corner. Accept the times you have, for you are human. But do not accept them as your destiny. Be an orb of light in the darkness of night, guiding yourself, and all others who wish for a kinder world. And when the end of your time— the best friend and greatest enemy of us all—does come closer to your eyes still, blind him with a greeting. Be bright to the last breath. Let your love for humanity, in all its human imperfections, shine for tomorrows of tomorrow. This, I ask from you. This, I demand of myself.
A Heart Called Maybe

Present Day:
"Twenty eight years, it's hard to believe that it's been that long since Thomas died. He lost too much—too much of his innocence when he was a child, too much love when he was an adult, and too much blood on that living room floor. All I've lost is my time and sanity."
Beep. Beep. Beep.

She can see him. Even when her eyes are closed, she can see him, and she always has. He comes with the old man—his father. He whispers in the old man's wrinkled ears as he reads to her. Thomas tells him the story, and so his father follows, reading the book. Each flip of the page is a new breath, a new voice, another story changing each time told, yet, every story is still the same. They struggle, agonize, survive and die in death and life, and they love—always, for all of all.

Listening in silence as the old man speaks, Maybe's grateful for him. The old man has come to her, stayed with her, even when she hasn't spoken, he has always been there. Whatever the past, whatever the future, she loves him for it all.

"Not all heroes die in the light of a bright sun— perhaps your father was wiser than Thomas or I ever gave him credit. He was right. Most of us slither away from the light by way of machine or man, in senility rather than divinity, never to resurrect ourselves, as if unable to climb up the mountain. We fade away in the depth of our souls, here one moment, gone the next. How tragic. How beautiful. How human."
Beep. Beep. Beep.

Maybe knows it's time, even without the old man telling her. She feels it. Her body is letting go. Not giving up, but giving it the peace to rest, renew, and be with him—the one who makes death shine. Still, she worries about how her death is going to affect them all, but in her last moments, she thinks of Mumma and Daddy.

It has been a year since the debilitating heart attacks had started to come, leaving her in the constant care of the nursing home. She didn't quite understand why she couldn't come home from the hospital at first, all she knew was that she had a broken heart, but she liked the nursing home, so Maybe made the best of it.

"Her hearts damaged from years of overuse," her father would tell the nurses when he and Mumma came, flirting with them, though harmlessly. That side of Willy had been gone as long as Thomas. Maybe always liked when her father said it, though, she knew using a heart too much could never truly happen.

While the old man speaks and reads to her during his visits, Maybe's father only sits on the side of her bed, holding Maybe's hand while never saying a word to her. Wanting only to comfort him, she imagines her father is a man who has always been this kind. No matter what the past had brought, there is love in his palms and fingers now, and she can feel it. *Perhaps*, she thinks, *I always have*. What Maybe does know for sure, is that she loves being with both of them; and even in their differences, that both men cry—always.

Mumma cries every time she comes, as well. Maybe used to tell her stop. "Stop it, Mumma. I'm going home to Jesus and that isn't anything to cry about." But Maybe could still see the pain in her mother's eyes. Most of all, Mumma would cry when she looked at the dolls on Maybe's nightstand—My Buddy and My Kid Sister.

"Talk to us, Mumma, and we will never leave you, ever," Maybe had told her when she caught her mother's eyes drifting to them, but that only made Mumma cry more. Even trying to comfort her, Maybe understood why.

When Thomas had died, a part of Maybe had died with him. Maybe Baby had been left to face the world without her greatest protector, without her Thomas.

"I still miss him so much, Mumma," Maybe had cried over the years, Mumma right there by her side. Now, Mumma was going to be the one left to cry, though, if anyone could handle that fate, it was her. Mumma's entire life had been one loss after another; such was her destiny. But even past experience can't dull the pain. Mumma was aching, but where Mumma had always told Maybe that love could make a person blind, in Maybe's opinion, love could also help you see. Maybe wanted Mumma to see the happiness when she was gone; Maybe wanted Mumma to talk to her in the rain.

Nothing is ever perfect—it never has been. But Maybe knew that Thomas would never leave her, and every time she had ever talked with My Buddy, she knew he never had. She wanted Mumma to have that feeling. No matter how it ends, or when, Maybe wanted Mumma to know that their lives were always worth living, even when dying was the cost.

Beep. Beep. Beep.

"What have you thought of me all these years, the old grey fool with no more relation to you than Adam, here crying over your bedside? They think I am at work. We know better though, don't we? We know the bond between us, between all of humanity, better than most, I'm afraid. Most people think it takes genius to solve the great problems the world has caused. They're wrong. It takes great heart. The closer we get to their forced knowledge, the greater the distance we are creating to wisdom, compassion, love. The greatest gift we are all given is so often the first forsaken."

Beep. Beep.

She was the last person in the world he was looking for, and the only person in the world who had ever taught him to see. She was his god to hold on high. She was the one, the creator of all. Made of her beauty, he prayed to her, for her, and with her. Even when she shouldn't have, she still and always believed.

"I have known you, without ever truly knowing. Your beautiful heart has been my flashlight in the dark of my days. When I was lost, I watched you, forever shining. I shall miss you, my friend. Even in death, I shall speak to you often. Hearts have ears, and with all the physical problems that came with the set you born with, I know, your heart heard more than the heavens and earth combined."

Beep.

"You may not die in the shimmering glow, my dear, we both know that. But you have lived in the light of one. For that, for showing me that it is possible, I thank you, Maybe. With all my heart and soul, thank you. Of all my actions, you were the greatness that came from my misfortunes. You were born into a world I could not stand, took care of him when I wouldn't, showed him more than he would have ever seen in my presence. For all of that, thank you. He was better for having known you, better than he ever would have been for knowing me. Thank you, for making him a part of your path, and for being the heart he needed most."

"Bless you. May god find your smile and see his own. I must go now. Your brother will be here soon. Thomas will show you the way."

He could barely finish his last sentence. Joseph had needed to tell Maybe the story, for her, for himself. But it was time to let it go—to let them both go. Closing the book, he places it on the nightstand next to Maybe, leaving it for the one who now needs it most.

With his hand on Maybe's hair, Joseph reaches down and kisses her forehead. While his lips meet her skin, he hears the heart monitor. Through his entire body, he feels her last beat.

Be.........

Removing the collar as he walks out of the nursing home, the one that was never his to wear, Joseph breathes deeply, the fresh daytime air playing with the tears on his skin. "Take her home with you," Joseph screams into the daylight. "Take her home."

Walking past her window for the final time, he sees the scuffle of activity inside. He can see in their faces what he already knew, that it is her time to pass. Thomas had told him in a dream. He had whispered of her death in his father's ear. Joseph had been right to listen. Thomas had been right to tell. Thomas was the one who told him to leave the book.

Looking out across the street, the dry red looking back, Joseph wondered if he would also die soon, or even worse, live forever. It was the thought of his time left alone that concerned him—his time left alone in the shadows—with no one to watch, care for. Until then, there was only one thing left for him to do, for all of all, and that was to follow the sign on the wall. The sign he himself had written.

Doubt like Thomas. Love like Jesus. And forever say Maybe.

~ ~ ~ ~

She knew losing people was an occupational hazard that she would have to endure when she took the job. Yet, losing a younger patient, which was anyone under fifty—no matter who they were—had a way of adding an extra burden to the heart. Knowing Maybe however, only made it that much more difficult.

She had taken the job after Roger had passed away. Liam was only eight years-old when it happened. He was still just a little boy when the only father he had ever known took a bullet to the head in Iraq. She knew then that she was going to have to take on the task of raising Liam on her own, so, after a year and a half of school, LPN M.S. Burdick began working at Henderson Health Care, a nursing home/rehabilitation center on the outskirts of Hayward.

The nature of the job burnt out most nurses within a year to two, but for Mary-Sue, it was her calling. Every patient was a survivor, first of life, and then from the damage of being lost and forgotten. Mary-Sue understood that way of life. Mary-Sue had always survived. After everything she had been through, there she was, still breathing, still roaming the halls on her own two feet. Some people have a way rising to the top in the worst of occasions, and for Mary-Sue, that was her true gift in life. She went to work, cared for her patients, held it all together, only to go home and do the same for herself and her son.

She had spent the twenty years after Roger's death telling people how devastated she was when she had gotten the call, though, behind closed doors, Mary-Sue never shed a tear. It wasn't that she didn't care for Roger. He had been a good man, a good provider, a good father to Liam, and she loved him for all of it. Yet, Mary-Sue had accepted a life without passion long ago. As she saw it, it was for the best. There would never be another man in Mary-Sue's life after Roger, and while others praised her for never settling after her one true love died, Mary-Sue knew the truth.

Liam wasn't exactly sure why his mother had called him over. A grown man of twenty-eight, now with a wife and child of his own, Liam didn't get many calls from his mother. Especially ones telling him that "they needed to talk," and that it was "important." He also knew his mother wasn't a woman that you said, "No," to. When Mary-Sue Burdick told you to "Get over here," you did it.

She wasn't exactly sure when the first time she noticed it was. All she could remember was that the boy was young. *He'll look like my father, and everyone will pass it off for genetics,* Mary-Sue had thought. The truth, she believed, would fade into the casual recognition. But by the grace of God, Daddy wasn't her father's child, and the more time that passed, Mary-Sue knew that he wasn't Rogers either.

Looking at him, she thought she knew Liam's true maker. The body was all too familiar, *and the eyes*, she began to think. Each day became a new recognition, a new confirmation. Yet, the true giveaway, the one that finally convinced Mary-Sue for good, was the boy's smell. It was the same smell that had lingered on her nose every time the old man came to visit Maybe, the same smell and memory that still lived her in head, the sweet smell of something different from herself that had forever permeated from the old man's son.

She didn't have any plans on taking anything from the room. Normally, a patient's belongings were boxed up and given back to the family. Yet, gathering Maybe's things for Prudie and Willy, Mary-Sue saw the book. The title said it all, but upon opening it, all it took was a few passages to recognize the story the same way she remembered the smell.

What good would telling him do? What good was it to tell him that his entire life had been a lie? Would it be for him or for her? Perhaps, Mary-Sue decided, *it would be best to believe that she was doing it for the memory of Thomas.*

"What are you saying?"

Mary-Sue had watched her son grow, held him, and looking at the man now, she handed him the book. She wasn't sure who had written it, not that it truly mattered, though she suspected it was the old man, adding his own perception and life into the mix. Mary-Sue didn't hold it against him. She had done the same when she read it. When every story has already been told, what is left but to add our own piece of life among it?

"Your real father died twenty-eight years ago, not twenty. This book is the story of his life."

Liam looked at the bound pages, felt the thin leather cover—it reminded him of a bible cover, yet it was imperfect, worn, the outer edges of the pages, stained, as if it had been read daily for the last thousand years. Holding it, breezing the pages like a deck of cards, Liam had no doubt it was handmade. He took a second to think about it, his finger running over the title, which appeared to Liam, to have been gently scratched into the leather with a knife.

Believing Thomas.

Mary-Sue had past transgressions, demons that upon reading the story, her son would know. Perhaps, this was the only way she could tell Liam. Maybe this is how he was meant to find out. She had given him the book, handed him a piece of both of their lives. It was up to him to find the light in it now, but she had faith. What else do we have at the end of the day, but that belief in something—something more powerful than any of us combined.

She watched her son open the first page. Reading aloud, Liam began his journey into the world he had never known.

"In the name of the Father, and of the Son, and of the Holy Ghost."

THE END

A new beginning

Book two in the Hayward Series

BETWEEN THE HEAVENS

By

Thurman P. Banks Jr.

CHAPTER ONE

New York City, New York

"When the wind of time has blown and we are each reduced to sand, the true God will be the one that lies within the grain of us. For we are all gods, mastered by no false creations, as equal to any Jesus, as any Jesus is equal to us. Man created religion. Religion created not one man. Stand up to false myth! Use science and common sense as the pew. Be as united in peace and beauty as the sand on the beach. Let religion be what it has become—the lonely old stick in the mud—too unmoving to change its failed ways, too self-captured to be free and true."

"You don't really believe that crap, do you?"

Love him or hate him, everybody knew what an asshole Riley Todd could be.

"I am here with L.B. Thompson, author of 3 bestselling books. His latest book, titled—Dog in Rewind—is available now in bookstores all across the country. Now, you L.B.— Liam—if you don't mind me calling you by your actual name?"

"Of course not."

"You sir, proclaim yourself to be an atheist, and as far as I'm concerned, all atheists really are, are just religious pessimists looking for an excuse to bash God for the turmoil they have experienced in their own life," Riley, in his usual cock of the walk, intellectually condescending, tone argued.

"There's no looking for excuses on my end, just look at the world Riley—poverty, famine, horrendous amounts of abuse. If there is a God, he's failing miserably."

"But what I don't think you understand, Thompson, is that faith for many is hope, and what you're offering is, for lack of a better term, nothing." Todd responded, foregoing the use of Liam's first name, and simplistically stating an anything but simple problem.

"It bothers me when people say that Riley. It's just like when someone writes a post on social media asking for you to pray for *one* particular sick child. Doesn't the fact that they are singling out one person mean they are spiritually neglecting all others? Shouldn't we *always* be—whether it's praying for religious believers or thinking happy thoughts for those of us with a different noetic based outlook—have our thoughts on everyone, all the time, not just the one that has been chosen to be looked at. I don't think I am asking people to do rocket science here, and furthermore, by asking for someone to pray for someone who is sick, aren't people really just asking for someone to help them accept that they can't control whether or not the other person dies, which even with the proper medicine, we can't do always do. Why are they so worried about them dying anyway if they believe in a wonderful place after death? Shouldn't they—I don't want to say 'be happy for them'—but at least be accepting that there is no finality. Isn't that what heaven was invented for? If they truly loved them they would be accepting, but they aren't, because they don't truly love others. People love themselves, and care only about themselves and the people who massage their egos and beliefs when it's convenient for them. And anytime someone disagrees, that person is the one painted the bad guy or heathen, even if that person is the only one who truly cares about everyone. If *your* Jesus did come back, I would hope he'd be pretty pissed off with all of you."

"You're aggrandizing an utterly useless point Thompson. Believers, which you know I am one, believe that God takes care of us all, even you. People need to connect at times with that *one*. What you're not getting, and most atheists don't get, is that it's that connection that brings us closer to each other." Todd's words flowed smoother than Johnnie Walker on a hot summer day.

"How convenient your faith is to the argument, Riley. Look, when a child gets sick, what do you do? You give it to God that his faith is getting him through it, but never once put any of the actual illness on God's shoulders. Doesn't it all seem a little silly? God only does what suits us, at the moment it suits us or our beliefs. What that tells me is that God wants people to be selfish and self-inflating, because that's the behavior he really seems to support—it's idiotic. I find a lot more comfort in saying I don't think that's how it works, and I'm also not going to sit here and claim I do, just to say I have all the answers. If there is a God, as I believe great men like Paul Tillich would have agreed, I don't think our little brains are anywhere close enough to grasping what he is all about. So rather than believe what human beings thousands of years ago created with their own purpose in mind, I'll gladly sit here and say, 'I don't know, but I certainly don't think it's that'."

Liam had no intention of getting angry, he had gone through this all before with Riley Todd, it was the same dance they had engaged in several times already when Liam had appeared on the show. Riley would win some points, Liam would do the same, and they both would walk away with a greater number of followers.

Something was out of balance however, and he was stepping on his own feet, getting irritated, and lacing his words with a sarcasm that was rarely brought out by most of those he argued with. Todd, however, was different than most. The man was genuinely kind when the cameras were off, which made the smug on screen demeanor and confidence he exuded, as if he knew God personally, a grating on Liam's nerves; match that with a patronizingly egotistical voice, and what you had was the equivalent of fingernails on a chalkboard.

"Who are we to judge an almighty deity, who I'm sure has a plan." Riley was goading Liam. He knew that using "God's plan" as an excuse was a personal pet peeve for Liam, and Riley knowingly smiled while riling up his guest.

"Oh come off it, that's the oldest excuse in the book, and an easy one for someone in your position to fall on. Let's face it Riley, while you're home in your cushy million dollar house thanking a lord for giving you a life that leaves you sitting here like you've been touched by an angel, there are poor young children in places like Ethiopia, starving, because their life has been a lot more like getting tea-bagged by God. What kind of a plan is that?"

Liam knew he shouldn't have said it the minute it came out, but in his defense, he thought, Riley Todd brought out the asshole in others as well as he let it escape from himself.

"I think that's about enough. You sir, need to take a closer look at your life," Todd directed his statement at Liam, before turning to the camera and informing the audience, "We'll be back with our America's Hidden Corner segment, right after this."

"We're clear," the producer of The Point yelled.

"What, that's it?" Liam asked Riley, who was hurriedly shuffling his papers.

The smug look on Riley's face dissipated. Raising his eyes while lifting himself off his seat, not because he had to go anywhere—there was still the rest of his show to do—but needing to get away from his guest, he said, "Really, Liam, tea-bagged by God? I have children who watch this show with their parents."

On the verge of a soft stuttering, Liam replied clumsily, "With parents who enjoy a healthy dose of right wing news propaganda, no different than religion," he semi-yelled the last part at Riley, who was walking away while shaking his head. Before Riley could get too far away, however, the man who lived on portraying himself as ever intelligent, showed the level of childishness that Liam had brought him to, and left the author with one last thought.

"By the way, Thompson, your haircut looks stupid."

"Fuck off, Riley! Thanks for having me on, though," Liam finished pathetically, knowing that having his face on a show like Riley's often sparked sales, most often from diehard fans of The Point who loved to purchase his books just for a chance to dissect and insult every line written.

"Achuuu." The sneeze came from somewhere behind the cameras.

"Bless you," Liam said instinctively. No matter what his religious beliefs, no matter what Riley had pushed him to, at the heart of it all, Liam L.B. Thompson truly cared about others.

Riley Todd may be an asshole, Liam thought, *but at times, it was like looking in a mirror.*

~ ~ ~ ~

Between The Heavens

Coming Soon

About the Author

Thurman P. Banks Jr. lives with his wife Jen, their two sons, and wildly loved family beasts—Max and Rusafee—in coastal Connecticut.

Painting Courtesy of Charlie Dale

Acknowledgments

A special thanks to all my family and friends, especially my wife and children, who patiently put up with me while I indulge the madness called writing. For my two major editors (Bonnie Banks and Ann Oviatt), as well as all of those who offered to take on the daunting task, thank you for showing me that great acts of kindness are still very much alive—I hope I didn't "finger fault" too much of your hard work away during formatting. For Charlie Dale, a fan turned friend who has been an incredible support, I thank you with all my heart for the beautiful painting. To my father-in-law (Gary Bergeson), who provided the cover photo, I am so grateful to have both you and Marge in my life. I also owe a big thank you to Andrew Stoner, for the humor, the jokes, and all the conversations we shared—I'll miss you most of all Scarecrow. I would like to give a great big shout out to Kim, AKA SlayerOf Gildamesh, for her generosity of time and support. Most importantly, I would like to give a most special thank you to Phyllis Williams, for opening her heart with stories of herself and her sister. For the letters, the inspiration, and the always kind words, I will forever be grateful.

I love you all,

Thurman

Made in the USA
San Bernardino, CA
12 February 2014